A Blue Moon in

VERMONT

New England Mysteries

Book #1   **_A Cold Morning in MAINE,_**
published in October 2014.
ISBN 978-0-9962397-0-7

Book #2   **_A Quiet Evening in CONNECTICUT,_**
published in April 2015.
ISBN 978-0-9962397-1-4

Book #3   **_A Bad Night in NEW HAMPSHIRE,_**
published in November 2015.
ISBN 978-0-9962397-2-1

Book #4   **_a PIZZA NIGHT in the BAHAMAS,_**
published in November 2016.
ISBN 978-0-9962397-3-8

Book #5   **_A Hot Afternoon in MASSACHUSETTS,_**
published in May 2017.
ISBN 978-0-9962397-4-5

Book #6   **_A Rainy Weekend in RHODE ISLAND,_**
published in November 2018.
ISBN 978-0-9962397-5-2

Book #7   **_GO DEEP: A Sinister Plot Is Afoot . . ._**
published in July 2019.
ISBN 978-0-9962397-7-6

Bookstores, kindle and amazon – audio books
available from audible.com and iTunes.

A Blue Moon in

VERMONT

MYSTERY NOVEL

Terry Boone

Published by **THREE RIVERS GROUP**
Contact: threeriversgroupvt@gmail.com

ISBN: 978-0-9962397-6-9

Interior design by Creative Publishing Book Design
Cover design by Harp & Company Graphic Design
Cover photo by the author.
Map: Copyright © 2021 Maps of the USA

In memory of Henry Scheier.
And for all the kids,
volunteers, and staff of
Everybody Wins! Vermont.

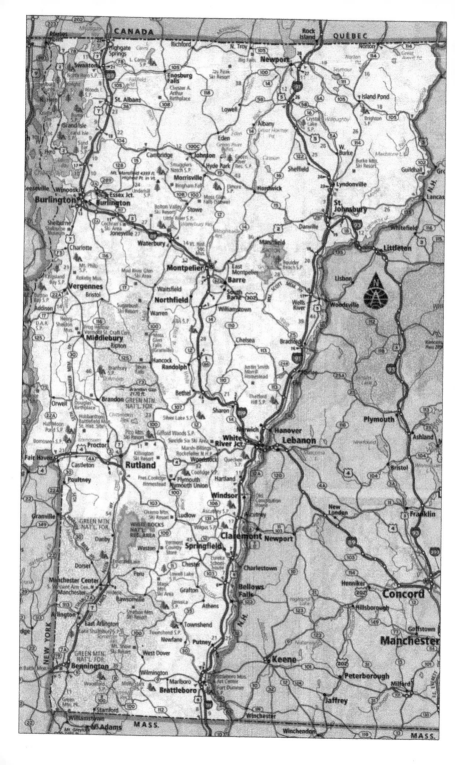

One

Probably never heard the shot. Doubtful that he felt any pain from the impact of the bullet. Now, he would not feel anything ever again.

At the age of sixty-five, retired only a month, a career US intelligence officer was dead. A 'hunting accident' in northern New Hampshire. The shooter turned himself in to Fish and Game authorities, paid a $500 fine and lost his hunting license for ten years.

Media coverage lasted just about as long as it took for the last of the autumn leaves to drop and for the first accumulation of snow in the White Mountains.

The victim's family 'accepted that it was an accident,' or so wrote a colleague in a memoir privately published years later after his own death in 2018.

A lifelong friend of the shooting victim, however, has a different view. And he believes that he has a way to prove that it was a 'contract hit'. He has *almost* enough information to identify who arranged the assassination.

Now, twenty years into a new century and just over a decade shy of this friend's' own century mark, chasing down facts possibly ignored by investigators, along with amassing information that was dismissed as not being relevant at the time, getting to the *real* story has become a mission for one old man determined to 'get it right.'

Back in time well before YouTube, social media, and online blogs — produced by seemingly more people than populated the US just a hundred years ago — back around the period when cable TV networks were being launched, 1980, one Stephen Winthrop Callahan was that shooting victim in the woods of northern New Hampshire.

Actually, it occurred in his backyard, adjacent to the woods. The hunter who fired the shot was off in the forest approximately a hundred and ten yards away.

Only minutes earlier, the victim had apparently gone outside, mug of coffee in hand, to watch the early morning full moon setting off to the southwest.

The hunter's statement, given to Game Wardens and the New Hampshire State Police immediately following the incident, was tenable. He claimed that he'd been tracking a large buck since daybreak, that the deer had gone down a gully, crossed a brook and that he had lost sight of it. A noise from behind had startled him. He turned, saw movement off to the left and believed that the deer had circled behind him.

Shortly before sunrise, the hunter said, there was another quick movement through the trees, he raised his rifle and fired.

A Fish and Game press release later the same day stated that serious hunting incidents such as this one was rare, listing only five hunting-related fatalities in the Granite State over the previous 15 years.

There was no arrest, therefore no trial. The resulting fine plus the loss of a hunting license for the man who admittedly fired the shot, was imposed in a citation for 'negligence in the discharge of a firearm while hunting.'

Nonetheless, 'Win' Callahan was still dead.

Two

The phone call came a little after ten o'clock on a Monday morning. I'd just come back into the house from thirty minutes of walking, running, and throwing a sun-bleached, well-chewed yellow tennis ball for Rocco, my Golden Retriever.

The caller ID showed an 802 number that I didn't recognize.

"Michael Hanlon," I answered.

"Is this Michael Hanlon the former radio news reporter?" a man's voice asked.

Some state rep who still has a bone to pick?

"Yep. That's me. May I ask who I'm speaking with?"

"Mister Hanlon, you don't know me. My name is Frank Marino. But I feel as though *I know you*. I listened to you when you were on the radio. And I've read some of the material that fellow's been writing about you."

"Yeah, well, not sure how far I'd go with *that*. Fiction, non-fiction. People write all kinds of things."

The response was a laugh with a just hint of mischief. The man's opening delivery, soft-spoken, reminded me of my late father. I made a quick guess that he was an older type.

"What can I do for you, Mister Marino?" I asked.

"If you have the time, I would like for you to come visit me. I have a story that I would like to share. And I believe that it is something that you will find . . . *intriguing*. It is a project that I have researched for years and now I could use some help."

Switching the phone to my left hand while opening the refrigerator, I listened without comment as he continued. My intrigue 'at the moment' was Rocco, who was on high alert as to what might come out of the fridge.

"It is my understanding that you really *do* private investigation work, is that accurate?" he added.

"It is," I said.

Most of what I 'do' is nowhere near anyone's radar, perhaps with the exception of a few municipal and state police departments, which made me wonder if this call was a referral. I would find out soon enough.

"When you say, 'come visit you,' where are you?"

"About an hour from White River Junction, not far from Norwich University," he said. "A couple of miles over the hill from the interstate, in Williamstown."

I could see the I-89 exit ramp in my mind. Turn left to Northfield and the Norwich U campus, or, take a right, up over the ridge and you're in Williamstown. A more scenic route was to follow a state highway along the Second Branch of the

White River, then continue through the valley, a drive that I knew well.

"When did you have in mind?" I said.

"That's completely up to you. I'm retired. No pressing schedule. So, if you can find the time, I am completely flexible." Before I could respond, he added, "It might be better if we could try for late in the afternoon or in the evening."

We talked for another minute and settled on two days from now, Wednesday evening, September 30th at 5:30. I made a mental note to look online at the Norwich U calendar to see if there might be a home soccer match scheduled for that afternoon and if the public could 'social distance' near the field.

We didn't get around to how Marino found me. Despite regular, sarcastic taunting from my pal Louie Ragsdale, an undercover drug cop, I deliberately had no internet presence, at least none of my own creation, and embraced a selective, minimalist approach to finding clients.

On a few occasions my name had surfaced in news stories relating to law enforcement investigations, including a somewhat high-profile case a few years back. Fortunately, the accounts had spelled my name correctly and, equally important, I had been on the right side of the incidents being reported.

Louie routinely suggested that I have a hotshot web designer create a flashy site that advertised my *Private Investigation/ Background Security Services.*

"You could insert links to old TV episodes of *Paladin*. Go a little artsy, start wearing all black. You kinda' look like him, same nose," was one of the more recent marketing inspirations from Ragsdale.

Both of us were old radio guys; Louie had been a DJ in his college days at UMass Amherst before becoming a soldier and then a cop, and I had worked for many years as a small market news reporter. Quite accustomed to the frequent wiseass needling, I never missed a chance to hit the ball right back at him.

"Tell you what, Captain," I had replied. "I will get a website when *you* start hosting that Oldies show up there in the Northeast Kingdom."

This only produced a smirk, but it temporarily shut down Louie's creative concepts offered up unsolicited. Fact of the matter was that I really *liked* being low-profile. *And*, selective about the jobs that I take on and who is picking up the tab.

Three

It was a pleasantly warm evening, and we were sitting on a wooden bench in a small park in Williamstown. During the short walk from Frank Marino's apartment we had talked about the weather and the changing color of the leaves.

I watched the old man reach down and pick a speck of lint from one of his socks. He flicked it away into the grass, made two quick inward swipes with his right hand across the bottom of a pant leg, then sat up straight and looked directly at me.

"Much better here than back at Camp Keyhole," he said, followed by a short chuckle.

"You're not crazy about being there?" I said.

He shook his head, quickly raising both hands in a gesture of 'hold it just a second.'

"Truth is, I like it there very much. Didn't think that I would. Knew I couldn't live alone any longer," he said, gazing at the few cars travelling along Route 14 through the center of town.

"And I've been coming to Vermont practically every summer since I was ten years old." He watched me take this in. Again, the chuckle and he added, "If you want some help with the math, that's seventy-five years now."

"On the phone, when you called to ask me to come visit," I said, "you implied that you needed some help with a project."

He nodded. "That I did. And I *do*."

I waited. He waited. It took me all of five seconds to accept that I would lose at playing poker with this man.

"You also said that there's an intriguing story. Could I ask for the Executive Summary?" I asked.

He studied me for a beat, leaned backward, stretched a long, left arm along the top of the bench, crossed his legs and raised his right hand up to his chest as though he were about to pledge allegiance. Instead, he softly patted his hand a couple of times on his breastbone, still watching me.

If we were playing cards here, I was going to stick with the hand dealt. He could be bluffing. I said nothing.

"It's a project about . . . getting at the *truth* of something that happened forty years ago," he said. "Really, it was something set in motion long before that."

The sun was dropping below the ridge behind us as he began the story. I had been ambivalent about taking notes, so I didn't. That could be done later.

"One of the things I learned as a young man," he said, "was to be very skeptical of coincidences. Yes, they do happen, I

9

accept that." He let out the soft chuckle. "What's the disclaimer they use in books and movies? 'Any similarity to real people and real events is coincidental.'"

"Sounds right," I said.

Marino shifted on the bench and placed his right leg over his left, glanced across the street at a young couple out for an early evening stroll. They were pushing one of those combo child car seat/stroller rigs.

Once again, he brought himself to an erect position. On the walk here to the park I had noticed that for a guy his age, standing approximately six foot-two, he had impressive, ramrod-straight posture.

Back with the direct eye contact, he took a deep breath and with the soft, clear voice, commenced his tale.

"When I was four-years old, I spent a year with my maternal grand-parents, living in Greece. It was before the US entered the war, from the autumn of 1940 until early the following summer. My mother wanted to be with her own mother who was in frail health.

"At the time, my grandfather was on the staff at the US Embassy in Athens. I think that he was glad to have my mother's help, but my memory is that he spent very little time with us. My own father was serving in the Army back at Fort Holabird in Baltimore," he said.

Holabird, I knew, had been a sprawling army base not far from Washington, DC. As a kid growing up in Pennsylvania, we had an old guy in town who used to tell stories about being stationed there and working on the development of the original Jeep vehicle, which he claimed had been called a 'Peep'.

I did not share this anecdote with Marino. He was just warming up.

"I spent a lot of my time," he continued, "in the company of a young Greek woman who was then a first-year student at the American College of Greece. She wasn't my nanny, per se, but she watched over me a few evenings during the week and most weekends."

Marino smiled, shook his head slowly and took in a breath. "Selene Stavrakis. An absolutely beautiful young woman *then*, and just as lovely when I last saw her not long before she died at the age of 84.

"October 2004, following the Summer Olympics in Athens. I had gone back to Greece for a month. Selene died shortly after I returned to the states."

For the next twenty-minutes, I listened, without interrupting, as he added layer upon layer of a story that introduced me to much of his early life, his career working for the US State Department, including numerous trips to Greece, and a carefully developed conviction that he knew who killed, or had *arranged* to have killed, Win Callahan way back in 1980.

"This is where the intrigue comes into play," he said, again with the smile. He wore a corduroy Norfolk jacket and reaching inside the breast pocket, he pulled out a fat, number 10 envelope.

He handed the envelope to me. My name was printed on it in blue ink.

"Most of the story is there, eight pages, the 'condensed' version," he said. "I have thought about it for years. In recent weeks I've focused on putting it all down while all my marbles are still rolling in the right direction.

"I would like you to read it. Then, if you want, come back and interview me. I can fill in a lot more detail than what is included there," he added, gesturing toward the envelope.

Dusk was settling in. The young couple with the stroller had crossed over and were now coming back on our side of the highway. They turned into a driveway just before reaching us. I started to open the envelope and take out the sheets of paper.

Marino placed a hand on my right forearm. "Wait," he said. "You can read it when you get home. Might put you right to sleep. Or . . . I hope to the contrary, you will find it to be something of genuine interest. And that you can help prove the real story of what happened."

Four

After escorting **Marino** back to his apartment at the retirement community, I drove I-89 south and got off the exit at Route 4. My home is seven miles west of the Connecticut River in the small village of Quechee, next to White River Junction.

Rocco was enthusiastic to see me, as though he hadn't peed in a few hours. Placing the collar on him for the pet containment fence around the property, I gave him a biscuit and let him go out to bark at the deer and any other ferocious actors hanging around in the woods. All the veteran critters knew by now that he was not coming in to find them.

Left-over smoked pulled pork, red skin potato salad, half a baguette and a bottle of Landshark Lager would be dinner. Before the microwave beeped, Rocco was back at the door. Even with another biscuit for the prompt return to the house his focus would stay on me as I got ready to eat, so I fed him first.

Standing at the kitchen counter, I took a swig of beer and settled onto a stool. Having already removed the typed pages from the envelope I spread them out where I could read while eating.

Neatly spaced margins and, what I guessed from my days writing news stories, approximately 500 words per page, which would bring it in somewhere around 4,000 words. At the top of the first page he'd given his story a title: Win Callahan's Death — *Not An Accident.*

The first two pages incorporated much of what Marino had told me about being in Greece as a young boy and his days with Selene Stavrakis. The transition in the story came with the introduction of Selene's boyfriend, a young American soldier stationed at the US Embassy. His name was Stephen Callahan. Family and friends called him 'Win', a nickname bestowed on him by his grandfather.

The narrative continued with Marino telling how much he came to adore Callahan, always excited when Selene and Win took him along on afternoon walks into the city center of Athens.

"I was impressed by his uniform and the spit-shined shoes he wore," Marino had written. "*And* he treated me like a grown up. Years later, when I was in my first year of college, I realized that my childhood affection for Win had much to do with the absence of my own father during that period."

While a sophomore at American University in Washington, DC, Marino wrote, he learned that Callahan lived in the city and was working for the federal government. With assistance from his mother, he was able to contact Callahan and arranged to have him meet them for dinner. It was the spring of 1955.

"From that very evening, for the next twenty-five years, Win Callahan was a mentor and an older brother to me. I was devastated when he was killed.

"Many of the interests and experiences that I've had," Marino wrote, "are directly attributable to the influence of Win. Hiking, travel, reading history, spending time with *women* — Win mentored me through the early stages of my life." I continued eating my dinner, reading, and placing each page face down on the counter before moving onto the next. Skimming through passages about Callahan and his wife visiting the Marino family summer cottage in Vermont in the 1960s and 70s, my eyes locked on a paragraph in the middle of the page.

"Someday, if you read about my death and it is reported as an *accident*, don't be fooled," Win had stated. "After more than thirty years of travelling in circles that do not get much sunlight, unfortunately, people like me have more than a few enemies."

"Win said that" Marino wrote, "to my father and me late one night as we sat on the screened-porch of our cottage in Chelsea. It was the fall of 1976, shortly after my own 40th birthday, and *four years* before he was shot by a deer hunter in the White Mountains."

Reading the paragraph for a second time, I upended the bottle to finish the beer, placed my plate on the floor for Rocco's pre-rinse, waited 'til he'd finished, then put everything in the sink and returned to Frank Marino's essay.

The last two pages summarized Callahan's career, at least as much as Marino could piece together from personal knowledge and references to newspaper stories and periodical accounts of Callahan, including the news reports following his death. "Speculation, for certain," Marino wrote, "not just my own, but lavish helpings from one of Win's old colleagues still working at NSA."

The acronym got my attention.

"Win was scheduled to testify at a closed congressional hearing in December 1980. His death came two weeks before he was to appear," Marino wrote. "One could believe that had there been *any* substance about the non-accidental nature of the shooting, something would have leaked during the intervening years. To the best of my knowledge, that has not happened.

"However, as a lifelong friend, after many, many years of trying to convince myself that it was, as reported, an accident, I am still unpersuaded. It was the posthumous publication two years ago of a memoir by another career NSA employee that makes me even more determined than ever to get to the truth.

"Why was Win Callahan murdered?"

Five

Putting the pages together in proper sequence, I stuffed them back in the envelope, got a second beer from the fridge and went to the laptop computer on a desk in my combo office/guest bedroom.

Rocco was happy to stay stretched out asleep on the rug in the living room; he would be good until his last outside visit of the night, usually around 11 o'clock.

It took me only a couple of minutes to find stories about the death of Stephen W. Callahan. First up was a digitized version from a New York Times print article in their archives, long before the start of the paper's online publication. It was dated November 23, 1980, and included a photo of Callahan.

The story gave the name of the *shooter,* Ronald Davis, a twenty-year old hunter from Massachusetts, who immediately contacted Fish and Game when he realized what had happened. A high-ranking F & G officer said the shooting was under investigation and that no charges had been filed.

The five-paragraph account outlined Callahan's career working for US Government Agencies beginning at the end of World War II, through various posts within the domestic intelligence operations of the National Security Agency, some liaison work with the FBI, and concluding with his retirement just weeks before the shooting.

A Washington Post story, also dated November 23, 1980, went on for twenty paragraphs and offered more about specific points throughout Callahan's career and concluded with the mention that he was still party to "various civil suits growing out of alleged government abuses involving private citizens."

It made sense to me that the story would have gotten more play in DC as clearly Callahan had been a 'Washington guy' for most of his professional life. I printed both stories and bookmarked the links for future reference.

Just as I walked back to the kitchen my smartphone buzzed. It was on the counter next to the key fob to my car.

Tapping the screen to bring it to life I saw a text message from Louie Ragsdale. *Still on for brkfst tomorrow—8:30 at 4 Aces?*

He was driving down from the Northeast Kingdom for an appointment at the Dartmouth-Hitchcock Medical Center in Lebanon, New Hampshire, twenty minutes from where I lived.

Yep. Pretty sure that it is your turn to buy. I hit send.

At the diner, I got a booth in the corner as far away from the ceiling speakers as possible. Louie hadn't arrived yet. Depending on what was on the playlist, neither of us was a big fan of 'music too loud to enjoy your breakfast.'

A waitress asked if I wanted coffee. I told her yes and that I was expecting a friend. She left two menus on the table and went to fetch the coffee. Louie came through the door as she went behind the counter.

"I wasn't sure you remembered this place," I said as he settled into the bench across from me. Offering up a modified smirk, he simply nodded in the affirmative. It's an authentic diner dating back to the early 50s. Swivel stools up against a long counter, six booths, plus four more and a table located in an addition at one end of the diner.

"Came through here when I was a kid with my father and uncle. We stopped at the original 4 Aces," he said, gesturing with his thumb back toward the entrance. "Used to be up on the corner of Main Street."

"Right. Before my time," I said. "They moved the diner here and added the extra room in 1986."

The waitress returned with a mug of coffee for me and a handful of the little half-ounce creamers. Louie asked for decaf. She told us about breakfast specials listed on the whiteboard behind the counter and said she would be back to take our order.

"So, what's up with your medical appointment?" I said. "You still having the lower back issues?" He shook his head and started to answer just as the waitress brought his coffee. We hadn't looked at the menus.

19

"I'd like the mushroom spinach omelette special," Louie said. She scribbled on a pad and looked at me.

"Two eggs over easy, home fries, homemade toast, please."

"White or whole wheat?" she said.

"White, I think. Those are the thick slices, yes? Same as you use for French toast?"

She nodded and held up a thumb and index finger to indicate about a full inch.

"Great."

Ragsdale waited until she'd gone before he replied to my question.

"I have a meeting with the head of Emergency Management at DHMC. Used to be a cop back in the day. We worked a couple of drug cases, maybe 15 years ago," he said. "Good guy. *And* he's a native woodchuck."

The Dartmouth-Hitchcock Medical Center, I knew, is a major institution in Northern New England. The Lebanon facility is close to two million square feet in multiple buildings on 225 acres, with more than 7,500 employees, plus over a thousand health care providers.

I also knew not to press Louie now that he had told me about the appointment. One of the unspoken terms in our friendship was a mutual embrace of, 'If I want you to know more, I will tell you.' That often got thrown out the window when it was *he* snooping about my personal life, or just yanking my chain for his own amusement.

"Did you know there's a weather/traffic website 'Woodchuck Central'? I said. He nodded. "Yeah. Some guy in Montpelier, I think."

"And Becky is well?" I asked about Louie's wife.

"Fit as a fiddle. Out doing something every day, taking another evening class over at Lyndon State."

"Didn't they rename it Northern Vermont University?" I said.

"Yeah, yeah. Northern Vermont U-*Lyndon*. Northern Vermont U-*Johnson*. And NVU *online*. Next time you visit, she can tell you all about it. If they're still in business."

The waitress was back with our breakfast, carefully placing the plates on the table in front of us. "Would you like ketchup?" she asked.

"I would, please," I said. She retrieved an upside-down plastic container of Heinz aux tomates from the next table and placed it between us.

"And you, Hanlon. What's happening down here in the metroplex?" He cut the omelette with a fork and tested a small bite.

"Interesting you should ask," I said. "Got a call from a guy about a cold case that's been in the freezer for about forty years."

Louie's eyebrows went up as he chewed his food.

"Technically *not* a cold case, at least as far as I know. Only found out about it last night." I dabbed a piece of toast in the center of one of my eggs and took a bite. He waited for me to go on.

21

"Got a phone call out of the blue. An old guy living in a retirement community up in Williamstown. A friend of his was killed in a hunting accident long time ago, but he doesn't believe that it was an accident."

Louie was now eating like he'd just come off a fast. I took a sip of coffee.

"So I went up to see this codger last night. Seems like a nice enough guy, thoughtful, articulate. Not a flamer. Pretty sharp, in fact, considering that he's in his eighties. *Impeccable* dresser. Maybe tailor-made wardrobe far as I could tell."

"My grandfather," Louie said, "at *ninety-four*, was sharper than half the people I work with. Steel-trap mind."

As we ate, I laid out much of what I had learned from Frank Marino's eight-page essay and the online research. Another thing Louie was good at, much like a shrink, I suspected, was allowing the person talking to keep going. And I did, for several minutes.

When we were finished, he paid for breakfast, we went out to the parking lot and sat in the cab of his crossover pickup, the always shined-up Honda Ridgeline that he treated as though it was going to be a collector's vehicle at an auction someday.

"How are you for time," I said, looking at my watch.

"Good. My meeting's not until eleven. By all means, continue," he said, with just a hint of sarcasm.

Six

After extracting all that I'd learned so far, expressing both curiosity and skepticism, Ragsdale pulled out his phone, touched the screen, swiped twice and tapped the screen again.

"Let me give you a contact. New Hampshire Fish & Game," he said. "Probably makes sense to get your hands on the actual report from the incident."

Naturally it made sense. It had already occurred to me. Louie was just going to help move it along at a faster clip. He handed me his phone. I wrote down the name and phone number for a Lieutenant Heidi Murrough.

Louie pointed at the phone. "Talk to Murrough. She can help cut through any red tape. Use my name when you call."

"Great." I handed the phone back.

We talked for a minute about the possibility of a quick trip down to the south shore of Long Island later in October for a final day or two of striped bass fishing, agreeing that we could decide in couple of weeks subject to the weather forecast and our respective calendars.

"Thanks for breakfast," I said, climbing out of his rig. "I'll let you know how things go."

Before heading home, I spent 15 minutes grocery-shopping at the White River Co Op, then made the short trip back to Quechee. It was one of those spectacular fall mornings with blue sky and a lot of sun, a good excuse to get out with Rocco on a trail that ran through the woods directly behind my house.

At the retirement community in Williamstown, Frank Marino's apartment was small. A single bedroom, bathroom, one closet, a kitchenette, and a tiny dining area next to a 12 x 14 living room.

When he learned that he'd been accepted by the facility, he had been happy to get independent quarters. However, he didn't kid himself. A move to 'assisted living' units next door could happen in a heartbeat. It occurred every day with someone, somewhere.

Rising from the sofa, he got down on both knees to study a map of Greece that he'd unfolded and spread open on the carpet. It was a newer edition showing more detail than an aged geographic design that he'd also spread open.

The older map, dating back to the 1960s, was worn and creased. It had numerous pen markings of different colors with circles hand-drawn around several towns and cities, some on the mainland and others on a couple of the islands.

Now that he was about to engage, or so he hoped, someone to follow the story that had been developing in his mind for years, refreshing his memory of the places he'd once known was crucial.

Whatever time he had left, Marino would make the best of it. He was more fortunate than many.

And he knew it.

Barely shy of five-thousand miles east of Vermont — in an arc from the 44th parallel across the Atlantic and down the middle of the Mediterranean to the 35th parallel — on the island of Crete, another old man lives alone. It is in the coastal harbor village of Matala on the Bay of Messara.

Sitting at an outdoor table of a taverna that he owns, Nikolaos Andreadakis, 79, watched for tourists and locals that he knew would be joining him shortly. Late September, the summer crowds and the buses were gone. The employees at Pithari Taverna could set their watch by the old man's evening ritual during the slower winter months.

Smoking a cigarette and sipping strong black coffee from a small cup, Nikos had reached an age where he frequently re-played memories of his youth growing up in the mountain village of Amari, two hours north of Matala. That's what he was doing at this moment.

As a teenager he first visited the mainland, then went to Athens to live. Other travel opportunities came along. In his late 20s, he went back to Crete and visited Matala to check out the 'hippie lifestyle' that had been widely discussed among friends. Subsequent stays in Athens and travel abroad expanded his horizons.

Inspiration for much of the travel was to 'party'. His first trip to North America was at the invitation of rich American college kids that he'd met on Crete. He spent two weeks with them in and around New York City before returning to Athens. But on a second trip to the US, in the summer of 1980 — he was still a young man not yet 40 — Nikos had been single-mindedly absorbed with a task assigned to him by his uncle.

It was that second journey that proved to be life-changing. Having completed the 'task' and made an immediate return to Greece, a course was set that brought Nikos to this table on this evening, dredging up images and conversations from the past.

His own father had died in his late 40s, one of the reasons Nikos fell under the influence of others, especially his Uncle Hektor. After a hastily arranged marriage to a younger woman in Athens and the subsequent birth of a daughter, Nikos was adrift.

Largely irresponsible, without steady employment and shirking family obligations, Nikos had been encouraged to move back to Crete by his Uncle Hektor.

The purchase of a small restaurant was financed by Hektor. Nikos later expanded it, changed the name, and it became a popular taverna busy ten months of the year. Matala shuts down completely for two months every winter.

More and more tourists found their way to the coastal village. The business thrived. And for more than thirty years,

Nikos worked long hours, smoked too much, but led a relatively contented life.

The birth of a granddaughter in Athens came as a surprise. Long estranged from his wife and daughter, he'd made little effort to keep up with family relationships and events outside the immediate surroundings and the acquaintances that he'd made in this small village.

A change in attitude began to surface in Nikos the first time his daughter and granddaughter came to visit Matala. It had not been a complete reconciliation, but it had initiated annual visits by the two. In more recent years, the granddaughter came alone to spend time with him, visits that both treasured.

Pushing aside old memories, Nikos smoked, sipped the coffee, and thought about his granddaughter now. He felt an urgent need to talk to her.

There were things that he needed to tell her about, things that she needed to know.

Seven

Following a brief, late afternoon phone conversation with Lieutenant Murrough at the New Hampshire Fish & Game Department, I received via email a Right to Know request form to obtain info on the hunting fatality of 1980.

Using Marino's eight-pager *Not An Accident*, I was able to fill in the date and location of Win Callahan's death. In the section labeled 'Information Requested' I typed; All information and reports pertaining to the hunting fatality of Stephen W. Callahan — 11/21/80 in Bethlehem, NH.

To my amazement, the very next morning, my inbox had a short email reply with a PDF attachment; four-pages of a Uniform Hunter Casualty Report Form. It was obvious that it had been copied from an older paper document, date stamped at the bottom — Nov. 28, 1980, a week after the shooting.

Under the heading that recorded the state, county, date, time and description of injuries, and listing the Medical Referee, there were three sections to the first page: SHOOTER, VICTIM and CASUALTY FACTS.

In all, with the appropriate boxes checked and 27 lines to cover pertinent details, it concluded with 'Investigator's Remarks' at the bottom of the page, two short sentences from a Conservation Officer: *Victim was partially obscured by a rise in the field. Shoulders, neck and head only parts of victim visible to shooter.*

The entire second page, running eight paragraphs and maybe 450 words, was a more detailed summary from the same Conservation Officer. I focused on reading this section carefully, then went to the last two pages, a statement written by the SHOOTER.

At the top was the date, time and location (Nov. 22, 1980— 11:30 a.m.—Bethlehem) of the 'Voluntary Statement' and the verbatim Miranda warning:

1. I have the right to remain silent;
2. Anything I say can and will be used against me in a court of law;
3. I have the right to talk to a lawyer for advice before any questioning and to have one with me during questioning;
4. If I cannot afford a lawyer, one will be appointed for me; and
5. If I decide to answer questions now without a lawyer present, I still have the right to stop answering at any time.

What followed, printed in block, all upper case letters, were 22 lines covering the time from when he woke up the morning of the shooting, 4:30, all the way through the time of his phone call to the state police at approximately 7:15. He detailed *everything* that occurred during the two-hours, forty-five minute time period. He signed his name at the bottom of the statement and wrote in the date.

The incident occurred in the small hillside town of Bethlehem in Grafton County, right on the western edge of the White Mountain National Forest — November 21, 1980. The report included a summary of facts as reported by the Fish & Game Conservation Officer who was first on the scene.

Typed, it ran eight paragraphs, listing tagged and secured physical evidence, the time of death declaration by a medical referee, and concluding with a statement that the body had been transported from the hospital in Littleton, to the Mary Hitchcock Memorial Hospital in Hanover for a postmortem examination.

When I'd finished reading the report, I phoned Frank Marino. He had previously mentioned that he could refer me to 'other material'.

"If you access the online archives of the Washington Post," he began, "you will find reporting on the story."

"Did that already," I said. "They have two stories, a short one the day after Callahan was shot and a longer follow-up three days later. I also found a story in the New York Times."

"I have clippings of the Post stories in my files," he said. "I must have read the Times story at some point."

"It doesn't have the extensive detail of Callahan's career as reported by the Post, but the same account of the accident, including the hunter's name . . ."

"Ronald Davis," Marino interrupted.

"The Fish & Game report shows that Davis lived in Massachusetts. But that was a long time ago."

"I have the name in my files," Marino said. "But he was twenty years old as I recall. I was never able to get an address for him."

"In your writing, the fat envelope you gave me, you refer to one of Callahan's 'old colleagues at the NSA'. Is that the same person whose memoir was published two years ago?"

"No, different man," he said. "The memoir was by J.A. Hilling. His son found the manuscript after Hilling died. I have a copy."

"So, the 'lavish helpings' you mention that support your speculation, they came from Hilling?"

"No again. That was from another man who worked closely with Win at the end of his tenure in DC. He was convinced the shooting was not an accident."

"Sorry. I'm getting confused here. The other man . . ."

"John Willard," he said. "He's been dead for about 20 years now."

I had this vision of a line of old guys stumbling off a cliff, Frank Marino just sitting there in a recliner watching them go.

"Okay. I think you're gonna have to help me sort some of that out," I said. "Maybe let me borrow the Hilling memoir."

"Mister Hanlon, you are starting to sound *interested*. Does this mean that you're prepared to help?"

"I'm certainly willing to nose it along some. *But,* considering that it is a closed incident, at least as far as law enforcement in New Hampshire is concerned, I'm a bit skeptical. Forty years is a long time."

"A long time, indeed," he said. "However, I once read about a cold case of a kidnapping and murder in Illinois that took more than 50 years to solve."

I also knew there were cases all over the country that went unsolved, as well as instances where new information surfaced, especially with DNA evidence, and occasions where imprisoned people were set free and the real perpetrators never found.

"How about I take a run up and get the Hilling book from you?" I said.

"That would be fine. When did you have in mind?"

Eight

A very close friend and next-door neighbor, Virginia Jackson, faculty member at the Vermont Law School just up the road in South Royalton — same direction as Williamstown — accepted my invitation for a leisurely foliage drive, roadside picnic lunch and a brief stop to fetch the J.A. Hilling memoir from Frank Marino.

Virginia bought sandwiches, a salad, chips, and soft drinks. She was waiting out in front of RB's Delicatessen. Rocco was in the backseat and gave her a quick sniff, then a lick. She scratched his ears and gave him a nuzzle.

I crossed the White River and drove north, first through the town of Bethel, then Randolph, and eventually stopped just outside the village at a pull over with a picnic table. It was a nice spot situated on the bank along the Third Branch.

"The water looks beautiful," Virginia said. "Thank you for getting me out of the office." She was unpacking sandwiches and placing the food and drinks on the table.

Rocco raced to the edge of the river and within seconds was standing in water up to his chest, lapping away. I hoped that a fish might leap and give him a thrill.

"You have a day like this, you *better* find an excuse to get outside."

"Absolutely," she said.

"Not a lot of traffic yet," I added. "This weekend, lookout. It'll be bumper to bumper through the valley and over on Route 100. A bunch of people have been cooped up for more than a year."

"Yeah. When I lived in New York, I must have known a hundred different people who made a point of driving to Vermont every fall just for the leaves."

We took our time eating, talking about the smaller number of students at the VLS campus and online classes available; all the strangeness with the imposed Covid 19 restrictions; and discussed only a little bit of the nastiness in the current national political scene. We agreed that some of the blatantly partisan characters and their routine, self-serving pronouncements had become an embarrassment.

After small bites of the sandwiches given to him away from the table, Rocco had stretched out and closed his eyes. In that position, tail curled under his hind legs, he was over three feet long. The sun on his reddish fur made him look more like an Irish Setter than a Golden Retriever.

"The stop we're gonna make in Williamstown," I said. "There's an old guy who has asked for a little help in finding, what *he says*, is the 'real story' in the death of a friend 40 years ago. He has a book that apparently supports his belief that the hunting accident that killed the friend was not an accident."

Virginia told me a story about a cousin of her late husband who had been killed in a hunting accident back in the 60s, adding that the friend who shot him "never really got over the incident."

Then I recounted an incident from my youth when a kid I knew had been blinded as the result of a shotgun misfiring when he was hunting with friends.

"Maybe we can find something more pleasant to talk about," she said, clearing the table, putting our trash into a small canvas tote bag.

As soon as I got up, Rocco was back on his feet and alert.

"How about I give you an update on Ragsdale?" I said. "He's going through all kinds of contortions trying to find ways *not* to completely retire."

"Can't say that I blame him," she said. "If you're lucky enough to have good health , stay active. They don't have grandchildren or parents to take care of?"

"Correct. Becky wants to travel. Louie doesn't seem quite ready to sign on to that plan."

In the car we kept the conversation going, circling back around to advantages and disadvantages of online classes, and the prospects of how education at all levels was changing as a result of the pandemic and its impact on schools.

The side route I took eventually got us to I-89, then a 20-minute drive to Williamstown. The dashboard clock showed

2:11. We would be very close to the 2:30 ETA that I'd given Frank Marino.

Nine

Virginia stayed in the car with Rocco while I went to Marino's apartment. A few seconds after I knocked, he opened the door. Reading glasses were on a waxed cord string hanging around his neck and he was holding a book in his left hand.

"Mister Hanlon do come in," he said. "You are indeed punctual."

"Not always," I said, looking at my watch: two-twenty-eight. "Just by accident this time."

"Tsk, tsk," he said. "When someone offers you a compliment, accept it with a smile." He'd turned and made his way back to an easy chair on the other side of the small living room. I followed.

On the floor next to the chair was another book and what looked like a couple of folded maps. He reached down, got the book and handed it to me.

"Please, have a seat," he said, gesturing to a sofa.

"Thank you, but I can't stay. I have a friend waiting in the car. She has to get back to her office."

His eyebrows went up. "Of course. I won't keep you, then." He pointed at the book that he'd given me. "A lot of interesting reading there. Much of it sour grapes, I'm afraid. I knew Hilling. He was an unhappy man." He fluttered his right hand again and added, "I've marked the section where he talks about a conversation with Win not long before he died."

I looked at the book, powder blue paperback cover. *Need to Know: My Life Keeping Secrets* by J.A. Hilling in burgundy type across the cover. It looked like an Annual Report one might expect to find in the business reference section of a library. A yellow tab protruded from one of the pages.

"I'll start reading this evening. By the way, could we drop the 'Mister Hanlon' and just go with Michael?" I added. "You know the old joke — that was my *father's* name."

Marino nodded. "Call me when you are ready to discuss more," he said. "I'm not going anywhere."

Back in South Royalton, with a light kiss to my cheek and one for Rocco on his nose, Virginia unhitched her seat belt and got out of the car.

"Nice to see you, stranger," she said. "That was fun."

"*Yeah?* Maybe you can come along when we do recycling on Saturday. That'll blow your socks off."

She gave me a look and a shake of the head, then started across the street to where her office was located on the second floor of a nineteenth century clapboard building.

"Thanks for the lunch," I yelled.

She gave a backward wave and kept walking.

I punched up 96.5 for Royalton Community Radio, a low power FM station with limited range but good, eclectic programming. Back Roads, Bluegrass and Beyond was the program of the moment. The track just finishing was the Dry Branch Fire Squad and their version of *Golden Ring*. Next up, *Love at the Five and Dime* by Nanci Griffith. Pretty good stuff.

No phone messages when we got home. Rocco was content to again stretch out in the sun while I poured a glass of apple cider. Settling into a deck chair I started reading *Need to Know*. First, I turned to the page near the end that Frank Marino had flagged with a yellow sticky note.

It began, "Win Callahan was a man who didn't particularly care for me and I was not crazy about him. He was at NSA — sometimes FBI — during a long run in DC and a lot of time in Europe. Before he retired, he came by to make a peace offering for some long ago slight. I barely recalled the episode.

"We drank a little port and I mostly listened," Hilling wrote. "Callahan seemed to be in the mood to offer a long, rambling apology for things that I either previously had not been aware of or had long ago purged from my memory.

"The apology wasn't aimed directly at me, more of a blanket confession that ended with him rolling out the old truism,

39

'We have to *do* what we have to do.' In hindsight, it was all a little puzzling."

"Then he died in that hunting incident up in New Hampshire," Hilling wrote. "I remembered another thing that Callahan dropped toward the end of his monologue. He said something to the effect of, 'One of these days you will read about my death in some form of an accident. *Don't* believe it for a minute.'"

Rereading the last paragraph, I tried to imagine two old guys sitting in a dark office, speaking in hushed tones. And sipping port, no less.

Flipping to the front of Hilling's book, I read the foreword written by his son. It was succinct to the point of suggesting emotional detachment between the two men. There was an obituary style accounting of the author's birth and death dates, a one sentence reference to a career in 'intelligence work,' followed by the statement, 'This is my father's story as he wrote it in the year before he died. It has been edited for punctuation and spelling. I have not changed a word.'

The title page of the book showed that it had been privately published in 2018, no indication by *whom* or where. Hilling's son, or the unknown editor, did declare a copyright in the author's name.

No table of contents, no chapter titles, just numbers. The story opened with the senior Hilling reminiscing about career choices that he had considered as a young man before settling into 'Global Intelligence work.'

He wrote, "Like most idealistic young men at the time — this was the early 1950s — for those who aspired to a career in government service, I was an eager beaver. After initial training, we started out as entry level Staff Operations Officers. I was one of the lucky ones who got an overseas assignment right out of the gate."

Describing his first posting in Germany, he wrote several pages about things that he learned, mistakes made — none of them major — and how he met the woman who would become his first wife, Miriam. At that early spot of the narrative he made a point of stating that there would be 'very little of a personal nature' in this book.

After finishing the first chapter, which went on for 17 pages, I marked my spot with a paper clip and turned to the end to see how long it was: 297 pages, plus three pages of endnotes and attributions.

Okay, I can do this. A bit of a slog maybe, certainly not Robert Ludlum or Daniel Silva, but I can at least skim through it.

Ten

The 'SHOOTER' was not *now* and had never meant to be a killer. In fact, having missed military training as a young man — the US Selective Service draft lotteries ended when he was only sixteen — his interest in target shooting came from the enthusiasm of a high school friend who had inherited a collection of firearms.

On weekends during the late 70s, when other teenagers were going to malls, or driving an hour to learn about skydiving at a small airport, or participating in 'normal' outdoor activities and team sports, two young men from a Boston suburb instead drove to a farm in New Hampshire where they would blast through boxes of shells.

Both of them became proficient at hitting a variety of targets.

In addition to enthusiasm, the shooter's friend had more pocket money than possibly the rest of their entire high school class combined. The kid was flat-out rich. And he didn't give a shit what others thought about that, or much of anything else.

They had no burning interest in girls, but they weren't fags. The term 'gay' was still working its way into mainstream vocabulary. It was years later when the friend, aka 'the rich kid', began to spend more time with women. Eventually, it pretty much did him in. He was taken to the cleaners by a vindictive ex-wife. Or that was *his* spin. Others, including the ex, may have had a different take on who did what and why.

But the shooter — a prophetic moniker bestowed on him by the rich kid — *almost* had a normal life. If a vocational evaluator were to use the employment record of the shooter as offering a good example of job stability and remuneration, the line was unswerving. A reliable, financially prudent industrial manufacturing worker for nearly 40 years, he reflected the best traits of a blue-collar work ethic.

Now, at 61, he was living on a modest pension and anxious to make changes in his life.

Somewhat different, to the point of being ironic, Win Callahan had come to disdain firearms of all types. This despite his own military training and a subsequent career in the 'spook' business.

Shortly before his retirement, Callahan had conveyed his views on the subject in a lengthy memorandum circulated to a select group of colleagues. A few thought it nothing more than a rant from an 'old man about to hang it up.'

The gist of Callahan's missive boiled down to the easy access and totally inadequate training related to the *responsibilities* of owning and using a gun of any type. For good measure, he had included a few paragraphs citing statistics and the excessive profits reaped by the firearm industry. He was not a fan.

If read today, 40 years after it came off the electric typewriter in his Washington office, Callahan's memorandum might be considered prescient, even by some who had so easily dismissed it at the time.

But just like Callahan, most of those guys were dead, too.

So, that memo never went far, before or after November 21, 1980. It is *possible* that someone from within the US Intelligence community gave it another look. The *public* never heard about it. The *media* never carried any reporting on it. And the New Hampshire Fish and Game Department never saw it, for sure.

Only one NSA associate saw fit to mention it in his memoir, written prior to his own demise, and privately published.

Charles Hilling of Tacoma Park, Maryland, found an editor for his father's unfinished memoir. It was published under the title, *Need to Know: My Life Keeping Secrets*. To date, the book has had limited circulation and no professional reviews. Copies have made it into the hands of individuals on a short list composed by the author before he died.

Hilling, the son, still anticipates some push back from agencies of the US Government. How much of the material in the book might be classified is uncertain, but he knew that his father was bitter about the way he and others were treated at the end of their careers. So far, no calls from the Feds.

Out of 300 pages from the memoir, only one page addresses a conversation the author had with Stephen 'Win' Callahan. It was in August of 1980, shortly before Callahan's retirement. Toward the end of the manuscript there is also reference to the 'questionable circumstances in the death of Win Callahan and the likelihood that additional information will come to light at some future date.'

Eleven

I was beginning to nod off. My phone played the opening of *Once in a Lifetime*, the current ringtone downloaded on a whim. I placed the Hilling memoir on the deck next to my feet and reached for the phone.

The screen showed Ragsdale, L.J.

Huh. He's using his 'domestic' smartphone, not one of the undercover androids that only tells me that a 'wireless caller' is at the other end.

"Let me guess," I answered, "You're calling to tell me that Becky has booked an Alaskan cruise and that you can't wait to start packing."

"Better than that. *She* is going to Arizona to help a cousin get settled in a new house," he said.

"And you are *not* going, I take it."

"You take it correctly, Kemosabe."

"How'd you wiggle out of it?" I said.

"*She* wiggled me out on her own. Said that I would be bored when I wasn't getting in the way. Said they could manage very well without me, thank you."

"D'you give her a hug for such clever forethought?"

"Not yet," he said. "I did volunteer to drive her to the airport."

"When's she going?"

"Not for a couple of weeks. But . . . she *needs* this trip. Been cooped up for months. And might slow down all the chatter about 'other places' we could go."

"Brother Ragsdale, better stay on top of it. Before you know, she's gonna be taking trips without you, tagging along with her quilting pals and leaving you back on the farm."

"Wouldn't that be just *so-o-o* traumatic?" he said.

Like an overzealous and somewhat annoying telemarketing survey caller, Louie, predictably, launched into questions about where I was with the 'new project'.

'Did you get what you needed from New Hampshire Fish & Game? Anything there? You really *believe* this old bird's story that it wasn't an accident? What's next? You know, some who originally worked that case are probably out hunting the big woods in the sky by now.'

"I'm making a list," I lied. It was my intention to start with a few notes and questions. But, so far, nothing on the yellow pad in the kitchen.

"Marino loaned me a book by an old spy guy," I said. "A memoir published a two years ago, shortly after the man died. There's a very brief reference in the middle of the book about a conversation the guy had with Callahan. He *claims* that Callahan alluded to future reports of his own death as 'a result of some accident' and went on to say don't believe it."

"C'mon, Hanlon. Half those guys — if they did any heavy lifting at all — gotta have *somebody* out there hoping they get whacked," Louie said. "And the *other* half, when they're sober, probably afraid to sleep without a night light."

"Bit of a broad brush you're painting with there, Jules," I said.

"Maybe. But more than a few of my old Army buddies went in that direction. I've heard *their* stories. I can only imagine what it's like with the generation from back in the so-called 'cold war' era. Who knows how many are still around?"

"Roger that. Marino's 85. And he was a young apprentice to Callahan's bunch."

Louie chuckled. "Geez Louise. You watch some of these old movie guys, moving *real-l-l-y* slow. Same thing. Spooks may *think* they still have it, but you put a young gun on 'em, game's up."

"So, is that Captain Ragsdale's current take, official like? A young guy, 40 years-ago, 'accidentally' dropped an old guy out in the woods. With a single shot. And maybe the young one was another spook?" I waited for his reply.

"I think that's *why* your friend over there at 'retirement village' called you in the first place, yes? *Go find out.* Get the 'real story'."

"That's exactly what he said, the 'real story'."

48

"I know," Louie said. "You already told me that."

"It's been a thrill visiting with you."

"The pleasure's all mine. Let me know if I need to watch Channel 3 news, huh?"

Twelve

Late morning on Thursday I concluded that there had been a series of events over a period of years, offering sufficient fragments of information — scant as they might be — regarding people that I'd read about so far, that did warrant more of my time and effort. *Let's see where this goes.*

One thought noodling around in the back of my mind since the first meeting with Frank Marino, was that he already had his idea of how this should be pursued.

Before calling him, I needed to think about what terms would be in play. Specifically, how we would handle my compensation. Having danced around the edges of 'PI' type work for a few years now, terms with clients had been either a flat fee plus expenses, or, more often, a per diem arrangement, with a minimum amount set, plus travel and any out of the ordinary expenses.

My preference was the daily rate, one-thousand-dollars, minimum set at three days. Might not be three consecutive days, but I always told prospective clients that if it wasn't working, either party could say so and we would go our separate ways. And for that reason, fifteen hundred was the deposit required to get it in gear.

"Sorry I missed your call," Marino's voice said, via a phone answering device. "Please leave a brief message and I will return your call before the next full moon."

Beep.

"That gives you nearly a month," I said, knowing the moon had been full three nights ago. "Frank, it's Michael Hanlon. *Yes*, I am prepared to give this a run. Let me know when I can come back up. We can decide what the next step should be." Click.

Thursdays. For those fortunate enough to have a place to live — and who do their own housework — I wonder how many designate *Thursday* as their cleaning day? Sweep the kitchen, clean the bathroom, vacuum the living room and bedrooms, bag up trash and recyclables, do the laundry.

Domestic multi-tasking. *Somebody call Martha Stewart.*

While swapping a load of wet towels and sheets to the dryer, entertaining mundane thoughts about who does what on which day of the week, I recalled that back in my married days, as a young couple, we shared the household chores.

As a kid, it had been my grandmother, my mother and my sister who initially roped me into daily washing the dishes routine. They later introduced me to ironing my own clothes.

These habits turned out to be a real hit with my former wife, who was more than happy to handle shopping and most of the cooking.

Coming back up the steps into the kitchen, I laughed at a memory of some kids in junior high school who every week, proclaimed that if boys wore anything *green* on Thursday, it signified that they were queers. *Where did that nonsense start?* I never found out if kids at other schools prattled the same dumb notion. This was before the advent of social media.

My friend Virginia is older than I am. She grew up here in Vermont, 500 miles from central Pennsylvania and my hometown. I went to the pad next to my kitchen phone and made a note to ask her about 'green on Thursday'.

No blinking light, no new messages on the phone. Good.

"Rocco, time for a good pee," I said.

He rose slowly and stretched. Taking two biscuits from the box under the sink, I snapped on his 'stay alert' collar so he wouldn't try to head for the woods, gave him a biscuit and let him go out. He always expected the second biscuit when he came back to the door.

"Lucky the collar's not green," I said. He ambled off the deck, tail and ears up. Gender didn't always seem to be the deciding factor when some dogs felt the urge to go for a little humping.

The silence didn't last long. The landline phone on the counter began to chirp, incoming ID showed that it was the same number that I'd called earlier, Frank Marino.

Thirteen

On the island of Crete, it was coming up on ten o'clock. The last few diners of the evening at *Pithari Taverna* were clearing out, much earlier than was the norm on busy nights when lots of people are around.

Nikos Andreadakis was having his last cigarette of the day, a Superior Virginia short, manufactured by George Karelias and Sons of Kalamata. Sixty-years of addiction and he'd recently cut his two-pack-a-day habit down to just one pack, 20 smokes. And they were *filtered*, unlike the cigarettes of his youth.

His granddaughter, Melissa, nagged at him about the smoking. When he spent any time in her company, he could force himself to go more than an hour without a cigarette, as he had done for most of the day on a visit to The Holy Monastery of Preveli.

It was on that excursion, a drive north from Matala, when Melissa had informed him that she was about to make her first trip to the US. Observing her enthusiasm brought back long-ago memories, not all of them good.

Until recently, Andreadakis had managed most of his life avoiding ruminations of 'things done in another time.' A change in thinking accelerated on that afternoon of the trip to Preveli. A visit to the chapel there had provoked an onset of daily memory flashes — and recurring dreams — about the secret task handled for his uncle on Nikos' visit to the US 40 years ago.

A meeting with a Greek living in the US, phone calls that led to another hastily scheduled meeting, a bundle of US currency, a newspaper clipping to take back to Greece confirming the 'task completed.'

Now, Andreadakis found himself viewing the decades-old scenes with a clearer focus each time the reel played in his mind.

It had become a nightly occurrence. And very unsettling.

A two-generation age differential can make it difficult for many people to relate to life experiences. Melissa Lambros, at 21, had cleared that hurdle when she was a teenager.

'Papou' was the first name she used in addressing her grandfather. Then at 14, she began calling him 'Papouli'. Five years running — travelling from her home in Athens — the annual spring and summer trips to Crete and spending time in Matala had brought them closer as Melissa grew older.

Preparing for her trip to America she had a fear that Papouli might not be here when she returned. She wanted to spend as much time with him as possible. The recent outing to the historical Monastery had been her idea.

Two summers before, Papouli had told her about the important role the monastery had played in the Battle of Crete in the early days of World War II, when he was an infant. The stories he told came down from his own grandfather.

After visiting the main chapel at Preveli, while they had sat on a stone bench in the courtyard, she listened again to her grandfather tell how the monks and local citizens helped to feed and hide stranded allied soldiers from an invading German army.

At one point while he was telling the story, Papouli went silent. He remained that way for several minutes. Melissa feared that he'd had a stroke.

When he finally resumed talking, the words came more slowly, with long pauses. The old man's eyes were teared-up throughout the afternoon and into the evening. Back at the taverna, each time she asked what he was thinking, her grandfather would close his eyes, bow his head slightly and run a hand through his short, gray hair. But he did not tell her more.

In a conversation with her mother, she learned that Papouli had called twice in the last week to ask when Melissa was coming back to Crete. That surprised her as she was certain that she'd told him.

She hadn't called her grandfather in days but now felt that she had to before going abroad. It was urgent that she speak with him.

Fourteen

Marino and I talked for a few minutes and agreed that I would swing back to his apartment tomorrow, Friday, and that we would pin down the arrangement. I told him that the next steps I had in mind would dictate the calendar, and then we could establish a preliminary timeline to see if I could actually make any progress.

What I *didn't say* was "sufficient progress" that might warrant staying with his 'project'. No sense wasting anybody's time or money; I had little interest in being a research assistant.

I'd barely put the phone down and was going to the door to call Rocco when I spotted Virginia coming up the road, Rocco in front of her doing a circling around, tail-wagging routine that showed how much he liked attention. He would bolt ahead a few yards, then double-back to make sure that she was still with him.

How in the hell did he get over to her property?

The pet containment system strung around my land had always worked, i.e. kept him contained. The special collar emits first an audible signal, then a mild shock if he goes through the barrier. It's really not invisible — being stretched along the perimeter under leaves and branches — with little blue flags every few yards to remind him of the boundary. To my knowledge, he'd never gotten through before.

"Handsome boy here seems to have found an opening," Virginia said, coming up the steps behind him onto the deck. Rocco was now circling around me as if to indicate, 'Is this great or what?' No sign that he felt any remorse, or that he'd recently been juiced by the system.

I raised my hands skyward and looked down at him. Then I checked to be sure that he was still wearing the red collar. He was.

"What's the story, Rockethead?" I looked at Virginia. "You didn't call him over?"

"I did not. I was in the kitchen, he came to the back door," she said, a hand now on top of his head. "At first, I thought it was a squirrel. Too big for a *squirrel*," she added, bending over to take his ears and rub noses with him.

"He's never done that," I said. "How did he get *through*? You didn't hear him yelp from a shock?"

She was shaking her head and continued to ruffle the fur around his neck.

"Inside, hot dog," I held the door open. He went into the kitchen and straight for the water bowl.

"Want a beer?" I said.

"Sure."

"Hang on a second. We can sit out here. Let's try to figure this out," I said.

Opening two bottles of Landshark and getting a bag of pretzels from the cupboard above the fridge, I went back outside. Rocco followed me and positioned himself at Virginia's feet.

"That's about six-hundred yards of wire," I said, waving out toward the edge of the trees along the backyard. "It's buried in a couple of spots, but mostly above ground."

She took a sip of beer, looked at Rocco, then at me. "Guess you will have to retrace where the wire is and see if there's a break. You don't have flags everywhere."

"Nah," I said. "The guy who installed it and helped me train Bozo here, he ran out of flags, so had to get strategic. The flags are just to keep him alert. Until now, seemed to have worked fine. Maybe I need to check the control in the garage. If there's a break in the wire, a light will show that."

By the time we finished our beer, having yakked about canine behavior and the variety of wild animals inhabiting the local forest, Rocco was sound asleep, occasionally moving his paws in a dream of who knows what.

Virginia stood, stretched and twisted her upper torso left, then right. She bent at the waist, touched her toes and held the position for a few seconds.

Pay attention here, Hanlon.

When she'd finished the routine, she knelt-down and scratched Rocco's ears again. The eyes opened but he made no move to get up, clearly happy to be right where he was.

"I was peeling apples for a pie when he came to the door," she said, looking up at me but still giving the affection to Rocco. "Would you like to come over later when it comes out of the oven?"

"You have ice cream?"

"Yes, but some of us prefer freshly baked apple pie without extra calories. And the *fat*."

"Will you show me yoga positions after the pie?" I said, adding, "I kinda' like that cat cow pose. Or the squat palm press maneuver."

She looked at me, then at her watch.

"We'll see. How about eight-thirty?"

Fifteen

US Intelligence services have expanded and evolved over more than a century. There are not many people who know that better than Frank Marino.

In conversations with Hanlon, he'd briefly mentioned having 'worked with various government agencies' in Washington, DC and in the tidewater area of Virginia — dating back from the days of the Eisenhower administration in the 50s, up to and including time in the second Bush presidency fifteen years ago — plus occasional consulting during the first term of the Obama administration.

Like many working within the intelligence community, conversations with anyone *outside* that community tended to be anchored in vagueness.

Certainly, older veterans of government service generally were not shy about letting on when they recognized a name or had previously worked with an individual. They might even share an amusing anecdote or two about such a person. But offering *specifics* on dates, duties, locations, or other details, that was a 'no go' area left entirely to the listener's imagination.

Now, Marino was going to have to open up just a bit more with Hanlon and make his best case.

Like an old prospector from the storied days of searching for gold, Marino had cached bits of information he'd found over four decades of trying to prove or disprove that Win Callahan's death was a 'hunting accident.'

A recent television series that he had watched looked back at the 1980's professional basketball rivalry between the Boston Celtics and the Los Angeles Lakers. Marino was amused by the hyperbole of the LA owner in promoting his team, spouting bluster that reminded him of Michael Keaton's role in the film *Beetlejuice*.

"Showtime," he said to himself.

Placing a large paperclip on some faded newspaper articles, Marino shoved them back into a pressboard file folder, wrapped the security cord around twice and tied it closed. He was ready for Hanlon's next visit.

'**Golden handcuffs**' was one view held by cynics who had worked for the Central Intelligence Agency, a reference to their perception of the pension plan that made it difficult for one to retire at a date of one's choosing.

An unnamed Senior Operations officer in DC opined that the income *might* be adequate, but the uncertainty of future politics could threaten a cut in benefits. It was not an issue for Marino. Never mind that few people stayed on the job into their late 70s and still received a paycheck.

A careful, thoughtful, frugal man, from the day he turned twenty-one, and likely going back to his teens when he had a daily paper route and sold wreaths every Christmas season, he salted away the bulk of his earnings. Always.

Remaining a bachelor — of the heterosexual variety — probably helped. He was spared the normal ongoing expenses faced by most families. Not once in his life had he made a tuition payment, nor sent a check to a divorce attorney.

Frugal, yes. Cheap, no.

Marino had several charitable organizations that he supported in amounts well above biblical tithing. During the last twenty-five years, he'd spent no small sum on personal travel. But it was beginning to wind down and he knew it.

The move to Vermont had adjusted his focus. While he enjoyed, for the most part, 'good health' today, the calendar was not in his favor. Numerous friends, acquaintances and former colleagues were fine when they went to bed, only to awake and discover a serious malady the next day.

Looking out a window above the sink in his tiny kitchen, watching for two chipmunks that played chase every morning, he mumbled to himself, "You're either wrong, or you are right. Just get it done."

At this late stage, Hanlon was his best hope.

Sixteen

Living comfortably is a relative term. A quarter of a century younger than Frank Marino, 'The Shooter' was getting by with a meager retirement income derived from his manufacturing job. He was not yet eligible for a monthly Social Security check.

Cash from the occasional sale of firearms remaining in his possession had provided supplemental income. Unlike the old high school pal who introduced him to shooting, these guns were not inherited. They came from years of purchases and trading, a couple before 1980, but most had been acquired as he got older.

All in all, the cache of more than 30 rifles and shotguns included a few prized collectibles, some of which he knew would command top dollar.

There are gun enthusiasts who will pay a quarter-of-a-million dollars and higher, for custom-made, perfectly crafted firearms. While none of those were in *this* collection, he did own some that could bring ten to fifteen thousand dollars each and one, with custom engraving, that could bring twenty-five thousand.

Rarely did he fire any of the guns. After he'd lost interest in shooting, either targets or wildlife, he kept them clean and locked away. These days he spent most afternoons and evenings in a tidy woodworking shop in his basement.

The shooter's live-in companion, a woman ten years younger than himself, knew nothing of the long-ago incident up in the woods of the North Country. Yes, his late wife had known some of the story, but it was never discussed. A cancer victim in her 50's, she'd gone to her grave *not* knowing the truth behind what had really happened 'back then'.

It was information best not shared or re-examined. It was over. A long-ago story not fully recorded anywhere.

On average, there are just shy of one-hundred gun shows every week in the US. Many of these events are held in smaller towns and might draw a couple thousand people on a weekend.

Smaller shows could have a hundred or so dealers set up in a gymnasium or a civic arena. Larger venues, hosting upwards of seven hundred dealers, could draw tens-of-thousands of people over a two-day period. The largest gun trade event in the country is the annual SHOT Show held every January in Las Vegas. In recent years, it has drawn 60,000-plus attendees.

Sell 'em all, or sell a few?

The shooter had contemplated this numerous times. While he had not explored either option in much depth, he knew that there were several gun shows scheduled around the Northeast between now and Christmas. One event slated for mid-November was to be held at the Shriner's Auditorium in Wilmington, Massachusetts, a twenty-minute drive from his home.

There had been lot in the news over the past few years about selling and buying guns. He would need to get up-to-speed and talk with one of the more experienced dealers. He recalled that a few of those guys sometimes functioned as a middleman, putting the seller in contact with a buyer, then taking a percentage of the purchase price.

The few sales that he had handled himself to other small-time collectors had been of guns that were similar to another weapon that he already owned. One firearm he had resisted parting with was a Winchester Model 70 rifle. It was listed in that 40-year-old Uniform Hunter Casualty Report Form in New Hampshire.

He was uncertain if that would cause a problem in a potential sale.

Seventeen

Louie Ragsdale had been considering retirement going on five years now. Each time he got closer to pulling the cord, it seemed as though some new assignment was so vital that his superiors, as well as some other undercover cops, felt that the job of the moment really needed Ragsdale's participation.

'Packing it in' had been the topic of an ongoing discussion — once or twice an extended, intense debate — with his wife Becky. But now he was ready. He knew it, his immediate supervisor knew it, and quite possibly a few of the characters that he had arrested knew it.

Having the good sense to take Becky out for dinner, Louie had been prepping himself for a couple of days on just how to make his announcement sound convincing.

In an attempt not to prematurely reveal his decision, he'd told Becky that he wanted to talk about Hanlon and it might be nice if they ate out this evening.

"He's going to marry Virginia," she said. To which Louie rolled his eyes and smirked.

"That's *exactly* it. How did you know?"

"Now you're being a smartass."

"Hanlon's gonna get married again about the same time I take up quilting," he said.

"You don't know that."

"Yes, I think I *do* know that. Course, I could be wrong. Happened once before."

"Where do you want to go?" she said.

"Nova Scotia. The salmon rivers are open until mid-October. Maybe call John and meet him on Long Island for stripers . . ."

"For dinner. Where?"

"How about The Scale House over in Hardwick?"

"What time? Do we need a reservation?"

He shook his head. "I doubt it, but I'll call. Seven o'clock?"

"Okay. I have to put some fabric together for tomorrow's quilting group, but I can be ready by 6:30."

The restaurant was nearly full when they arrived. Some wore face masks. Good thing that he had called ahead, or they might have been stuck at the bar for a while.

Once they were seated, Becky ordered a glass of Pinot Grigio. Louie asked for a pint of von Trapp Lager.

"And could we have two shrimp cocktails to start?" Louie asked the server.

Becky tried not to show surprise at her husband's initiative.

As soon as the waitress was gone, Louie raised his butt enough to allow him to reposition his chair, got comfortable, then propped his elbows on the table and clasped his hands together under his chin. And stared at his wife.

"What?" she said, grinning.

Stretching the silence for as long as he could, like five whole seconds, he took in a deep breath and reached for Becky's hand. Her smile gave way to a look of puzzled concern.

"I'm done, January 1st. That's it. Already told 'em. No going back this time."

Becky knew that this wasn't like previous occasions. From the look in his eyes and the tone of voice, she realized that Louie was absolutely serious. She squeezed his hand.

The waitress returned with the drinks, carefully positioning them on the table.

"The shrimp cocktail will be out in just a sec," she said. "Do you need time to decide on your selection?" Both menus were still on the table where she'd placed them two minutes earlier. "I can tell you about this evening's specials."

"Thank you. When you bring the shrimp," Becky said.

Their leisurely paced dinner was about to pass the two-hour mark. Becky was still working on the house-made Herbed Fettuccine, while Louie had completed another Clean Plate Ranger performance with the fried Fisherman's Platter.

The rhythm of the conversation had flowed to match the consumption of their meal, allowing the food to set the pace.

There were stories about Louie's days as a local cop, colleagues long gone, people they'd known who had moved away. They shared two different toasts in tribute to both the pending retirement and to so many memories of the early days of their marriage.

Louie took a sip of wine and put his almost empty glass back on the table.

"You've heard me talk about the old radio guys, Bob and Ray," he said.

"Of course. Bob was the father of the actor Chris Elliott."

"Yep. Anyway, they had one routine," he said, "about . . . the . . . Slow . . . Talkers . . . of . . . America." Now he laughed out loud, then added, "We could be the . . . Slow . . . Eaters . . . of . . ."

"The Northeast Kingdom," Becky finished the sentence.

"Nah. I was gonna say . . . *all* . . . of . . . Vermont."

They were still laughing when the waitress came to ask about dessert.

Sharing an amazing bread pudding and sipping decaf coffee, Becky, having allowed Louie to guide much of the discussion to this point, decided that she had at least *two* questions for her husband.

"January 1*st* is still more than two months away," she began. "What is your plan between now and then?"

"That's the first piece of good news," Louie said. "Starting next week, I have 30-days minimum, with nothing to do. No office time, no trips down to Albany, no road rage out chasing bad news clowns who are selling drugs. Zip!"

"So, you're going to be home? *Then* what? What happens after 30 days?"

"Sometime mid-November, I agreed to help with a few training sessions. Not sure where yet, probably just in Vermont and New Hampshire. Maybe a couple of days in Albany. *Whatever* we come up with, it'll all be finished before Christmas."

Becky let that information settle in and took a sip of her coffee.

"Okay," she resumed, pausing to laugh and shake her head, "we have talked about this *so often* in the past, you will be able to stay home, *fulltime*, for about three days." She stared at him. "Now that you are 'pulling the cord' as you say, what do you think you are going to do next? And please, Louie, be serious."

"Serious, huh?"

"Just like your mother taught you. Pretend you're in Sunday School."

The smirk appeared in the same way another person might blink their eyes.

"We'll see," Louie began, shrugging his shoulders and holding his hands up. "No shortage of things that need attention at home. *You* know that. Honestly, I can imagine, at this point, doing *absolutely nothing* before next spring or summer."

Becky watched him, not fully convinced, but not fully disbelieving, either.

"You are lucky to have good health," she said. "I know you've scaled back over the past two years, but probably not a good idea to go from 65 miles an hour down to zero."

"Not gonna happen," Louie said.

"I know. But we've known too many people who haven't been as fortunate. Retire one month, discover some major illness the next, dead six months later."

"By the way, one of the benefits of this Task Force; I get a full physical before I walk out the door."

"Good."

"You know that John's got eighty-seven different projects he wants help with in North Carolina. We could drive down, hang out for a couple of weeks."

"If we do that," Becky said, "better to think about March."

"Sure. That can work."

"Have you told Michael?" she said.

"About January 1st?"

Becky nodded. "Yes, that you are really doing this."

"We had breakfast last week when I drove down to Lebanon. I told him that I was going to visit with an old acquaintance who now works at Dartmouth-Hitchcock, maybe explore future employment opportunities there."

"You mean *part-time* opportunities? Future as in *a year from now*, right?"

"Right. Nothing immediate," he said.

"But you didn't tell Michael that you will finish up the end of December."

Louie shook his head. "I did not."

"Don't you think that you should tell him?"

"I thought I'd wait until after their engagement announcement."

Eighteen

When Melissa called her grandfather, it was a few minutes after midnight in Virginia, where she was visiting. The time difference made it a little after 7:00 in the morning in Greece.

"Papouli, it's Melissa." She knew that he would be drinking coffee and reading the newspaper.

"You are back in Athens?" he said.

"No. I am with my friend Emma. We are at her home, it is very close to Washington, DC. She lives in Richmond. Do you know where that is?"

"I did not go there," he said.

"It is beautiful. She lives on a horse . . ." With a slight delay in the phone transmission, he talked over her.

"When are you coming back?"

"We will be in Athens one week from tomorrow. October 20th. Don't you remember? We talked about when I could see you again."

"Yes. I want you to come to Matala. Can you do that?" he said.

"I can. Emma will come with me. Would that be OK?"

Nikos needed to speak with his granddaughter privately. He didn't want to do it on a mobile phone. He'd read stories about phones being tracked and calls monitored. It was something that he believed was likely with the Greek government, perhaps with assistance from Americans. He didn't like phones.

"Is it possible for only you to come?" he said.

Melissa was puzzled by the question, as she had told him prior to her departure from Greece that her friend would be returning with her. She wanted Emma to see some of the sites on Crete.

"She can stay at Effie's. You could arrange to get us a room, yes?" she said.

He thought about that. He could certainly arrange for a guest to lodge at the home of his longtime employee, Zephyra — also known as 'Effie. It was only a five-minute walk from Pithari Taverna and would still allow Nikos to have time alone with his granddaughter.

"Yes. I will do that."

"Great. We can take Emma to the monastery. You can tell some of the stories for her. She will love that."

The idea startled Andreadakis. It was the last trip to the holy site that had provoked the memories and feelings that he was now experiencing.

"Ισως," he replied in Greek, sounding like 'Ee-soss' in English, 'maybe.'

"Are you busy at the taverna? Are tourists still coming in the evening?"

"There are some. Not as many," he said.

"Will you be able to have time away when we visit?"

"That will not be a problem."

"When we come to Crete, Emma will rent a car so we can visit other parts of the island," she said.

"That would be good."

"I love you. You take care of yourself."

"I love you, too. You be very careful. American boys may be like Albanians, chasing after beautiful Greek women."

"*Papouli*, I will be careful."

Nineteen

Indigenous Peoples' Day, or as many auto dealers and furniture outlets still call it in their ads, Columbus Day — both observed on the second Monday of October — generally brings a lot of traffic to Vermont's secondary roads.

The preceding weekend could be hectic on the highway, particularly in the central and southern parts of the state. It was an outstanding reason *not* to drive anywhere. And that was exactly my plan.

Then I got a text from Ragsdale on Friday afternoon, five minutes before I was heading up to Williamstown to see Marino.

'Nice wthr tomorrow. Maybe hit the White for couple hrs in the morning?'

We had missed fishing the White River back in the spring. I had promised to show him a stretch of water known to a few as the Broken Glass Pool.

'Sure. Meet at Irving station Exit 3, 10 o'clock?'

'*Ten-4*'.

Might make sense to get a room and not drive up and back, up and back. With a little forewarning, that would've been a good idea. I considered it for two minutes, then decided that I would be more comfortable in my own bed. And that Rocco would be happier, too.

This was my second real visit with Frank Marino, not counting when I saw him briefly to pick up the Hilling memoir. Instead of walking to the park bench that we'd used a week earlier, we now sat in two composite wicker chairs on the back lawn of his retirement community complex.

"I found some of the other articles you mentioned," I said, maneuvering my chair around so I would face him. He held up a hand to stop me.

"Before we discuss any of that, Mister Hanlon, may I ask, do you have a passport?"

"I thought we'd established that we would *drop* the Mister?"

"Beg your pardon. We did indeed establish that, Michael."

I nodded in the affirmative, "Yes, I have a passport. Renewed just last year."

"That's good. If we can agree on what I'm about to propose, there will be some travel."

This comment piqued my interest as I was under the impression that we had already agreed to my proposed plan; more digging, attempt to track down a New Hampshire Game Warden from 40 years ago, if he was still alive, and see if there were any non-classified documents that might be obtained from the CIA or the NSA.

"Travel to where?" I said.

"We'll get to that."

Might be my imagination, but Frank Marino had ratcheted things up a notch or two. Since we'd spoken on the phone just a day earlier, his demeanor at the moment conveyed a 'no-nonsense, let's move this along' attitude.

"I wasn't sure that you would agree to help me. As we discussed, forty-years is a long time," he said. "I'm an old man on a mission. Which doesn't necessarily mean that I am right. And it doesn't mean that you have to play along."

Never miss an opportunity to keep your mouth shut, Hanlon.

He studied me for a few seconds, then continued.

"You don't strike me as one who willingly participates in boondoggles. And, as you told me about how you would like to get started, if there's no indication of progress in the first week, we can take another look, decide to continue, or just shake hands and let it go."

I nodded. "Yes. That makes the most sense to me. Happy to work for you, but no interest in going on a snipe hunt."

That brought a smile from Marino.

"Who do you suppose organized the very first snipe hunt?" he said.

"Don't know. But some of the older kids I grew up with, they sure had a lot of fun with it. My sister saw through it early on. I was a bit slower."

He laughed. "Most everyone gets duped with some form of a practical joke at one time or another."

Rising from his chair — I'd swear he'd lost 10 years since our first meeting — he motioned for me to follow. "Let's go inside. I have more material for you to look through."

On the floor next to his recliner was a stack of books, maybe seven or eight in all, including a large format coffee table volume at the bottom of the stack. I could read the title on its spine, *ATLAS OF THE WORLD*.

Marino motioned for me to have a seat. I settled into a navy canvas Director's chair opposite him. He stooped to pick up one of the books, then eased himself into the chair.

Flipping the book open to a place that he'd marked he tapped the page.

"Do you know who Moe Berg was?" he said.

"Nope."

"He was a professional baseball player. And a lawyer. *And* . . . a spy." He held the book up for me to see the cover, *The Catcher Was A Spy*.

Turning the book back so he could look at the section he'd marked, he ran a finger down the page and stopped.

"This was also a long time ago," he began. "Before World War II. And before Win Callahan apprenticed to become a . . . shall we say, an intelligence officer of the United States government."

He stretched to hand me the book, his index finger holding a section open.

"Read the bottom half of the page on the right," he said.

The passage was about Berg being sent, incognito, to Zurich in December 1944, to attend a lecture to be given by a German physicist. Berg carried a gun hidden in his suit coat. The orders were clear; if he heard *anything* in the speaker's remarks that convinced him that the Germans were close to having a nuclear bomb, he was to shoot the lecturer right there on the spot.

Berg had a lethal cyanide tablet to dispose of himself, as well.

I looked at Marino. "Better than calling pitches in both ends of a double-header," I said.

"Perhaps. Berg was only *one* of the people brought on board at the OSS by the infamous Wild Bill Donovan. A bit later, Win Callahan joined the ranks."

We talked for another hour, exploring the life and times of Morris Berg, aka Moe, the spy who spoke several languages, had a 15-year run in the Majors and was on the roster of the Boston Red Sox for the last five, ending with the 1939 season.

"If you bother to read up on him — I did a long time ago — you will find that he was one of those 'journeyman' ball players," Marino said. "Not Hall of Fame caliber, perhaps, but a solid position player.

"Fifteen years is pretty good. Especially considering his avocational pursuits. What is the average career for a baseball player these days?" he added.

"Ah-h-h, maybe 5 or 6 years," I said. 'Not sure. My buddy Ragsdale probably knows. I'll check."

"My point is, some people lead mysterious lives. I would be surprised to learn if many players back in Berg's era knew, or even speculated, about his spy work. Then, *after* the war, with the formation of the CIA during the Truman Administration, the recruitment of individuals might have been, as the current expression goes, more transparent."

I laughed. Marino looked puzzled.

"Wonder if any opposing teams stole Berg's signals?" I said.

"There is that. Pundits say stealing signs in baseball has been around since the beginning of the game."

Stretching my legs and doing an isometric neck roll, I fought off a yawn.

"Would you like coffee, or something to drink?" he said.

"No, I'm good. Thanks."

"**Now, about the travel**," Marino resumed.

"You're not going to ask me to go hang out in some European lecture hall and wait for the chance to shoot somebody."

"The shooting part is unlikely," he said. "But, go to Europe, yes." He watched for my reaction.

Never miss an opportunity . . .

"I really can't travel the way that I used to," he said. "Not alone, anyway. And, this won't surprise you, there is more information that I need to confirm. Apart from what you will be looking into."

The question had been nagging me almost from the first minutes I'd spent in his company, yet I had not found a satisfactory way to frame it. Here was as good a time as any.

"I'm sure that you've heard more than your share of bad jokes on 'let's be frank', huh?" Marino nodded that he had.

"But Frank, I am genuinely curious about exactly what *you* did all those years in Washington. Especially since you are . . . so *knowledgeable*. Plus, you're still reading this *stuff* . . . about *spies*! I mean aside from your friend Win Callahan."

The smile. And the eyes, conveying a mix of bemusement and self-satisfaction.

"I was beginning to fear that you would never ask, Michael," he said. "Tell you what," he went on, "I will provide you with a thorough disquisition when we next meet. Afraid that some of it might, in fact, put you to sleep."

"Doubtful," I said, getting up from my chair and handing back the Moe Berg book. "Next week sometime?" I added.

"Yes. Why don't you call me, say . . . on Wednesday? In the afternoon."

"Yep. I can do that."

He reached into his shirt pocket, pulled out a folded check and handed it to me. "That makes us official," he said.

"Thank you," I said, slipping the check into a pocket of my fleece vest. I didn't look at it; should be for our agreed upon $1,500 retainer. We shook hands.

"Wait," Marino said. I'd started for the door but turned around. He had his back to me and was kneeling in front of the shelves behind his chair. When he stood up, he held two more books and gave me one of them.

"Read that one first. He provides an excellent account of what's going on today with all this cyber war we hear about. But there's also an overview on the origins of the NSA."

I looked at the cover — *Dark Territory: The Secret History of Cyber War* by Fred Kaplan. Just over one inch thick, maybe 250 pages or so. I flipped to the back cover to see who Fred Kaplan was. Marino thrust the second book in my direction.

"This one is more recent," he said. "She offers insight previously not very well known about the Clandestine Service agents of today, somewhat different from Callahan's work years ago. More diverse crowd, bigger stakes," he added.

The second book was titled *Life Undercover: Coming of Age in the CIA* by Amaryllis Fox. Unusual name. Almost made you believe that it was a pseudonym. But I recalled seeing her on TV once offering commentary on a CNN program.

"A lot to read," I said.

"You can skim much of it. I won't give you a test."

.

Twenty

'The Shooter' parallel parked in one of the few spaces allotted for a small mixed-use commercial center in Stoneham, Massachusetts.

Three abutting duplex buildings with a muted red brick façade; business suites on the street level with residential/office space on the second floor. Hand-carved wooden signs above each door featured the business name in gold leaf lettering. Over the second door from the left the sign read *Weapons, Ltd.*

The man he'd spoken with on the phone, Armando, had acknowledged that with an inventory of more than 300 guns, his privately owned company did cater to collectors nationwide. 'Yes, on a selective basis', he'd replied to the question. And he also accepted firearms for consignment sale.

That's why the shooter was here, it was a test. Offer the Winchester Model 70 rifle with Leupold vari-scope and see what happens. He knew that it was a popular, top-tier hunting rifle and could sell quickly. Let the dealer do the paperwork and, more importantly, determine if any red flags popped up regarding the gun's history.

There would be no attempt at deception. He planned to provide the dealer with verifiable identification, knowing that the 1980 incident would certainly show up in a background check. Would that put off the dealer, or a prospective buyer?

A gun like this one would not command a big price, maybe $1,250 tops. If no issues surfaced on this sale, and if he *liked* and *trusted* Armando, the more valuable guns in the collection could be offered later.

He climbed out of the car and stood looking at the building. Standing five-four and weighing a hundred-thirty pounds, the shooter had likely never been perceived as 'imposing' by any definition. It was his visual acuity, and a stone-cold emotional discipline when handling a firearm, that made him more of a threat than one might imagine at first glance.

That was not part of today's test. Opening the trunk of his car, he removed a faded green nylon travel case with the old rifle zipped inside, then walked across the blacktop to the entrance of *Weapons, Ltd.*

Inside, a soft chime sounded somewhere in the rear of the business. Before he had released the door handle a man appeared from behind a sliding bamboo door in the far corner of the room.

"Hello," the man said.

Along the far wall were six identical wooden gun cabinets made of cherry with glass paneled doors. About four feet wide and over six feet tall, each cabinet held twelve weapons, shotguns and rifles.

"Armando?"

"That's me."

"I'm the guy who called yesterday about the old Model 70." He placed the gun travel case on a coffee table that was positioned in front of a sofa and two wingback chairs.

"Let's have a look," Armando said.

Twenty One

"**I brought you** the leftover pie," Virginia said. She wore jeans, a loose-fitting man's flannel shirt that looked as though it could have belonged to her father, and Bean boots with no socks. She was standing on the deck just outside my kitchen door.

It was 7:25 Saturday morning. I was having coffee and reading the Valley News. I looked at the glass dish that held a single slice of apple pie.

"Wow. That's all that's *left*?" I said.

"Sorry. I couldn't get to sleep last night, so I ate the rest of it." She pushed the pie toward me. "*No-o-o*, that is *not* all that's left. But it is all that *you* get."

Rocco managed to get around me and was going through the sniff check. As he did circles in the doorway, she scratched his ears, gently nudging him with a knee so she could come inside.

"Want some coffee?" I said.

"Sure."

I turned on the range-top element under the tea kettle, went to the fridge for a bag of ground coffee, then put a scoop in the previously used pour-thru filter that was on a paper towel next to the sink.

Virginia picked up the newspaper while I waited for the kettle. She drank her morning coffee black and had a self-imposed two cup limit. I presumed that she'd already had the first one. From the cabinet above the toaster oven, I pulled out another mug and placed it next to the stove.

"Do you read Gina Barreca?" she said.

"You know that I do. I just haven't read yesterday's column."

She flipped the paper back and looked at the front page.

"Of course. You're reading yesterday's paper," she said.

"I'm pretty sure that you also know *that*. Carryover from radio days," I said, fitting the filter onto the clean mug. "I want to go through it slowly. See which stories they got. And what they missed."

She shook her head and flipped the paper back to the Opinion page.

"Old habits die hard," I said. "I'm not a wham bam, ten minutes and zip, straight to the recycling tub."

"Yes, I have noticed. You *do* like to take your time with all manner of things."

After a minute, she handed the paper to me. "Read this column when you think you can handle it."

"Will do. Thank you." The kettle whistled. I removed it from the burner and poured a little water into the coffee and waited.

Rocco was drinking from his water bowl. He'd had breakfast shortly after we'd gotten up. Now he would need to go out again. I got the alert collar from the bench next to the door and clipped it around his neck.

"Would you please let him go out?" I said. "He knows that you're here, maybe he won't head for the slip-through spot."

"You found the break in the wire?" she said, opening the door for Rocco.

I poured more water into the filter.

"Yeah. Dumb. I should've spotted it sooner. Back behind the compost bin."

"An animal chewed through it?" she said.

"I don't think so. More likely that I hit it with a shovel or a rake when I was cleaning up in the spring."

"By the way, I just bought a battery-powered leaf blower," she said. "It weighs almost nothing. You're welcome to borrow it when all the leaves are down."

I handed her the mug of coffee.

"Might be more than I can cope with. The guy who mows the lawn does a fall cleanup that takes him about 20 minutes. Thanks, anyway."

We sat at the kitchen island and talked in short bursts. Virginia flipping through the newspaper and drinking coffee, me eating the apple pie slowly and watching her, with an occasional glance out the door to keep an eye on Rocco.

"Sorry to run you off," I said, getting up and rinsing the glass dish.

She drooped the paper down so she could look at me.

"Was it the pie, or something I said?"

"The pie was outstanding, maybe better without the ice cream. Thank you.

No, I'm driving up to Bethel to meet Louie at 10 o'clock. We're going to fish for a couple of hours."

"Supposed to be a lovely day," she said.

"Ragsdale would tell you, Bill Withers. I don't know the year, but he would."

She offered a 'you got me, there' expression, head cocked, eyebrows up.

"The song, *Lovely Day*. Big hit for Bill Withers. He died last year."

"Oh."

"Yes, forecast calling for sun and maybe mid-sixties this afternoon. It would actually be better fishing if we had some overcast," I said.

"Won't the water be cold?"

"Probably. But I wear long underwear and sweatpants under my waders. And wool ski socks."

Rocco was back at the door with a small tree branch in his mouth. Virginia got up to let him come in.

"Leave it," I said, pointing to the deck. Dropping the branch, he stood over it, tail wagging and hesitated to come inside.

"No sticks in the house, thank you." I removed the shock collar, tugged on his regular collar and he went in front of me.

"Should handsome boy stay with me today?" she said.

"He'd love that," I said. "We'll get something to eat after fishing. I should be home by 4:30 or so."

"Whenever. I don't have to go anywhere."

Louie was parked next to the air pump at the gas station-convenience store right off Exit 3. It was 9:55. The driver door was open. I pulled up next to him and lowered my window. He was listening to a call-in show on the radio.

"Do we need to go find 'em and blow up the transmitter?" I said.

He shook his head. "Nah, this is good. 'DEV out of Waterbury. Ken Squier and Farmer Dave."

"*Music to Go to the Dump By*," I said.

"Yep."

"What year did Bill Withers record *Lovely Day*?"

"1977. Not long before he took a hiatus from recording. Why?"

"I was telling Virginia about it this morning. Told her you would know the year." The radio show was ending, Louie turned it off, got out and gave me the smirk.

"So, where is this . . . Broken Glass Pool?" he said.

"Get your gear and we'll go in my car."

"Let me ask inside if I can leave it here." He pointed across the lot beyond the gas pumps to additional parking spaces.

"Maybe pull over there," he added. He went in to ask permission and was back out a minute later.

After putting waders, vest and flyrod on my backseat, he locked his SUV and climbed in next to me.

"Okay, head out, Private," he said. Still the smirk.

"First, I will have to blindfold you."

Twenty Two

5:08 pm on Crete, European Time Zone +3. Nikos Andreadakis was about to do something quite out of the ordinary,
at least for him. He was going to take a long walk.

At 250 meters, the beach at Matala is longer than two
football fields — that is FIFA official length soccer fields of 100
to 110 meters — and Nikos had not walked the full distance
in more than 20 years.

Wearing old, leather weave sneakers and shuffling along
slightly faster than a spur-thighed tortoise, it took him ten
minutes just to be out of sight of the taverna. He finished his
cigarette and told himself that he would make the walk down
and back without having another.

The late afternoon light on the harbor reflected across the
bay. He thought that he could be back before sunset still more
than an hour from now.

A few people were on the beach, not many, mostly at
the end close to the village. There were scattered chaises and

umbrellas out. An artist he knew was under a canopy packing up for the day. He waved. Only three boats anchored offshore and one small boat pulled up on the sand.

Removing the sneakers, he left them next to a cement breaker wall. He rolled the bottom of his pants part way up his calves and set off, slowly. It has been said that there are so many Greek myths that it is impossible to count all of them. One legend has Zeus swimming ashore in the guise of a bull . . . on this very beach.

After only a few steps, Nikos stopped and looked back at the breaker wall. There were splotches of graffiti along one section of the concrete. Another space had large blue words painted in English: TODAY IS LIFE. TOMORROW NEVER COMES.

He resumed walking toward the stone cliffs and caves at the far end of the beach, an area he knew from his youth. Recent disturbing dreams had dredged up the memory of a young woman he'd known half a lifetime ago. Along with others, they'd spent many nights under the stars at the mouth of those caves.

What motivated this walk was the recollection of a long-ago conversation about dreams. The young woman — she was French, Yvette was her name — had gone on about different theories of dreaming. She seemed to know a good deal about the subject and Nikos recalled having been completely enthralled.

A recurring dream that he had had frequently, for over a month now, involved his granddaughter being shot by an American assassin. Sometimes she was alone, walking along a city street. Other times she was in a large crowd at a concert. Once it happened when she was walking through a busy airport. In all the dreams, Nikos could see his granddaughter's face just before she was shot. Only a silhouette of the gunman appeared as he raised the rifle.

His heart rate quickened, and he was breathing faster. Trying to see Melissa *now* as she appeared during her visit a month ago, he stopped at the edge of the water. Muffled sounds from the village were barely audible.

When he got his breathing under control and heart rate back to normal, he stood in silence and stared out across the sea.

Twenty Three

I did not really make Ragsdale wear a blindfold. This beautiful stretch of water is likely known to many who fish the White River. The only people who refer to it as 'Broken Glass Pool' are me and a couple of friends.

Its main feature is a long, deep run against the far bank with good spots for fish to hide, fast riffles at the head of the pool, a few large boulders scattered over 30 yards or more, and submerged flat-surfaced rocks at the tail end. Over more than 25 years I had probably fished it a hundred times and had *never* failed to catch at least one trout, from May right through to mid-October.

The record continued. We caught three fish between us, two nice rainbows over 12 inches, both scrappy in the cool water, and a smaller rainbow that likely had not been in the river a year. No clipped fins, so all three fish were 'wild', even though not too far back they could have come from hatchery-stocked ancestors.

Barely two hours was enough and we headed back to the car. Going up the steep bank, Louie tapped me on the shoulder with the tip of his flyrod. I turned around.

"So, tell me the story," he said. "The broken glass bit."

"When we get up top," I said, and kept going.

As we broke down our gear and stowed it in the back of my car, I launched into a Reader's Digest version of how the name came into existence.

"Mid-July, during the 1994 World Cup," I began. "First time the US hosted the tournament. Soccer was new to me and I watched or recorded every game. *VHS tapes*, if you can believe it?"

"Wonderful," he said.

"I was here fishing with a friend, a Trout Unlimited guy from Burlington. He didn't give a shit about soccer and would have fished all night if his wife hadn't established a curfew for him. I left the river early, wanted to get back. He was still out there up to his chest, flailing away." Louie twisted the cap onto his fly rod tube.

"When I got up here to my car, my key was in the ignition. Doors locked, no spare," I added.

Starting to pull off his waders, he stopped and stared at me.

"Yeah, I know. *Not too swift*. But the driver side window was open maybe an inch at the top. I frigged around with the tip of my rod, tried to use a piece of fly line to lasso the key, got a small tree branch to poke around. Nothing worked."

Now Louie was giving me the 'you really are dumb' smile and shaking his head.

"It was the final, Italy versus Brazil, playing in the Rose Bowl. My wife was visiting her mother and I wanted to watch this match live. So, I got a softball sized rock from right over there," I pointed at the bank, "and smashed the passenger side window."

"Brilliant," he said.

"Hey, it worked. Most of the glass went on the front seat, just a little on the ground."

"And you got home in time to see the game." He folded his arms and leaned against the car.

"Yep. And it was *one great game*. First time ever the championship was decided in a penalty shootout after overtime. Brazil won 3-2.

"I found out the next day — my TU pal from Burlington called — to tell me what happened. He heard the window smashing, I'd been up here for a while trying to get into my car, which he didn't know and thought I was long gone, and he was certain that somebody was breaking into his pickup. Said he damn near had a heart attack scrambling up the bank to find nothing but one or two fragments of glass that I missed.

"So, he's the one who came up with the name. Pretty sure that he told a few mutual friends about it. Hell, if it happened today, he'd put it on facebook."

"Fascinating," Louie said.

"I can tell that you are truly excited to have had the opportunity to hear the story a second time."

"Maybe not. That was a page longer than a 'Reader's Digest' version."

Louie had caught and released the largest fish, but I had caught two, which made me top rod and meant that *he* would buy lunch. We were in his SUV heading for downtown Bethel.

"Turn right," I said, "and follow 107 for a couple of miles."

He did as instructed, crossing a bridge and heading southwest along the river, past the White River National Fish Hatchery.

"There," I pointed, "on the right." We pulled in front of a central Vermont landmark, Tozier's Restaurant.

"Good homemade chowder. *Great* onion rings," I said.

"Works for me."

We both ordered a bowl of clam chowder, a toasted lobster salad roll and a side of fried onion rings.

A little yuk, yuk about the fishing, how nice that section of the river is, and that he was glad I had finally shown him the spot, including a sarcastic crack that he had started to believe I'd made it up. I was about to explain my procrastination when the waitress brought the chowder.

Ragsdale held up a hand. "Hold on, Radio Rick. I've got some real news to share. Save the BS for the ride back." The waitress stifled a laugh as she placed the bowls on the table in front of us.

It was always a little fuzzy as to when Louie was about to be serious, or just setting the hook, with a solemn opening comment that eventually played out to a smartass lecture. Although *he* never thought of it as a 'lecture', rather simply 'trying to help out a friend.' *Sure.*

"Let's hear it," I said, picking up a spoon and bracing myself.

"I'm done. It's time. Fully retired as of January 1st."

I waited a beat and studied his face. No smirk, just a smile. And a slight nod.

"Huh! Becky finally got you to act," I said. "Good for her."

"Yeah, she'd gone low-key on it for almost a year now. Gave me some room. It had to be *my* decision."

"I'll save the interview questions for later, but January 1st is just a couple of months away. What's the plan? Give me an overview."

And for the next 20 minutes, that's what I got, the executive summary of L. James Ragsdale's 'short term' plan for retirement, with repeated and varied flourishes on 'lots of time to be outdoors'.

When we had finished eating — and Louie was winding down — I held up my right hand like a kid in class and waved it back and forth.

"Yes?" he said.

"Mind if I get my notebook out? I'm gonna have lots to ask you."

"Save it. We'll have time later."

"By all means."

Twenty Four

Writing a memoir held little appeal for Frank Marino. No immediate family to consider, no former colleagues who might find interest from the 'less than exciting' years he served as an overpaid scribe for a band of spooks.

Recalling the alcoholic haze frequently on display with his first boss, Marino could hear the man laughing at him shortly after he'd started the new job.

'You are going to find yourself, Marino, skipping back-and-forth between the role of an alert, but powerless amanuensis, and that of an archivist that nobody really likes to have around. Or *worse*.'

Fifty-plus years of reviewing, organizing — and on occasion, *revising* — written documents and related media which comprised background source material for countless US intelligence operatives. He had done his share. Others had the responsibility of the actual filing and storing of the records.

That was beneath his jurisdiction, just as gaining *access* to the more sensitive material was above his pay grade.

Initially, Marino's work was for the Central Intelligence Agency. Possessing a combination of impeccable professionalism and natural affability, he soon acquired the reputation of being a trusted, knowledgeable civil servant. Others soon recognized value beyond his working with the primary analytic agency for human intelligence in the US.

About mid-way through his career he was tapped to lend guidance to younger personnel not just at the CIA, but with the National Security Agency (NSA) at Fort Meade, Maryland, and at the newer National Reconnaissance Office headquartered in nearby Chantilly, Virginia. Virtually all the people Marino tutored, like himself, came under the 'Excepted Service' category of federal employees.

While he had no intention of loading a half-a-century's worth of professional activities into book form, he had habitually and methodically kept track of the waypoints from his journey. He had chronicled them, succinctly, in a collection of journals.

Those journals were now stacked on a table in his dining room where Marino leafed through them and made notes for what he was going to share with Michael Hanlon.

Printing block style with a blue ballpoint pen across the pages of a yellow legal pad, he noted a range of dates — 6/59 to 3/70, 4/70 to 1/81 — up to and including his last stint in government service, May 2015, or as he labeled it on the pad, 5/15.

Beginning with the first decade, under each heading Marino wrote a terse description of where he'd been and what he'd done, as though he were compiling a short-hand curriculum vitae to be embellished at a later date.

The exercise took most of the morning. He would leave it for now, subject to still another read-through, and probable additional reminders to himself, before concluding that he had all he would need to answer the question '*And what have you been doing all these years, Frank Marino?*'

Only when he paused for a snack and to take a short nap did it occur to him that he was preparing far more than was necessary. Michael Hanlon was primarily interested in *why* he was obsessed with this 'Not An Accident' endeavor. All the life and times recitation would merely serve as an attempt to legitimate the story about Win Callahan's death.

One fact unrelated to anything that Hanlon, or for that matter, anyone else, could influence was precisely how much time Marino had left on this earth. It was not something that worried him. The question of his own mortality — especially in light of the recent Coronavirus pandemic — just waltzed in from time to time. And then it stuck around for a spell, sometimes for hours.

It was more of a feeling, he thought. No muscle or joint aches, or symptoms of some form of illness. Just out of nowhere, the sensation would come to him that time was running short.

So, the best approach was to go with the thoughts of the moment. *None of us is leaving here alive.*

Frank Marino did not fret.

Twenty Five

Transporting firearms across state lines could be problematic. The Shooter had quickly dismissed that idea once he made the decision to leave New England for good. He planned to move to Arizona.

Sell 'em all.

Not a word from Armando at the gun gallery in Stoneham.

No news is good news.

He could remember the interview that was conducted later the same morning of the incident. It had been handled by the NH Conservation Officer. There had been a second phone interview two days later with a state police Commander.

A week after the incident, he had been notified by registered mail of the penalty: the $500 fine and suspension of a hunting license for ten years.

After the rifle had been confiscated as evidence, the shooter — with the help of his pal the 'rich kid' — was able to repurchase the gun years later at a state auction.

Sitting at a small folding card table in his basement, he removed a single sheet of paper from an envelope. He pressed it flat on the table. The paper was aged brown at the creases where it had been folded.

Handwritten on the paper was a list of all the guns he owned, including serial numbers and the date they were acquired and how much he'd paid for each. The guns were stored in two metal vault-style cabinets, secured by combination locks, and positioned out of sight behind a rack of random length boards that he used in his woodshop.

On the table in front of him was a cheap portable typewriter rarely used in thirty years. He inserted a clean sheet of paper and tested some keys to see if the ribbon was any good. It was a dual black and red ribbon common for this model.

Then he typed out O C T — 12 — 2020. Weak, but usable. You could read it.

Looking at the handwritten list, he slowly began typing information from his firearm inventory.

Ruger #1 Single Shot Falling Block rifle

Sharps Model 1874 Sporting rifle

F. Smith Percussion Drilling 16-gauge shotgun

It took the shooter more than an hour to compile the new list, double-spaced on two pages. There were a few typos. He had backspaced and x-ed out the mistake, then corrected the entry. It was good enough. He would make a copy at the speedy office/shipping center in a retail plaza two blocks from his home.

Reading down the original purchase prices and making a rough calculation in his head, the collection should easily bring over a hundred grand. The three prized shotguns alone would go for at least forty-thousand.

The conversation with Armando at Weapons, Ltd. had been of a general nature, more along the line of the models of guns much in demand, and those that didn't sell quickly. This list would help determine consignment versus outright sale.

It had not been discussed, but the shooter believed that any trader worth his powder would purchase an entire collection if it included some primo guns that the dealer coveted. And knew that he could easily sell with a nice profit.

Sell 'em all.

He closed the cover on the typewriter, placed the hand-written list back in its envelope, stood up and pushed the metal folding chair tight to the table. Taking the envelope and the two sheets of the newly typed list with him, the shooter headed upstairs to his kitchen.

Twenty Six

"Emergency. **Someone stole** my dog!" I blurted into the phone.

"How *awful*. When did this happen?" Virginia said.

"This morning, after I left to go fishing."

"Oh, wait. Can you describe the mutt?"

"Reddish coat, close to two-feet high. Bushy tail. *Great* brown eyes."

"And he would be wearing the Grateful Dead collar?"

"Not sure that's how I'd describe it. Multi-color stripes, actually."

"Likes to sleep on any comfy surface he can find, right?" she said. "Well, lucky for you that he is stretched out — at this very minute — on *my* sofa."

"Good. I'll come and fetch him."

"Do I get a reward?"

"Sure. How about I take you to dinner?"

"*Tonight?*"

"Unless you have other plans," I said.

"Once again, you luck out. My dance card is open."

"Did you ever really *have* a dance card?" I said. "Growing up, you took ballroom lessons or something?"

"Of course. Part of our 4-H winter program at the Hartland Middle School."

"Something tells me that you are not being entirely truthful, Ms. Jackson."

"Come get your dog. We'll talk about dinner."

"Have any pie left?"

Click. She was already gone.

What we agreed on was that we would go to Skunk Hollow Tavern in Hartland Four Corners, less than 20 minutes away. And that Virginia would drive.

I was able to get a reservation for 7:30 in the upstairs dining room. I called Virginia back to let her know. She said that she would come get me at 7:05.

After a shower, I got a beer from the fridge and sat down to resume reading the books Marino had loaned me. Putting the Moe Berg book aside, I got back into *Dark Territory*, the one about the history of cyber war.

Early in the book, the author, columnist Fred Kaplan, told how the NSA evolved from American intelligence activities of more than a century ago, toward the end of World War I. It was a US government branch labeled MI-8, that focused on German telegraph signals. The unit continued operation well after Armistice Day, 11/11/1918, conducting secret work for both the war and the state departments.

In a fast forward to the end of the 20th century, circa 1991 and the beginning of Operation Desert Storm, I read about the creation of a newer NSA office of Information Warfare and the man appointed to head that division. Kaplan wrote that what the US could do with its spying on other countries, those countries very soon would be able to do the same to us.

Anyone paying attention to the current news about cyber-attacks?

Clearly, Kaplan had done a ton of research. I flipped to the back of the book. *Thirty-one pages* of notes, chapter by chapter.

I was on page 141. Time for a break.

Dinner at Skunk Hollow was right up on the scale at a nine. Virginia had Chicken Czarina with zucchini, Parmesan cream and shrimp. I went for a baked manicotti entree, with portabella mushroom and ratatouille. An exceptional bottle of a Ferrari-Carano Reserve Chardonnay was the right selection, made by Virginia.

We were back at my house at 9:20. All rested up and ready for the Saturday night dance, Rocco met us at the door with a green heavy-duty plastic toy — it looked much like a cop's nightstick — and continued to make it squeak until I persuaded him to trade it for a bacon treat.

Virginia asked for tea, so I put the kettle on. I poured myself a couple ounces of Port from a new bottle given to me by a friend in Rhode Island.

"Any requests for music?" I said.

"Not really. Put on something you like."

Philip Glass, *Solo Piano* was an old CD that I had not listened to in years. I slipped it into the tray and tapped the play button.

The kettle whistled. Virginia poured water into a mug with a lemon ginger tea bag. She picked up the book I'd left on the counter earlier.

"The history of cyber war, huh?" she said. "Okay, so I guess it's about the internet and hackers and all that. But where does the word come from?"

"Cybernetics, I think. The scientific study of controlling and communicating with systems that use technology."

She lowered the book and looked at me. "Something you knew *before* you got this book?"

"Nope."

"I must say, Michael Hanlon, you still surprise me from time to time. Would never have guessed that this is a topic that interests you." She began dipping the tea bag in and out of the water, then placed it in the kitchen sink.

"Unlikely that I would have gone looking for it at the library. But . . . my new client loaned it to me."

"The older gentleman in Williamstown?"

"Yep. He sent me off with three more books last time I visited him."

We sat in the living room listening to Philip Glass.

"Those are really good speakers," Virginia said.

111

"Yeah. They're old Advents. A guy in Hanover rebuilt them for me."

"Michael's Audio," she said.

"How did you know that?" I asked.

"I think if you ask around — the owner, Frank, not Michael — is about the *only* person in this area who still does that kind of thing. A friend at the law school thinks the man should get a Nobel Prize. Takes all of his equipment there."

"I had those speakers downstairs in the media room. Louie suggested that I bring them up here. When he stops by he likes to crank 'em up," I said, adding, "Not sure that he would listen to this."

Solo Piano was now into a track titled *Wichita Sutra Vortex*. From a hymn-like intro it went through bursts of what sounded to me like gospel music. Only when I read the liner notes did I find out that it was inspired by an Allen Ginsberg poem.

Ragsdale would definitely pause this CD, then slip in something like The Delfonics from Hard-To-Find HITS.

"You might as well spend the night," I said. "Rocco's gonna be lonely when you leave."

"Rocco?"

"Well . . . look at him."

"You promise to wake me in the morning? Before seven o'clock?"

"I promise."

"Fortunate that I have VIP guest essentials in your bathroom."

"Aren't you glad that I encouraged you on that?" I asked.

"I'll be forever in your debt," she said, getting up and heading to the bathroom.

Twenty Seven

Forty-years ago, as he recalled it, the story was a matter of 'facts' according to his uncle. The American had misrepresented events, had lied to many people, and the deception had caused irreparable harm.

Nikos Andreadakis never learned more. But he never made the effort to do so. Back then, cavalier and irresponsible himself, he didn't try to get details. He took the money and, with the help of a few Greeks then living in the US, was able to make a necessary contact and assure that his uncle's task came to fruition.

In the years following his uncle's death, Nikos began piecing together bits of information that cast a new light on the American who had been deceptive. Much of the story was inconsistent and, depending on the people retelling it from their own sketchy memories, it was a contradictory tale.

Nikos was approaching the age when he believed that his days were numbered. His uncle, the more fortunate younger brother of Nikos' father who had died young, lived until he was 81, before he became a puff of wind and was headed for the 'Underworld.'

These days he was more aware than ever that just because the sun would rise tomorrow, there was no guarantee that one would be here to see it. Death comes in many guises and can slip in when least expected. Taking stories with you, *someone else's* story, was an increasingly worrisome burden.

The trip to the monastery — with reminders of the military battle of 80 years ago and learning of the recent death of a childhood friend — had rekindled his skepticism. And the dreaming.

Through the years, deliberately not wanting to reexamine the past, Nikos had allowed himself to believe that the 'deception' by the American was somehow connected to events at the end of the war.

That belief had become cloudy, much like his diminishing eyesight.

He needed to talk with his granddaughter.

Unrelated to the contemporary decline of the fertility rate in Greece, Nikos' family nearly a century ago had been among the smaller ones from the central part of the island.

He had a sister seven years older than himself and no brothers, unusual for his generation. When others from Crete had moved to Athens and elsewhere on the mainland, his parents remained in the village where they had been born and raised and where they had started their own family.

The surname Andreadakis shows Cretan roots. One of the stories is that Ottoman Turks added an *'aki'* suffix to insult or belittle Greek men from Crete. To them, it was Andread*aki*. But the Cretans made it masculine by adding the 's' and showing pride in the spelling with *-akis* that distinguishes them from everyone else.

The 'akis' stands for immortal, from Greek mythology in the Legend of Acis and Galatea.

Twenty Eight

At 7:20 Sunday morning Virginia went home. Rocco had been fed, gone outside for a bit, and was now lying on his side asleep next to the door. From the movement of his front paws, he could have been dreaming about wild turkeys not far away.

I settled into more reading, the *Life Undercover* book by Amaryllis Fox. She wrote about intensive training at the CIA and developing a good cover story for the role that she would play once out in the field, one convincing enough that even her immediate family believed it.

She told about recruiting arms dealers in Pakistan and using go-betweens to meet terrorists with the hope of negotiating ways to prevent suicide bomb attacks. And she did not hold back with detailed personal information, which surprised me. She had been *so young* when all of this was happening in her life.

Fox is a good writer. It is one of those books that as you get deeper into the story, you really don't want to stop reading. I stayed with it for two hours.

A light rain had begun which gave me a good excuse to stay inside. I got up, stretched, then went to the kitchen to fix something to eat. A cup of oats in a glass bowl with water and into the microwave. I sliced a banana, got a handful of raisins and some chopped walnuts to mix in with the oatmeal.

Carrying the bowl to my office/guest room — Rocco got up and followed — I went online to continue searching. At the very beginning of conversations with Marino, my focus had been on finding all that I could about Stephen 'Win' Callahan, primarily the newspaper accounts of his death and the hunting incident, plus a few snippets of his government career. But nothing about his early life. I decided that, at least for the moment, that information would have to come from Frank.

Taking a different angle, I decided to just go Google. Typing in different search references, beginning with 'veterans of the NSA,' brought up more than two-million results. *Right!*

Scrolling through the first page, I quickly saw that there was a mix of links to stories about *military* veterans as well as NSA veterans. Headlines such as, 'Veterans of the NSA's psychic wars' — 'NSA mystery case reaches the end' — 'Departing NSA veterans catch the eye of Silicon Valley investors' — 'NSA Veterans: The White House is hanging us out to dry' and more and more and more.

After half-an-hour of clicking and reading, I began to appreciate the adage about how the internet can lead you down a rabbit hole. So I just stopped. But not before bookmarking two different links to explore later. One, a Wikipedia page on an NSA whistleblower, and the other one, a 51-minute video from the Aspen Ideas Festival in 2018. The topic was listed as, *NSA: No Such Agency*.

A quick bathroom break, then a short walk out to the road to get the Sunday newspaper from the tube. Shift to a lower gear with maybe a little more casual reading that would prevent my brain from turning into cottage cheese.

Sunday afternoons at 'Camp Keyhole' — as Marino had dubbed the assisted living facility — could be slow and sleepy. Occasionally, however, things could be a bit more stimulating if there was a live musical performance.

It turned out that *this* Sunday was the latter.

Another resident, a 91-year-old man originally from the Long Island area of New York, was an accomplished violinist. His daughter, a pianist, was visiting. They were going to present a mini concert.

A dozen residents, along with three visitors, gathered in the large community room, seated in comfortable chairs carefully spaced apart, on a sofa, on padded folding chairs, and one woman in a wheelchair. Two of the facility's staff members stood against the wall near the entrance to the room.

The father adjusted pegs on the neck of the violin as he tuned it, while the daughter warmed up playing different scales in a moderate tempo. Out through the windows the sky was overcast and a light rain continued.

Ready to start, they opened with two Mozart sonatas, a Bach minuet, followed by *Ava Maria*, and then paused for a minute. The old violinist hammed it up for fellow residents, bowing deeply at the waist and clapping silently for his daughter. They resumed by playing Pachelbel's Canon in D.

Frank Marino closed his eyes. He brought up images of his grandmother playing the piano while he sat at the knees of his mother, listening. They were the only three in the room. It was from a long time ago. Yet the faces of his mother and grandmother were as fresh in his mind as the woman at the keyboard only 20 feet away.

When the performance ended, Marino stayed to visit with the father and daughter, complimenting their musical skills. He admired and commented on the old man's violin. "It came from Italy," he said. "Not a Stradivarius. But by a renowned twentieth century violin maker, Giampaolo Savini."

Back in his apartment, Marino listened to a message on his voicemail. A friend was in Vermont for a few days and would like to see him. He played the message again, thought for a minute, then called Michael Hanlon who answered on the second ring.

"I hope that I am not disturbing you," Marino said.

"Nope. Just reading the newspaper and watching the rain."

"Yes. If it continues, it will be a short foliage season I would imagine. Michael, are you up for a drive this week? I would like to go to Burlington."

"Probably. When did you want to go?"

Twenty Nine

Marino told me about a friend who was in Burlington for a brief visit with her niece, that he would like to see her and would be grateful if I could be his chauffeur. And plan to spend most of the day there.

"Not tomorrow. Tuesday would be good, or Wednesday," he said.

"Either day can work for me. What time are we talking about?"

"Leave here by 10, I would think. I would like to take her to lunch and have some of the afternoon to catch up," he said.

"Why don't you pin it down and let me know? The things I'm working on can be juggled. Still plowing my way through all these reading assignments that you gave me."

"I will call you back this evening. As soon as I have made a plan with Maggie." I assumed that Maggie was the friend, not the niece.

"If I'm not here, just leave a message. Or try my cell, although reception can be spotty. You have my cell number, yes?"

"I do. It's on your business card, I believe," he said.

"It is indeed. I'll wait to hear from you."

Less than an hour later, Marino called back.

"Maggie says that either Tuesday or Wednesday will be fine," he said. "I looked at the forecast. Wednesday looks like it will be the nicer day."

"Okay. It's maybe an hour from Williamstown to Burlington. We still thinking ten o'clock?"

"Ten-thirty should do it."

"Where in Burlington are we going?" I said.

"Stanbury Road. She says that it's close to the lake."

Lot of Lake Champlain waterfront in Burlington. Could be north, or down near Shelburne.

"Did she give you a street number?"

"No, but I will get it from her niece," he said.

"Yeah, that'll help. We can just plug it into the GPS and know where to get off the interstate."

"I truly appreciate this, Michael."

"Hey, I am working for you. Not a problem."

"But you didn't sign on to be my driver," he said. "We can talk on the way."

"Go ahead and confirm the address. Unless I hear differently, I will be at your apartment ten-fifteen Wednesday morning."

"Thank you."

I hadn't been to Burlington in nearly a year. Might be a good idea to check on the different places to eat, see who was still in business after the pandemic shutdown with many restaurants offering curbside pickup and takeout orders only.

Then again, maybe Marino's friend or her niece already had a place in mind. I wrote 'restaurants?' on the pad next to my phone to remind me to look anyway.

Leaving the newspaper on the kitchen counter, I put on boots and got my rainslicker from the closet. Rocco sat up to watch.

"Come on, champ. Let's go for a walk."

He stood and did the curtsy leg stretch routine, or downward dog.

"Something Virginia taught you?"

Biscuits in one pocket, leash in the other, I put his alert collar on so that he could run the perimeter of the backyard first. We headed out into the rain. After a minute, I removed the alert collar and placed it in my pocket, attached his leash and we started up a logging road that eventually intersects with the Appalachian Trail.

What I normally did on this kind of outing — if we didn't encounter other people — was to let him go off leash for the first part of the walk. As soon as I heard or saw someone, or as we got close to the AT, I would snap the leash back on.

The rain was a steady light drizzle. Rocco repeatedly stopped to sniff trees, grass, boulders and rotting logs.

"I'm tellin' you, kid, *bears*." It was my favorite taunt any time we got near the woods. He would look at me for a couple of seconds as though it was another code word for biscuit, then he would continue ahead, unfazed.

Back in the summer one afternoon, sitting on the deck having a beer, Ragsdale had heard me teasing Rocco. He shook his head.

"One of these days you're going to be out here reading, or cooking up some liberal bullshit to influence the less informed," he'd said, "and a bear is going to come up here, bend that bird feeder in half and kick your ass."

"I'll be sure to call should that occur."

Thirty

An hour after we'd left the house, Rocco and I made it back before dark. He smelled like a wet dog but was quite happy. I dried him off with a large towel and gave him a bacon treat.

The walk gave me a little time and quiet to process some of the reading from earlier. Ready for another hundred pages. Maybe watch the *No Such Agency* video clip *first* was a better idea. I got a beer from the fridge, some crackers, cheese, half of a yellow onion, opened a can of sardines and went to my office to go back online.

The Q & A session was part of the *Aspen Ideas Festival* recorded two years before. This portion featured a woman who was Assistant Deputy Director from the Operations Directorate at NSA. She offered an overview of the US intelligence community officially made up of sixteen different agencies.

Beginning with the national agencies, she explained that the CIA oversees 'human intelligence' from around the world, and NSA's responsibilities are focused on 'signals intelligence', listening to communications of all types from many different places. In addition, NSA is charged with building the cipher programs that protect the United States' most sensitive secrets.

Pausing the video, I put my earbuds in, tapped the play arrow again, leaned back and listened to audio only, as though I was listening to a radio interview. That worked much better.

The woman eventually talked about why people are drawn to work for NSA — and the federal government in general — noting that many individuals are drawn to a 'mission', being a part of something larger than themselves. About 30 minutes into the presentation with a few questions from the moderator, they shifted to questions from the audience. I opened my eyes to observe who was asking a question.

All in all, interesting, but it really did not help me learn much about the type of person who might have been drawn to this work before the days of the internet and before we began listening in on cellphone calls from around the world.

I decided that the Aspen session was perhaps a good faith effort to provide a broader view of NSA. It had offered a few nuggets of relatively minor detail that one might not otherwise learn. But any information on the messy or unpleasant stuff, that would have to come from another source.

Hanlon dives into 'human intelligence' gathering? We'll see.

"Ragsdale might know about 'signals' intelligence," I said to myself.

Louie, how about some help here?

127

Clicking out of the online recording, I went back to the living room and the book *Dark Territory*. Picking up where I'd left off earlier in the day but before I started reading again, another thought was whacking the back of my head.

All of this is fascinating. And well-written. But nothing here is going to tell me about people from three generations back, before cyber warfare.

People like Win Callahan.

Marino had told me that he had a longer story to share. I would have to listen carefully and see if there was anything that would get us to a motive of *why* Callahan's death might not have been an accident.

Thirty One

"**I honestly don't know** but let me speak with the Colonel. He will know for certain," Lieutenant Heidi Murrough said.

Tuesday morning after the holiday and I had her on the phone. My question went to the 1980 New Hampshire Fish and Game investigating Conservation Officer, Robert Dufresne. "Is he still alive?"

"I'd appreciate any information you come up with, either way," I said, "If he *is* still with us, could you also ask Colonel Gordon what is department protocol for me to contact Dufresne?"

"No problem. I will get back to you as soon as I know."

"Thanks for taking the time."

Experience with other law enforcement agencies in the past had taught me that you could not predict how quickly a request might get attention. Sometimes you were able to get answers on the spot or within hours. But there were instances when a query could float around out there for days on end. Plus, if you hoped for reasonable cooperation — especially if you were not a working reporter — there was a fine line between being persistent and being a real pain-in-the-ass nag.

As a rule, I avoided making follow-up phone calls too close together.

Contacting New Hampshire F & G to get a 'first person' line underway seemed to make sense. At the same time, I tried to work through the abstract data coming at me from books, video clips and old newspaper accounts. Good background and logical starting point, yes. But, so far, I was not getting the feeling of much forward movement.

I went back to my scribbled notes on the yellow pad from a few days earlier, reading through two pages of marginally legible shorthand: recorded facts, assumptions, speculation, and several questions. But the *real* starting point was underlined right there at the bottom of the second page: FM – why do you believe this? Please expand.

The phone chats and short, hit-and-run conversations seemed to have the same effect as keeping a trickle of water flowing through a long garden hose. What I really needed was to get the nozzle wide open. Soon.

Frank, give me all you got. No time for playing around with your 'intuition.'

The thought reflexively caused me to take a deep cleansing breath, inhale through the nose, hold it for a count of three, exhale slowly through the mouth. And that led me to the useful old radio technique of 'back timing' used by DJs and reporters. Establish the point you need to reach, consider the required steps between now and that point, make it all flow smoothly. Simple.

I had once explained it this way to my late friend, Bonnie Mackin.

"Good disc jockeys need to pull it off with music tracks, commercials and other announcements," I told her. "Knowing the exact length of time for each step and programming them in a sequence that hits the top of the hour right on the mark, 8:59:59.

"Reporters and news announcers have an easier time of it. They can pace their stories and audio cuts, with accurate timing, to get to the same spot."

Back timing. With Frank Marino. On Wednesday, the trip to Burlington. Drive up in the morning, come back in the evening. Whatever he wants to share on the drive up, fine. Go for 'all that he's got' on the drive home.

The phone rang. It was Lieutenant Murrough calling back.

"Mister Hanlon. Unfortunately, Officer Robert Dufresne is deceased," she said. "Colonel Gordon said that he'd been sick for a long time and that he passed away in 2017."

"I appreciate such a quick response," I said.

"Not a problem."

"If I think of anything else, I may call you again."

"We're happy to try to help," she said. "Have a good day."

Thirty Two

'The Shooter' parked in the very same spot on the street where he had parked on the previous trip to Weapons, Ltd. Just as he had on that occasion, he stared at the entrance. The shade on the door was pulled down.

It was 1:52pm. Armando had told him that he would be there after 2 o'clock.

The newly typed list of all the guns that he owned was lying on the seat next to him. The only firearm that he'd brought along was a Parker Brothers 12-gauge double shotgun, inside a two-tone brown leather case that was covered with a beach towel on the back seat.

This collector's shotgun had hunting scenes engraved on the breech face and both barrels, with a walnut stock that featured decorative checkering. Factory records from Parker — a copy of which was tucked inside the case — showed that this gun had originally been ordered by a wealthy New Yorker in 1903 and that it had been manufactured the following year.

The gun was worth a lot of money, possibly twenty-five-thousand dollars or more.

A slim-built, dark haired man wearing a navy windbreaker over gray corduroy slacks came from behind the building. It was Armando. He approached the front door, unlocked it and went inside.

Waiting a full minute, the shooter placed the folded list inside his jacket, got out and opened the rear driver's side door to remove the case with the shotgun. He adjusted the leather shoulder strap to go over his left arm and walked toward the entrance.

Inside, the faux hunting lodge parlor was darkened from afternoon shade, end table lamps not turned on. The soft chime of the bell in the back office sounded.

"Hello," Armando's voice said, then he appeared at the office door. "Come in. I just got here."

"Take your time," the Shooter said. He removed the strap from his shoulder and rested the butt of the case on the carpeted floor.

"Let me get some lights on," Armando said, stepping back inside the office. A few seconds later, both lamps next to the sofa came on, as well as the recessed lights above the gun cabinets along the wall.

"Thanks for coming," Armando said. "Would you like coffee? I have a Keurig machine in the office. Fresh brewed in no time, regular or decaf."

"I would take a cup of regular. Black, no sugar."

"Make yourself comfortable. I'll be right out."

The figure he had in mind was one-hundred thousand dollars, minimum. Thirty-one guns total. That would be for an outright sale to Armando, *no consignments.*

While the Parker 12-gauge was a special gun that would sell quickly, there was a rifle in the collection that could bring almost as much. It was not as old as the Parker, but the engraving was spectacular.

He laid the shotgun case on the sofa, unzipped his jacket and settled into a wing chair. The seven-foot high antique grandfather clock in the corner chimed twice.

The shooter glanced at his analog watch; four minutes after two.

Armando appeared carrying two mugs of coffee. He handed one to the shooter, placed the other one the table in front of the sofa and seated himself in a matching wing chair opposite the shooter.

"I have a buyer for the Springfield," he said. "No issues with the weapon. But we didn't expect any," a voice with the soft inflection of a Spanish accent.

"Good coffee," the shooter said. "Thanks." Placing the mug on the table, he added, "How much?"

"Eighteen hundred. No quibbling. He's ready to purchase others, depending on what you have to sell."

"I did what you suggested, made a full list." The shooter pulled it from an inside coat pocket and placed it on the table. Pointing at the list, he said, "Each weapon, date of purchase and the price paid."

"May I take a look?" Armando said. The shooter nodded.

Unfolding the two sheets of paper, Armando slowly read down the first page. Half-way down, he stopped, looked at the shooter and gave a soft whistle.

"When you came in last week, you did not tell me the age of the Parker," he said. "That is a very, *very* rare shotgun."

The shooter patted the gun case, then leaned forward to unzip it. Removing the double-barrel, he turned the butt end toward Armando and passed him the gun. After a couple minutes of gently handling and examining the gun — feeling its heft, squinting an eye on the sight, breaking the gun open and looking into each barrel — Armando rubbed the stock with his fingertips and admired the engraving.

"This is in remarkable condition," he said. "How long have you owned it?"

The shooter pointed at the two sheets of paper now resting on the table. "Almost 40 years. It was the first shotgun I purchased. Had a few rifles. This belonged to an old high school buddy who got it from his grandfather."

Armando handed the gun back across the table, picked up the list and resumed reading. Listed in parentheses next to the Parker 12-guage was the purchase date and price: (February 1981 - $7,500.00.)

"You got a deal," Armando said. The shooter nodded.

Three lines below the Parker was a listing for a Holland and Holland Super 275 rifle that included a Zeiss scope, with engraving by Frank Conroy.

Armando held up the page and tapped the paper. "This gun is worth twenty-grand," he said. "Conroy's engraving is among the best. *Really* excellent."

They spent another forty-five minutes going over the list and talking about the condition of most of the guns. When they finished, Armando asked if the list was his copy, the shooter said that it was.

"Give me a day or two," Armando said. "I will give you one price for everything here."

"Good. That's what I'm looking for."

Thirty Three

The long, slow walk on the beach at Matala helped to surface a name Nikos had long forgotten; Pavlos Astrinidis, an old man he believed to still be alive in a small village close to his own ancestral home.

The calendar showed that it was Tuesday, 13 October. Melissa had confirmed in their phone conversation that she would be back in Greece on Friday, staying in Athens for three days, then bringing her American friend to Matala in one week, 20 October.

Smoking a cigarette and drinking coffee at one of his outdoor tables, Nikos said in a loud voice, "Ari, come out here. I need to speak to you."

A tall, thin young man, possibly not yet 21, appeared at the door of the taverna. He wore denim blue jeans and a white shirt, longish brown hair down to the collar.

"Nikos, what is it?" the young man said. "Are you not feeling well?"

"Can you borrow your father's van? For one day."

The young man shrugged. "I think so, yes. What do you need me to pick up?" Nikos shook his head. "Nothing," he said, stubbing out his cigarette. Slowly pushing himself from the chair, he said, "*Me*," tapping the gray hair covering his head. "I need to go to Opsigias. Not on your scooter."

A fulltime employee at the taverna — daytime gofer and handyman, nighttime bartender — Ari was accustomed to running errands. He had never been asked to be his driver. Nikos no longer owned a car. But then, he never went anywhere.

"When do you need to go?"

"*Today*," Nikos said with a grunt, then added, "Tomorrow could be also good." Surprised by the sudden urgency of this request, Ari watched the old man shuffle past him and make his way through the empty taverna.

"I will go and ask my father," he said.

"Tell him that I will pay. It will be rental. And you the driver."

Leaving Matala a few minutes after eleven they arrived first in Amari, Andreadakis' native village, at 12:30 pm. Nikos was adamant that they would not spend more than one hour in Amari. This was not a trip to visit relatives, but a childhood friend named Kostas.

Kostas was surprised at the sudden appearance of Nikos, whom he had not seen in more than a decade. Their only contact was by phone, usually when someone in Amari had died.

Three years apart in age, Nikos the elder, they had been close growing up. That changed dramatically after they reached young adulthood when Nikos had travelled first to France, then to the US, and once back in Greece having spent two years in Athens before finally purchasing the taverna and settling at Matala.

"I saw him at Easter," Kostas said, responding to Nikos' question about Pavlos Astrinidis. "He is frail. Living with his daughter."

"She is in Opsigias?" Nikos asked.

"Yes. She was a school teacher there for many years. They still live in the village. Just ask, I am sure that you can find her."

With assistance from a middle-aged man sitting on a bench at a roadside pullover in the village, Nikos learned that Astrinidis and his daughter and son-in-law lived barely a kilometer up the road. "Look for the goats. And a blue truck. Next to the school," the man told him.

Five minutes later, the van stopped in front of a two-story building of yellow stucco with a red tiled roof. There was a faded blue pickup truck inside an attached garage. The sound of bells could be heard from a small herd of goats in the field behind the house.

Nikos and Ari went up the steps.

A woman at the door stared at Nikos as though she might recognize him.

It turned out that she was wrong, she didn't know him. But after listening to his introduction, she knew of his family and

139

she had heard his name. She invited the two men to come inside, then led them to a street level terrace at the rear of the house. In a winter coat with blanket pulled over his legs despite the mild weather, an old man wearing large black plastic frame sunglasses sat in a metal folding-chair, and appeared to be asleep.

"Papa," the woman said, tapping the man's shoulder. "You have visitors."

Nikos watched as the old man slowly raised his head, then turned to see who was speaking to him.

"Pavlos. It is Nikos Andreadakis," he said. He held out a hand to the old man. "You knew my father, Dimitri. And my uncle, Hektor."

The old man, hands trembling, removed his sunglasses and placed them on his lap. Looking at Nikos, he slowly accepted the extended right hand and, through bleary, limited vision, studied the stranger's face.

"I will bring out chairs," the woman said.

"Ari will help you," Nikos said. And he did, following the woman back inside, returning with two straight back chairs from the kitchen. Nikos sat close to the old man while Ari sat in the other chair off to one side.

Reaching inside his coat pocket, Nikos removed a rolled-up photograph held by a rubber band. Handwritten on the back of the photo was 'Chania 1946'. Unrolling it revealed a monochrome print in a panoramic format, nearly a meter in width and 250 millimeters high — eight inches by close to thirty-six inches.

It appeared to have been taken by a professional photographer. A group of more than one hundred-men, a few in military uniforms, but most others dressed in civilian clothes. They were 'at ease,' standing or kneeling in front of a long building, not assembled in a formal, rigid line up.

Three teen-aged boys were also in the photo, standing at the left end of the group, as though they were included as an afterthought.

Nikos spread the photo and motioned for Ari to help him hold it up in front of the old man. Stretching his neck to look over it and using his right index finger, he tapped the area of the photo near where the boys stood.

"This is my uncle, Hektor," Nikos said. "And that is *you*, in the middle."

The old man looked at the photo but offered no response.

"Who is the other boy?" Nikos asked.

The old man touched the photo. A full ten seconds passed. He tapped the image of the other boy in the photo. "Varnavas," he said in a soft whisper.

Nikos nodded to Ari to hold both ends of the photo. He shuffled around to lean forward next to the old man.

"Who is this?" Nikos said, pointing to one of the men standing close to the boys. A pen-drawn black circle was around the man's head. He wore the uniform of an American soldier.

Thirty Four

Nikos was quiet for most of the trip home. It was late, Ari driving, few other cars on the narrow pavement winding through small villages. Eventually they came to the lights of Matala.

They had been gone for more than 10 hours. A respite had come in the form of an earlier than usual diepnon put out by Pavlos' daughter — lemon chicken with potatoes, stuffed tomatoes and peppers, and glasses of a white retsina.

The conversation had been mostly about families of Opsigias and Amari, with the daughter asking Nikos questions about 'what Matala is like' these days. For his part, Pavlos ate like he was 22 rather than 92, not talking, but consuming nearly the same quantity of food as Ari.

After the meal, there were small glasses of Raki. It was at that point when Pavlos opened up with more stories about the photo and days spent in Chania a long time ago. Nikos had helped him back out onto the terrace, where the old man talked while Nikos smoked. And listened.

Back at the taverna now, climbing out of the van, Nikos gave Ari two €50 bills and a €20. "Efcharisto. Tell your father that he has a dinner on me. Anytime," Nikos said.

Alone at an outside table, having his last cigarette of the night and observing the crescent moon over the bay, Nikos sat ruminating over the information that he'd gotten from Pavlos.

Could he trust the old man's memory? How much of it was accurate, how much jumbled in with other people and other events?

How much could he share with Melissa?

Pavlos was still awake at midnight. Too much food, too much retsina, too much Raki. Restless in bed, his mind churning with the memories of the stories he'd told earlier in the evening.

His childhood friend, Hektor Andreadakis, had been gone for twenty years. Out of nowhere comes this nephew, Nikolaos, to ask too many questions, showing the old photograph.

Pavlos had nearly forgotten the American soldiers. It was *Hektor,* he now recalled, who had severely berated one of those same soldiers in a conversation not long before Hektor himself passed.

The occasion had been at a family gathering in Amari, Pavlos had gone to visit Hektor. It was shortly after the beginning of the twenty-first century. Greece was preparing to host the summer Olympics. Many Greek newspapers wrote about the money that would be spent, what it would mean for the country's infrastructure, and who would lose out.

Pavlos could still hear Hektor's voice. Off on a tangent about Americans, then quiet for a spell, only to resume with a long, disorderly recollection of that particular American soldier, the one whose head had been circled in the photograph taken in Chania so many years ago.

Shortly after sunrise on a cool October morning, the recurring bell-clapper sound of goats clinking across a field on the outskirts of Opsigias, and the buzzing of a single motor scooter winding its way through the village, the well of memories finally ran dry.

Pavlos Astrinidis, 92, died in his sleep.

Thirty Five

Wednesday morning. I was getting ready to drive to Williamstown to take Frank Marino to Burlington to meet his old friend for lunch.

After trimming my beard, shaving and a long shower, I got dressed, cleaned up the breakfast dishes, finished deleting and responding to email, took one more look at the forecast on my phone app, then roused Rocco. First stop, drop him off at Virginia's. She had agreed to take him along to her office later in the afternoon.

Frank was ready when I arrived. Spiffed up in a navy blazer, button-down navy and red tartan shirt, tan dress slacks and burgundy loafers. He presented the appearance of some old British actor right out of Masterpiece Theatre.

"Looking pretty sharp there, Frank. Nice aftershave," I said. "Subtle."

"Bay Rum," he said, locking the door to his apartment.

"I shaved, too." I patted my neck.

"And groomed the beard, I see. Must take extra time," he said.

"Only twice a month. I've got it down, not a big deal."

After we had crested the hill and got onto the interstate, Frank said that we would be looking for The Old Chittenden Inn off Stanbury Road when we got there.

"Okay," I said, thinking how to set up what I hoped would be a productive interview session later, on the way back.

"All this NSA, CIA reading you have me doing — some of it remarkably candid, if you believe what they're writing — makes me wonder about all the things they're *not* telling."

"Oh, I'm sure," he said. "A lot of ink by too many to count over a very long time. Some events will never see the light of day. Or, not a public, *declassified* light of day."

He told me about a 60th anniversary NSA Timeline project — dating from 1952 through the months just before he officially retired. Historical documents, audio files, and photographs from World War II up to and including activities in 2012. According to Frank, the treasure trove included more than 200 declassified documents, most of which were then released for the first time.

Clearly, I had hit the right play button. Frank talked for 50 miles, until we approached Exit 14W to downtown. I held up my hand as we looped the exit ramp.

"Maybe 10 minutes from here," I said. "You're on a roll. Save those thoughts. I have a bunch of questions about where *you* fit in with all that classified stuff."

Holding up fingers of both hands to form a V, he did a fair Richard Nixon imitation and said, "I am not a spy."

"But if what you told me a couple of weeks ago is on the level, you must've met old Tricky Dick."

"Fortunately, the answer is *no*, I did not. There was a lot going on back then. However, *my* expertise was not required. At least it was not needed by any of those closest to the President at that time."

At exactly 12:30, we pulled into the parking lot of the old inn.

"Maggie said that her niece would be driving a red Prius," Frank said.

I pointed to the right. "Might be that one up ahead," I said, moving slowly in the direction of the car I'd spotted. It was parked nose out, a woman behind the wheel and another passenger next to her.

We pulled in front of the car, Frank lowered his window and waved. The passenger, a woman, waved back.

Glancing at my outside mirrors, I hit the emergency flasher button and began backing toward an open space three slots back. The two women were getting out of the Prius.

By the time I had parked, Frank was unsnapping his seatbelt. The women were moving in our direction. The older one, I assumed to be Maggie, had short gray hair and was nearly as tall as Frank. The younger woman — also on the tall side, possibly six feet — walked a couple of feet behind her aunt.

Out of the car, Frank gave the older woman a bear hug, leaned his head back to look at her, then continued to embrace her. I could not hear what they said to each other. The younger woman had stopped and was smiling at the reunion.

I stepped past Frank, extending my right hand to the younger woman. "Hi. Michael Hanlon," I said. She shook my hand.

"Katherine Wolfe," she said. "Nice to meet you."

"Katherine, so nice to see you again. How long has it been?" Frank said, now embracing the younger woman.

"At least ten years," she said. "I believe that it was at Aunt Mags' birthday in Washington."

"We do not have to be talking about birthdays," the older woman interjected.

"Margaret Sanders, say hello to Michael Hanlon," Frank said. She took my hand in both of hers.

"It is a pleasure to meet you, Michael," she said.

"Very nice to meet you, Ms. Sanders."

"Please, everyone calls me Maggie. *Not* Margaret," she added, giving Frank a playful pat on the arm.

After another minute of chit chat, Katherine said that she would walk into the restaurant with Frank and Maggie, but then she was going to run errands. I said that I was going to go visit an old radio pal in South Burlington.

"If they don't kick us out," Frank said, "we'll settle in the lounge for a spell after lunch. No need to rush back . . ." he looked at his watch, "before 3:30 or so."

We agreed that 4 o'clock was a safe time to reconvene. Katherine told her aunt to call if she needed her to come back sooner.

So much for a surprise drop in. *Shoulda called ahead.* My old radio pal at WJOY was on vacation. As I didn't know any of the current staff, there was no need to stick around. I left my business card with the date and a short note on the back.

There was a slight breeze, but it was mostly sunny and would stay warm for a couple of hours. I decided to get a sandwich to go, find a bench somewhere near the lake to watch boats and read a book. I'd brought along *Dark Territory*, more to reread and learn, I hoped, about the culture from the early days of US intelligence agencies.

A little after three, I stopped reading, watched joggers and people out walking, a Lake Champlain ferry approaching, and two sail boats farther out. With the sun dropping, I got up and began a quick-paced, extended roundabout trek to the car.

At 3:55 I was back at the restaurant. The red Prius was one of a few cars in the lot, but Katherine apparently had gone inside. I parked and headed for the front door.

Much praise for the food and service at The Old Chittenden, Frank and Maggie both enthusiastic about the place. They were seated in side-by-side chairs in the lounge, empty teacups on a table in front of them. Sitting forward in a chair opposite the couple, Katherine was beaming.

"We've had a wonderful time," Maggie said. Frank patted her hand.

"I have tried to convince your 'Aunt Mags' that she should consider moving to Vermont," he said.

"Something that I have been telling her *for years*," Katherine said.

"The summers and fall are beautiful," Maggie said. "I don't think that I would enjoy the winter. And I love my little home. I can't imagine leaving Washington."

Holding her right hand and patting it again, Frank said, "We understand, dear. I hope that I can come visit you in the spring."

A slow amble to the parking lot, more hugs, 'hope to see you again' farewells for Katherine and me, all passengers back in their vehicles and synchronized departure from Burlington at 4:25.

There was a lot more traffic than one sees this time of day in Quechee. Commuters leaving downtown and the UVM campus, headed south on 89, with cars peeling off at the first few exits, then thinning out after we passed Waterbury.

Other than saying that it had been "heartwarming" and "just so good to see her," Frank had gone quiet. Not Ragsdale quiet, as in 'don't ask, Hanlon', but more of a serene state.

So, Radio Rick, how you gonna start this interview? Louie's voice in my head sometimes caused me to wonder if it was him or me? *Hypnosis, or reporter's anxiety?*

Thirty Six

Camel's Hump was behind us off to the west, the sun closer to the horizon, and cruise control locked in at 65 mph. I volleyed up a preamble to my first question.

"You know, Frank, about . . . let's see . . . maybe 12 years ago, I had a chance to interview a man who'd been caught up in a mess of unethical, and quite illegal, business activities.

"He'd been perceived as a 'community leader', was well liked by many; and on the surface, he appeared to be quite successful. By the time he agreed to talk with me, he had been charged, indicted, then *convicted* and sentenced to prison for two to five years." I could feel Frank's gaze, though he remained silent.

"My opening question to the man was, 'Tell me how you arrived at this point in your life?'"

Frank laughed. "Very good, Michael Hanlon. How, indeed, did I get to this point in my life?" He patted my right arm. "Do not worry. I have given much thought to all the 'strictly background' information that I think you need. And *deserve*, if we expect you to succeed with this assignment."

"Great. I'm going to shut up now," I said. "Go for it."

The traffic was perhaps only a car or two passing every minute or so. Checking the driver side mirror, I kept my eyes on the horizon.

Frank had clearly given it much thought. In a measured, often self-deprecating manner, for the next 45 minutes he doled out slices of his story.

Beginning with tales from an overly protected childhood through prep school and college years — including becoming reacquainted with Win Callahan — he was approaching the part about starting work for the US government just as we were approaching Williamstown.

Taking a longer route back, I turned off at Berlin and followed Route 14 south. Frank paused, looked at landmarks as we got closer to Williamstown, and seemed surprised that we were nearly home. He momentarily switched gears.

"You will be able to stay for a spell?" he said. "I'm not really hungry, but I am sure that I can find sufficient vittles to get you through the evening."

"I'm good. Maybe some cheese and crackers."

"Good. I can open a bottle of wine," he added.

"All that speculation about how so many old, confirmed bachelors like me are homosexual, is just that . . . *speculation*,"

Frank said. He had prepared a platter of garlic bagel chips, slices of cheese and some black olives, placing it on the coffee table in front of me.

"The spy business, as much as any profession, certainly has its share of men and women, who prefer the company of their own gender." Twisting the cap off a bottle of red wine, he poured equal amounts into two glasses. Laughing, he took a sip of wine, put down his glass and placed both hands on his thighs.

"Just this afternoon, Maggie and I were rekindling tales that might have come out of a Victorian novel. Unlike some of those 'gentlemen' who disliked and often avoided women," he said, "I can assure you that some of the most stellar times of my long life have been with the intimate companionship of the female gender." Another chuckle followed by another tip of the glass.

I was not clear about where this line of the conversation might be heading, afraid that Frank wouldn't get back to the earlier story that he had been telling so well during the drive home. Picking up on my puzzlement immediately, he clasped his hands together and leaned forward.

"The whole point here, Michael, is to assure you that my obsession with Win Callahan's death is *not* because we were an 'item,' as the old expression goes. We were not. If anything, during his lifetime good 'ol Win strayed many a day with a *lot* of women. Wouldn't be a complete surprise if one of them had him shot.

"He was far from perfect. He committed professional acts for which only he could have been held accountable and often times was not. By the way, he was not a pioneer in that regard. Some of the real stories likely will never be fully accounted for. But, let me reiterate, he was a mentor to me, and others. And, a lifelong friend."

"Frank, I believed you the first time."

He studied me for a beat, then said, "Thank you."

We were quiet, I had another piece of cheese and a sip of wine.

"And even though Win *may* have done some of those 'unpleasant things' that you have read about, he did not deserve to be murdered." Again, Frank watched me for a response. When I offered none, he continued. "And if I am right that he was *murdered*, the crime should not be lost in the incomplete and murky duplicity of secret intelligence history."

Did unpleasant things. Did not deserved to be murdered. Murky duplicity. Who is keeping that scorebook?

Frank got back on track with the story. Telling how it all related to his own career, then recalling numerous pivotal moments from the life of Win Callahan. And just as in the car an hour ago, once he began, the pacing was steady, without detectable gaps in the narrative or moments of hesitation in his commentary.

A review of selective assignments, in the States and abroad; climbing the bureaucratic ladder; feuding with superiors — Frank ticked off some names — who were serving at the pleasure of different presidents; and the inter-agency rivalries. All this making a lengthy, colorful account of what Frank referred to as, "a story of just one more minor cold warrior, doing his best for his country."

Finally, a long pause. I was pleased with myself that I had been able to keep my mouth shut. Louie would've been impressed.

Holding up the bottle to offer more wine, which I declined, Frank now appeared to be weary from all the talking. He took the empty glasses and the bottle to the kitchen, walking slowly, then came back and stood next to his chair. He had a tired smile on his face.

"I'm beat, Michael."

"I'll bet you are. Long day."

"Here is the good news," he said. "All of what I just told you — about Win and many other 'associates' — I believe is simply an overview to this story. And most of it unrelated to his death."

Guess that I was tired, too. I half expected Frank to throw up his hands and say something like, 'This really isn't going anywhere. Let's just stop right here."

But he didn't say that. Instead, he threw me a Bill Lee curveball.

Placing a hand on my shoulder, he gestured toward the door. I got up from the chair.

"Top of the next inning," he said, "I will tell you *why* I think Win was murdered. Something Moe Berg might've chased down if he were here."

155

Thirty Seven

Having absorbed and having quietly celebrated the news that yes, her husband was really and truly going to retire, Becky Ragsdale felt a profound sense of relief.

Louie was already showing signs of restlessness since giving her the news a week earlier: at his own initiative, taking on little tasks inside and outside their home, helping a friend with repairs to a barn, taking his SUV in for servicing early in the morning before the dealership opened, and a lot of activity that might be classified as 'fidgeting your way to tranquility.'

Thirty-one years in law enforcement. A long early run as a municipal policeman in a small Vermont town, years sprinkled with Becky's concern of what could happen on any given day. Subsequent work with a state level task force attempting to combat drug dealing and all its ugly waste. But it had been the last 10 years that had really made Becky anxious, even though she had done her best not to let it show.

A multi-state effort — known as the *Joint Northeast Counter-Drug Task Force* — first recruited and then kept Louis James Ragsdale as one of their best undercover agents. And he was *really good* at the job. That fact did not always provide solace for Becky.

Louie rarely shared stories with his wife about the work. Usually just a brief account about some of the funny or silly things that happened, none of the dangerous incidents. She accepted that. But being in the dark did not take her very far in eliminating the worry.

There had been many occasions when Louie was on assignment somewhere in New England and would be gone for a week or longer. Becky knew the state, sometimes the name of the town or city, and Louie regularly checked in with a text or short voice message. That helped, some of the time.

One of the ways that she coped was by avoiding the TV shows featuring cops, especially the trendy urban fare which frequently included cocaine and heroin busts and all the ancillary services to the world's drug thugs.

Now Becky was ready to accept that in just over two months, Louie would be home every day. The short weekend trips and rare vacations of the past could now be for as long as they wanted them to be. Didn't matter where to.

She had the germ of an idea about one way to help Louie make his transition into retirement. For her part, it would require more thought, a couple of phone calls, and some planning.

Michael might be willing to help.

The screen on the phone showed 'Name Unavailable'. I decided to answer anyway — too early in the day for robo calls. Maybe.

"Michael Hanlon," I said.

"Michael, it's Becky. Is this a good time?" The Ragsdales' had always had an unlisted number.

"Hey, Becky, how are ya? Sure. What's up?"

"Louie gave you the good news."

"In fact, he did. Is he really going to go through with it?" I asked.

"Oh yes. He showed me the letter from his boss in Albany accepting the date. December 31st."

"You making plans to go to Hawaii?" I said.

"Not yet. But I have a trip out west to help a cousin. Give Louie a chance to settle in here at home," she said. "He has all this earned leave right now. And is beginning to act as though we're about to get a new puppy. He can't sit still."

"You know my take on that. You guys *should* get a new dog. Maybe two."

"I'm sure we will, but not before spring."

"Good."

"I have a favor to ask," she said. "Louie told me about your fishing the other day. He had a good time. I could tell when he came home."

"Yeah. Took him to a spot that I'd been keeping secret for a long time. We had a nice lunch. It *was* a good day."

"Would you think about planning a short excursion to get Louie away for a few days? You know that John and Angie moved to North Carolina. Louie got used to the fishing jaunts down to Long Island that he did with John."

"Right. I went with them once," I said.

"He has a lot of time between now and the end of December. He told me no overnights, just occasional day training for new agents."

"Same thing he told me. I think he said nothing on the calendar again until middle of next month," I said.

"Think about it, would you? Who knows, he might even consider going back to the Bahamas."

"Unfortunately, *that* is not a possibility. At least not where we went in 2016. Abaco was devastated by Hurricane Dorian. And with the pandemic, I'm not sure they're letting people from the US visit yet."

"Just a thought. It probably wouldn't matter where you go, if you can do it. He's just happier when he can fish, but you know that," she said.

"I'm on a new project at the moment. Not sure where or how long it's going to go," I said. "Let me noodle it around for a couple of days, okay?"

"I really appreciate it, Michael. I won't call you back until this weekend. Let's not let the cat out of the bag until you know something."

"Got it. Dumb's the word. Take care, Becky."

Take Ragsdale on a trip? The thought spliced right into the ongoing chatter with Frank Marino and his early caveat, 'there will be some travel.'

Standing at the door of Marino's apartment two nights ago, both of us tired, he'd asked if I could come back sometime over the weekend, maybe Saturday.

"I have some thoughts about your next step," he'd said. "Too late to get into tonight."

"Sure. Let me check the weather. Maybe go for a short foliage drive. It's pretty near over," I'd said.

"That would be nice. I didn't pay much attention to the leaves on our travels today, I'm afraid."

"We could go south a bit, or out through Woodstock and Killington. There's still some color in other areas of the state."

"I would really enjoy that. Find a spot for lunch," he'd said. Before I departed, we had agreed that we would talk on the phone on Friday and pin it down.

Driving home late that night, jazz on the radio at low volume, one of the many pop-up questions I had regarding the next meeting with Frank was, '*What about the travel?*'

Thirty Eight

'The Shooter' was, for the moment, satisfied that Armando and Weapons, Ltd. had been the right choice. Maximum payout for selling all the guns, check in hand within three days of the completion of the sale.

Now everything would be about the calendar. First, what is the optimal date to leave Massachusetts? That would determine when to deliver the guns to Armando. Next, the Carolinas, Georgia, or Arizona? He was leaning to Arizona but would watch the pandemic map and see what was happening with new cases of Coronavirus.

The third — and most volatile consideration — was the timing of when to tell his housemate that she needed to make other plans.

It had been a convenient, mutually gratifying yet often mercurial relationship. They had met at work and clearly had what she had called 'good chemistry'. He wasn't so sure. She had been divorced just over a year. As far as he was concerned, the whole 'sex thing' had pretty much run its course.

By his way of thinking, it would be a straight-forward dissolution. No one owed anyone anything. In his head, the analogy was as though one of them had died or had developed amnesia. The other one simply needed to move on.

He would break the news this evening.

In Matala, when word reached Nikos about Pavlos' death, he went to his regular outside table at the taverna, sat and sipped cold, strong coffee. He smoked three cigarettes in a span of 20 minutes.

The news had come in a phone call from the cousin in Amari, whom he'd visited on his way to find Pavlos. The death did not surprise anyone. The man *was* 92. He had lived a long life with no major illnesses or suffering. And had died at home, in his sleep. *We all should be as fortunate.*

As though he needed still another reminder of his own mortality, Nikos contemplated the age difference, just as he had done during the drive back after visiting the old man.

Pavlos was born in 1928. Hektor, younger brother of Nikos' father, was three years older and much like a brother to him, Pavlos had said during the long, fragmented conversation of three nights ago. It was a sentiment shared by Nikos. When Hektor died, he also felt that he had lost an older brother, not an uncle.

Rising from his chair, Nikos shuffled back to the small office behind the kitchen and retrieved the old photo that he'd taken to show Pavlos. Back outside, he sat, lit a cigarette, and spread the print across the table. Using the nearly empty coffee cup as a paperweight, he placed the cup at one end of the long photo and a glass ashtray at the other end.

The photo had a crease near its center that would crack and tear through the paper with much continued handling. Nikos took a long time studying the faces, his eyes moving slowly right to left, fingers of his right hand barely touching the surface and sliding along as though he were reading a Braille transcript.

Reaching the spot in the group where Pavlos stood next to Hektor and the other boy, Nikos eyes locked on the soldier in the American uniform, the one standing next to the teenagers. He was the only person in the photo with a circle drawn around his head.

Nikos touched the image of the soldier, slowly running a finger back and forth, up and down, leaning closer to examine every detail of the face and the uniform.

The man was of medium build. His jacket had epaulets featuring shiny buttons with larger buttons on the lapels. Two small ribbons were attached just above the left breast pocket. The man's hat was a garrison cap, the soft style soldiers could fold and place inside a pocket.

The first time Nikos had ever seen this monochrome print was shortly after Hektor had died. It had been stored in a trunk along with some letters and a small box of mostly family photographs, now in the possession of Nikos' daughter living in Athens, Melissa's mother.

Moving the coffee cup and the ash tray caused the curled ends of the photo to spring back into a scroll. Nikos tightened the roll of the print and replaced the rubber band.

He would show the photo to Melissa. And he would share what he'd learned during his visit with the now dead Pavlos.

Thirty Nine

Saturday was the choice for the foliage drive with Frank. It would be my second in two weeks. Going to pick him up again made me wonder how many Uber drivers there might be these days in a small, mostly rural state.

People in cities have an Uber account and are quite accustomed to having a driver show up within minutes of their message that they need to go somewhere pronto.

All those national rankings on so many different statistics . . . how does Vermont stack up with, say, Wyoming? Or North Dakota? Uber drivers, or anything else, for that matter.

I began paying attention to the cars going in the opposite direction or passing me. Someone else riding in the car with the driver; is it a relative or a friend? Do Uber drivers require you to sit in the back, or is it your choice?

After forty minutes of watching traffic and looking for wildlife along the highway, I pulled into the parking area behind the 'continuing care retirement community.'

When he opened the door of his apartment, the room was filled with operatic music. By 'filled', I mean much like a car that pulls up next to you with its speakers dialed up to maybe a nine.

A woman singing — *amazing voice* — then a male that even I was pretty certain was Luciano Pavarotti.

Wonder what the neighbors think about this?

Marino went to a cabinet, opened a door and lowered the volume. His face had the appearance of a person recently informed that he was in excellent health and should approach each day accordingly.

"What are we listening to?" I asked.

He handed me a plastic CD case: *The Ultimate Puccini Collection.* A half a dozen names were listed on the cover, Pavarotti at the top. I flipped the case over to read the list of songs and performers.

"Before I moved in here, I culled my music collection. Just under 200 CDs and only 40 or so LP's came with me. *This,*" he motioned to the speakers behind him, "is my very favorite. I play it at least once a week."

I pointed at the cabinet that held his CD player and a turntable. "Bring the CD, we can listen on our drive."

"Wonderful idea," he said. "Let me get a coat."

In the car, now heading west, I started to slip the CD in for more opera.

"Could we listen to that on the way back?" Frank said, adding, "I have more to tell you from our conversation the other night."

"Sure." I inserted the disc but tapped the button to turn off the changer.

Earlier that morning I had decided on a route that would take us by side roads through Roxbury, then over the mountain to Route 100, one of the most traveled 'scenic' stretches of blacktop in the entire state.

Frank got right to it.

"I told you how great it was to spend the afternoon with Maggie on Wednesday. What I *failed* to tell you was that her granddaughter is going to Greece, this week."

I waited for the significance of this news.

"It came to me after you left when I went to bed. I was completely pooped. Not used to having two glasses of wine that late and then staying up," he said.

"Sorry."

"Not your fault. I was the one who brought out the bottle. And it was *me* doing all the talking."

"That's how I recall it, as well."

"The next morning, I called Maggie," he continued. "I asked her if she thought that her granddaughter would be willing to do me a small favor while she's in Greece."

Keep your mouth shut, Hanlon.

"You remember that I told you about living in Athens for a brief period with my grandparents when I was a small boy."

I nodded.

"And the woman who often looked after me, Selene."

167

"It's when you met Win Callahan," I said. "He was stationed there."

"Precisely. However, I don't recall that I told you of my last visit with Selene. It was . . . in 2004. I spent a month that fall in Greece."

He had, in fact, briefly mentioned this earlier, but I didn't interrupt.

"Selene died not long after that visit. Before she passed, she wrote me a letter. It was very touching. Things she recalled about the time looking after me, her memories of my grandmother.

"But the letter contained a real surprise. She just dropped it in, almost as a passing thought. She said that 'what had given her solace in recent weeks had been long conversations with her son.' And the time that he spent with her. In *Athens*."

I glanced over at Frank as he'd gone silent. He was looking at the scenery. I was about to make a right turn onto Warren Mountain Road.

"Until that letter," he resumed, "I had no knowledge — *whatsoever* — of Selene ever having a son."

Forty

Frank's story went on for another 20 minutes as we observed splotches of yellow, orange and red leaves along unpaved roads over the mountain to the town of Warren. Reminiscing at length about images stored in his memory from childhood, many of them from the days in Athens, he told me about how shortly after Selene died that he had been in touch with her sister. He said that he believed that the sister, though now elderly — "close to my age" — might still be alive.

That's when he came back around to Maggie's granddaughter 'doing a small favor while she is in Greece.'

"I gave Maggie a name and an address to pass along to her granddaughter," he said. "Selene's sister, Helen, if she's alive, may be living in Athens."

My mind flashed on the capital of Greece and the little I knew about it, mostly from movies and TV travel shows. Practically everyone has seen photos or video clips of the

Parthenon on the Acropolis, maybe a panoramic bird's eye view from a drone above the sprawling city. *But what do we know about the place?*

"I want her to try to find out if Helen is still there," he said.

"Small favor, perhaps," I said, "but *big request* for a young American woman travelling in a foreign country. Look up someone who may be *dead*?" My skepticism didn't seem to faze Frank.

"Aha," he said. "But Maggie's granddaughter, Emma, is travelling with a friend who grew up and still *lives* in Athens."

"That oughta' help."

"You bet. And if she *does* find Helen, I am hoping that we can learn more about Selene's estranged son."

Surely, he has not asked this young woman to pose questions about the son?

"Among the items that have been misplaced since my move to Vermont is an old Rolodex. Full of names and phone numbers. One of was for Helen. I haven't fooled with trying to go through 'information' in Athens," he added.

"But you do have an address," I said.

"Yes. From Selene's letter. She lived with Helen the final weeks of her life."

"Well, I hope that this Emma, Maggie's granddaughter, can find her. And that you can find the son," I said, still unclear about how it connected to what he was asking *me* to do: pin down why Win Callahan was murdered. If, in fact, he really was. We didn't talk for a few minutes as we drove through

Warren, heading south on 100. I was starting to look for some place to stop for lunch.

"I have no idea," Frank perked up, "how *old* Selene's son might be. I never knew that she was married. Complete surprise. Never, not *once*, until that letter, was there any mention. And I don't have his name."

"Maybe she never *was* married," I said.

"Yes, that's what I've been thinking. It kept me awake for quite a while," he said. "Middle of the night, Wednesday."

"Sorry about that. You seem to have recovered, though."

"It's another piece of the puzzle," he said, ignoring my comment.

"And how's that?"

"Until now, we had not arrived at that point of the story, Michael," he said. "I didn't want you to think that I was completely senile."

I lifted my right hand off the steering wheel and held it up.

"Frank, I told you that I believed you the first time," I said. "While I know nothing — until the last two weeks, anyway — about the 'spy business' as you call it, I do accept the possibility that Win Callahan *may* have done something, or may have *known* something . . . that got him murdered."

"Yes, thank you. Again," he said. "And that is why I have from the outset thought that you might have to go to Greece. But if Helen is alive, it could make it easier to *prove*, or, disprove my hunch."

Uh oh. Hunch? That's a trail we haven't followed yet.

We picked the Rochester Café and Country Store for a place to eat. The timing was good. Several people were leaving just as we arrived, so no waiting to get a table.

Frank ordered a sandwich called The Mansfield, grilled ham on multigrain bread, with grilled onions, melted cheddar, lettuce, tomato, and a honey Dijon dressing. I chose the Avocado Melt, an open-faced sandwich with cheddar, lettuce, tomato, and sprouts on top of the sliced avocado, served on whole wheat bread. We split a large order of fries.

"So, in the car, you were saying something about a *hunch*," I offered as we started to eat. Frank had taken a bite of his sandwich. "Is this something beyond what you wrote in the long essay. Or is it something new?"

He shook his head. When he'd finished chewing, he took a sip of water and put the glass back on the table.

"Yes, it is beyond what I wrote two years ago, what I gave you to read. *No*, it is not new. It came to me back in the summer when I was packing and getting ready to move," he said. "Looking back on it, I guess that it's what motivated me to consider hiring someone," he pointed at me, "who could follow it until we have definitive proof one way or the other."

"Okay, let's hear about the hunch."

He hesitated, looked across the room, then smiled. "Why don't we wait until we are back in the car? Let's enjoy our lunch. And admire the lovely young women at that table." His eyes shifted left with a furtive glance.

My glance was not as subtle. Then I laughed. "My pal Louie is regularly on my case about using the word 'lovely' in regard to women," I said. "Glad that we share the appreciation."

"I would like to meet your friend, Mister Ragsdale. From what you have told me, sounds like quite the character," Frank said.

"We'll make it happen. Get him beyond his 'oldies' taste in music, you can introduce him to Puccini."

Forty One

Melissa and her friend Emma Nestor arrived in Athens early in the afternoon on Saturday. It had been a long, 12-hour flight with a brief layover in Brussels.

Shortly after leaving the baggage claim area, Emma's phone chimed to indicate a new message. It was a text from her Aunt Katherine in Vermont.

'Em. Call me when you can. Message from Grandma Mags.'

Fearing that something had happened, Emma called before leaving the airport.

It was 7:45 a.m. back in the states.

On the phone, she was relieved to learn that all was well. Her grandmother just wanted to speak with her in person.

"Just a sec. Let me get her," Katherine said.

"Emma Jean, my dear. Thank you for calling," Maggie said.

"Hi, Gram. It's great to hear your voice."

"You must be so excited. Have you seen the Acropolis yet?"

"No, we just arrived. I'm at the airport."

"Oh, then I won't keep you," Maggie said. "Do you have a pen to write with? I have a name and an address in Athens that I want you to try to find."

Emma felt her pockets, no pen. Her backpack was on the floor ten feet away, next to Melissa and their luggage.

"Could you ask Aunt Kath to text it to me?" she said.

"Of course. It never occurred to me."

"That'll work better. Then I will have it on my phone. Whose address is it?"

"A long story, dear. It is an old friend of an old friend," Maggie said. "I will have Katherine explain in the email to you."

"No, she should send me a *text*."

"Yes, you said that. A text. Then we can talk after you receive it. No rush," Maggie said.

"Great. Love you, gramma."

"I love you too, sweety. Have a wonderful time."

Just over an hour after the phone call, Emma received a second text message from her aunt.

Helen Stavrakis, 11 Lampsakou. If she still lives at this address, ask for her phone number. It is on behalf of Mr. Frank Marino who was a friend of her sister, Selene.

Emma showed the text to Melissa. "Do you know where this is?"

"I know where that street is," Melissa said.

"Is it far? From your home?"

"Not very far. What's there?"

"It's the address for the woman my grandmother wants me to find that I told you about."

"We can go there," Melissa said. "Perhaps tomorrow."

"Excellent. Gram will be happy."

Forty Two

It turned out that, on the face of it, Frank's hunch seemed not unreasonable. *If* you believed that some of these people were still alive. And that they could remember any of the things that had Frank kicked-up a notch in solving 'the puzzle'.

What he explained at length on our drive home was, that he *knew* that Win Callahan had made many trips back to Greece between the end of the war and the early 1970s. There was a NATO base on Crete and Frank recalled hearing Callahan speak of it on at least two different occasions.

"Souda Bay Naval Base," Frank said. "It's a major facility at the western end of the island. US warships sail in and out of there frequently."

"But wasn't Callahan an army guy before he got into intelligence work?"

"Yes, he was. The base itself wasn't built until the early 50s. Win had gone back to Crete shortly after VE Day and at least one more time after that," he said. "A lot of younger people from Crete migrated to Athens. Selene's family did. And she had relatives I believe that lived near Chania. That's where Souda Bay is."

My imagination leap-frogged over the names and places as Frank spooled them out. I resisted saying, 'The hunch, please. Tell me about *the hunch*.'

"**You know** that I told you about my own work, primarily for NSA in the final years," Frank said. "With all the different intelligence activities — open and covert collection of information, foreign language specialists, analysts of every stripe — *my job* became what we would now refer to as a 'hybrid'.

"I never had the title 'Archivist' but essentially that's what I was. Universities have them, some of the older and larger non-profit organizations have them. Even with more recent attitudes about inter-agency cooperation, there is no single office that filters and stores the absolute, top secret intel. And the events that may, or may *not, have* occurred."

I think we've already plowed this ground, Frank.

"Before I contacted you, I was in touch with a trusted protégé at Fort Meade. He's in a position to help me wade through unclassified information relating to some of the documented assignments of Stephen W. Callahan. That's how I confirmed Win's travel from 70 years ago. The more I thought about Win and Selene from when I was a child, then learning about a son . . ."

"You think the son is Callahan's?" I interjected.

"Certainly a possibility," he said. "But not my hunch at the moment."

Here we go.

"You think that Selene was helping Callahan with, ah . . . reconnaissance activities that we're not gonna read about anytime soon." I said.

We were climbing the ridge from Randolph and heading toward Route 14, another 25-minute drive to Williamstown. Frank seemed to be considering my question about Selene' son.

Out of nowhere, pointing at the dashboard he said, "Perhaps now we can listen to some music."

I turned to look at him. Stoicism in spades.

It took the CD a couple of seconds to engage. As soon as the music began, Frank made a palm pushing up motion with his left hand.

As soon as I raised the volume, he leaned back on the headrest and closed his eyes.

The music was remarkable. For the final few miles getting old Frank back home, there was no further chatting about spies, analysts, or long-lost adult children of uncertain paternity.

Each time I glanced over at him, eyes still closed, his head and shoulders moved ever so slightly in sync with the operatic tempos.

Back at the parking lot near Frank's apartment, as soon as I stopped, he sat forward. He looked at the dashboard, spotted the eject button and tapped it, ending the male aria that was playing. Then he looked at me.

"Michael," he said, a soft tone just this side of drowsy, "I promise. As soon as we find out if Selene's sister is still alive, we can determine exactly where in Greece you will be going. And when."

Okay, this is progress. Maybe he'll pony up some intel from the DC protégé.

I began to remove the CD and put it back in its case. Frank stopped me.

"Why don't you take that with you?" he said. "Listen to all of it. Eighteen tracks, just a little more than an hour."

"Thank you, I will. Better to hear it on real speakers, I'm sure."

"If you don't *return* it, the Vermont State Police are just over the hill and only a phone call away."

"They'll know where to find me," I said. "But I will bring it back."

He took his time getting out of the car and held the door open.

"Do you want me to walk back with you?"

"That's not necessary. I'll be fine. Why don't you plan to call me on Monday?"

"Yep. I will," I said.

"And thank you for the lunch. Glad we stopped there."

Forty-five minutes later I was back in Quechee. Rocco was eager to get out of the house. And maybe a bit miffed that he had not gone along for the drive.

I wasn't really hungry, but a beer and pretzels seemed like a good idea.

As soon as Rocco was back inside, I called Virginia. No answer — 'please leave a message.'

"Hey. It's Enrico Caruso. Wanna come over later this evening and listen to this Pavarotti guy, see what he's got? Let me know and I'll rustle up some food. Rocket Boy misses you." Click.

I suspect that he *did* miss her. There was always a lot more tail wagging and enthusiasm around *her* than when he was just hanging out with me.

"Not an issue, champ. I'll still feed you," I said.

Mixing a cup of kibble in with two forks of canned food, I placed his bowl back in the elevated food stand next to the door, then refilled the water bowl.

The phone rang. *Jackson, V – 802.295.3093.*

"That was quick," I said.

"Nice to hear your well-timbered voice, Maestro."

"Thank you."

"Do you *really* have Pavarotti recordings that I don't know about?" she said.

"I do now."

"Flabbergasted would be an understatement," she said. "But yes, I just got out of the shower. What time should I arrive?"

"You could come straight over now."

"What time should I arrive *after* I dry my hair?"

"How about, say . . . 7:30?"

"That works. What can I bring?" she said.

181

"Maybe your bath towel? Don't need to bring anything. I'm all set."

"Don't start the music until I get there," she said.

"You're in for a real surprise."

"Can't wait."

Forty Three

Probably a mistake to have been blunt when informing his housemate that she had a short window to make 'alternative living arrangements'.

When the shooter arrived back from a trip to Home Depot, he found food from the refrigerator tossed onto the kitchen floor, a bathroom mirror smashed, and hunter orange paint sprayed in random swaths across a bare mattress of the bed they had shared.

The woman had 'anger management issues' beyond their sadomasochistic relationship. Reacting in kind, however, was not in the makeup of this man who had spent his entire life being as unflappable as one could be.

She and her possessions were gone. Good. A little cleanup work and he could get the house in condition before contacting a real estate agent. List it now, price it right, be done with it. Adios to inflated property taxes on a small, mid-century ranch house that no longer fit in a neighborhood racing to gentrification.

After cleaning up the kitchen and bathroom mess, he went to the basement workshop to finish three wooden crates that he'd built. They looked like small coffins; four-and-a-half feet long, eighteen inches wide, one foot in depth. The lid for each box had pre-drilled holes for wood screws to make a tight closure.

All that remained was to wipeout sawdust from the sanding, and then line the crates with shipping pads. Their single purpose was for transporting his firearms. Armando had said that the crates were not necessary, but the shooter wanted to do it his way. He would rent a 20-foot box truck to haul the shipment, along with two empty gun safes he'd thrown in to sweeten the deal.

His days of sporting clays and range shooting were over. He had had more than his share of sighting, breathe, squeeze, do it again. By this time next week, the only weapon that he would own would be a Sig Sauer M17 handgun. But he would have more cash than he had ever had at any one time in his life. Proceeds from the sale of the house would come later.

Adjusting a shipping pad to fit the corners of one of the boxes, the shooter paused. He looked at the door at the top of the stairs going from the basement to the kitchen.

Maybe just his imagination. Or a noise from somewhere outside.

She won't come back now. "She's not that stupid," he said to himself.

Motionless, he waited. Still watching the stairs, he silently counted to ten.

Nothing.

Using the fingers of his right hand, he ran them up and down to make a snug crease in the pad and press it tight against the inside of the crate, then repeated the maneuver at each corner.

Moving to the next one, he thought about the possibility of his ex-housemate going to the police. He could imagine her making up an overwrought story about the cache of firearms in the basement.

If that happened, he was confident that all the receipts, certificates of sale and permits in his possession, would satisfy any law enforcement queries. On the other hand, if it happened in the next few days, it could be a minor inconvenience.

When he'd finished padding the last crate, he walked across the basement to the gun safes. Some of the firearms had individual cases, some did not. He would load the ones with cases first, then wrap the others with an extra pad and place them on top. The crates were constructed to hold a minimum of twelve guns each.

Cradling two weapons at a time, he made repeated trips to the safes until they were empty, and the crates were nearly full. It dawned on him that he would also need to rent a hand truck to move the safes.

Smoothing and fitting a shipping pad on top of all of the guns, he put the lids in place but did not screw them closed.

He could do that with a battery-operated screwdriver before he loaded them into the truck.

Going up the steps and turning the basement light out, he repeated aloud to himself, "Nah. She's not that stupid."

Forty Four

Virginia had her back to me. She looked terrific. Mid-rise olive drab linen pants — *nice fit* — slingback leather sandals, ivory knit pullover sweater. And she had been considerate enough to bring along a chilled bottle of Prosecco.

Standing next to my audio receiver and CD changer, she was holding the plastic case for the Puccini CD that Frank had loaned me. Reading aloud the back cover, she gave me performers' names, track titles and each opera included in the collection.

"When *you* do this," she said, "you program the sequence of the CDs that are playing. Can you show me how to do that?"

"You're only playing a single CD. Just slip it into slot one, close it and hit play."

She turned to face me. Smiling, she said, "But that's not what I want to do. Can I set it to play in the order that I want selections to play?"

187

"Yes." I walked over, took the disc from its case, placed it in slot one and closed the tray.

"Not ready to go digital, get rid of all of these?" she said, waving a hand toward the shelves of CDs,

"Not a chance." I pushed the 'Program' button.

"Tell me the number of each track in the order that you want to hear them," I said.

Holding the case up to see it better, she read over the titles.

"I've already heard some of this in the car, by the way."

"Doesn't matter. They're *all* worth hearing again. Let's start with number . . . 5, 7, then 13, and 14. After that . . ."

"Hold on," I said. "Let me set those first. 5,7,13, 14."

"Yes."

"Go ahead."

"4, 9, 11 . . . and 16"

I programmed as instructed. She had called out eight tracks, about half of the selections. "The whole thing runs more than an hour, according to Frank," I said.

"Okay, you ready?"

"Yes, keep going."

"Next . . . 2, 3, 8." Pausing for me to stay with her, she then continued, "12, 6, 15 . . . 17, 18 . . . and 1."

As I finished up the personal request line, I scanned the screen grid showing the sequence Virginia had asked for.

"Track one is *last*?" I said.

"Yes. One should be last."

Tapping the play button, I stepped back. "Here we go."

"Thank you," she said, giving me a soft kiss on the lips. "I'll open the Prosecco."

"Pretty amazing voices," I said. "Think that I enjoyed it more this time." We had listened to all eighteen tracks over an hour-and-fourteen minutes.

"Did you listen to all of it before?" Virginia said. I refilled her glass and then my own.

"No, only about half. It was just during the last leg of our drive back."

All through this playing of the collection, the only commentary came from her, either offering up a title — *Tosca, La Boheme, Madame Butterfly* — or telling me the name of the artist performing in a particular role and from which opera.

Track one, *Nessun dorma*, was indeed Luciano Pavarotti. I certainly had heard it before today but could not have told you the title nor the opera.

"It's from *Turandot*," she said, adding, "probably the best-known tenor aria in all of opera."

"Must be why I remembered it. He performed it on the PBS broadcast *The Three Tenors*, yes?" I said.

"All three of them," she said, going on to enlighten me about other famous tenors in addition to Pavarotti and Caruso. She ticked off names the way Ragsdale often did when he quizzed me about Pop oldies.

This information on a quiet October evening and her knowledge of opera was new to me. She talked about when she lived in New York, either listening to radio broadcasts live, or on a few occasions attending performances at The Met.

I got up, went to the CD changer, raised the volume a notch and played track one again. As the music began, Rocco came from the kitchen, went over to Virginia and stood with his head on her knees waiting to be patted.

Certainly, Pavarotti's voice. But the orchestration, and the supporting chorus, were equally impressive. Seeing a live performance must be a really special event.

We were down to the last couple ounces of Prosecco and had finished all the crackers and smoked trout pate. I motioned for Virginia to follow me.

"Wait. It's not the 'want to see the new wallpaper in my bedroom' bit is it?"

"Nope. We're going downstairs," I said.

"New wallpaper in the *basement*? I'm not sure about this."

When we got to what I call my media room — various audio components, a turntable, smaller speakers than those upstairs, a flat screen TV, and more shelves of both vinyl LPs and compact discs — I removed a flannel bedsheet that was covering an antique floor-model record player.

"Look at that," she said when I pulled the sheet away.

The machine was spring-operated and over a hundred years old. It had been stored in the corner of the room since I had moved into the house eight years ago. Oak veneer, excellent condition, it stood four feet high, opened from the top like a trunk, and had an adjustable front baffle for volume control. A hand crank was on the right side.

"Wow," Virginia said, lifting out a record-cleaning brush positioned next to the ancient metal tone arm.

"1912 Columbia Grafonola," I said.

"Where did you find this?"

"It was a gift. An old broadcaster I worked for in Massachusetts years ago. He had a serious collection of old radios and early electronic equipment. A couple of months before he died, he gave this to me."

"Does it work?" she asked. I nodded.

Opening the storage compartment on the bottom, we got the musty attic smell that had been trapped inside. I pulled out a photo record sleeve which held a 78rpm disk and handed it to Virginia.

"Unbelievable!"

Right there on the label, *Enrico Caruso — O Sole Mio.*

"The real deal," I said. "Wanna hear it?"

"This actually *plays?*"

Might've been pushing my luck but I had to go for it. Carefully placing the disk onto the turntable, I slowly turned the crank three times, opened the baffle, moved a lever to start it up, then lifted the tone arm and gently lowered it onto the record.

The maestro's voice came to us accompanied by crackles and a little hiss caused by the old steel needle. It sounded much like one of those early radio broadcasts they dig up to use in movies.

Back upstairs, Rocket Boy was eager to go out again. I put the collar on him, turned on two outside lights, and threw a biscuit into the backyard. He lunged off the deck and was sniffing for it immediately.

I asked Virginia if she'd ever been to Greece.

"Yes. More than 20 years ago," she said. "Richard and I went for two weeks." Richard being her late husband. "Why?"

"Good chance that I'll be going there," I said. "Some research that a client thinks has to be done in person."

"The man in Williamstown?"

"Yep."

Without getting into names and specifics — in part because I *lacked* same — I gave her an overview of the 'assignment'. She listened patiently and did not probe for details.

Rocco was back at the door. Virginia went to let him inside. After giving him the 'nuzzle, nuzzle, you're such a good boy' treatment, she stood up and pulled on my right hand.

"Walk me home," she said. "I can show you the new lamp in my bedroom."

Forty Five

Matala, Crete — 4:45 on a Sunday morning. Nikos had had another dream, this one featuring Pavlos and Hektor.

Bare feet on the floor, he sat on the edge of his bed trying to bring back the images that had awakened him. Men running, maybe the men in the old photograph. A monk holding a machine gun. The bench outside the monastery. His granddaughter lighting a candle inside the chapel.

Reaching for the pack on a nightstand next to his bed, he shook out a cigarette, lighted it and took a deep drag, holding the smoke for several long seconds before exhaling through his nose.

The dream scenes were fading fast. Nikos tried hard to focus on the image of the American soldier. It was not the same man in the photo, but that of another young man, someone Nikos knew.

It was Tommy, an old hippie friend that he had visited in the US so many years ago. That had been on his first trip, not the time when he had to find someone else to carry out the task for his Uncle.

Now he struggled to bring up a glimpse of a meeting place. Two men, a terse conversation. The packet of US dollars that he carried with him. *Those* images came easily. He had recalled them numerous times in the past. In the most recent dreams, some things seemed to come into focus clearly, others would not.

An hour after he had awakened suddenly, trying to will these images to stay in his mind but instead watching them fade, Nikos was seated outside the taverna smoking and drinking coffee.

He had the panoramic monochrome print once again stretched across the table and, just as he'd done before, weighted the corners with his cup and the ash tray.

What was different this time was that *something* in the photograph demanded his attention. He studied the building directly behind where the group was assembled. Nothing. It was a long, flat-roofed structure that showed no recognizable markings, no name. Pavlos had told him that he, Hektor and the other young man had sometimes found work in Chania as laborers or errand boys.

Then it clicked. Nikos bent his head closer.

The soldier. It was the same man from another photograph, one given to Nikos along with a name that he had taken to the US. The difference was that in that *other* photo the American was older, and he had not been wearing a uniform.

Later the same day, on the mainland near the center of Athens, an old woman studied two young women standing at her front door. The shorter of the two — black hair, bright, brown eyes and a smile of kindness — spoke first, in Greek.

"Good morning. My name is Melissa Lambros. Are you Helen?

The woman nodded. She kept her hand on the doorknob. Barely over five feet tall she was stooped, making her appear to be even shorter.

"I am Helen," she said tentatively. Then asked, "Do I know you?"

The dark-haired younger woman shook her head. "No, you don't know me. This is my friend Emma." She gestured to the other woman, taller with light brown hair cut short, also smiling. "She is visiting from America. A friend of Emma's yaya knows you. Do you know the name Frank Marino? He knew your sister, Selene."

Opening the door, she motioned for the two to enter her apartment. Waddling behind, the old woman invited them to have a seat in the small living room.

"Selene has been gone for many years now," she said, still speaking Greek.

"Yes, we know," Melissa said, switching to English for her American friend.

The old woman hesitated, then in a thick accent, also responded in English.

195

"This gentleman . . . Frank. He was a friend with Selene," she said. "From the time he was very small." She held out a hand to indicate a toddler.

"Yes," the American woman offered. "And he is a friend of *my* gramma. She just visited with him. When he learned that I was coming to Athens, he asked if I could see if you were still living here. And if we could get your telephone number."

The old woman fiddled with a handkerchief, dabbing at her nose.

"I believe that Mister Marino would like to call you," the American woman added.

"Is he . . . coming to Athens?" Helen asked.

The younger Greek woman interjected, "I don't believe so. It is my impression that he only wants to speak with you on the telephone."

After talking about her own family and growing up in Athens, Melissa told Helen that she was taking her friend to Crete to meet her grandfather.

"My family is from Dramia," Helen said. "We have only cousins, one still living on Crete."

"I have heard so much about all of the Greek islands," Emma said.

Helen said that when she was a young girl she had visited Crete and spoke of the beauty of the sea.

When they stood to leave, the old woman moved slowly to a kitchen table. She found a piece of paper and wrote down her phone number.

"You will please tell Frank Marino . . . *yes*, Helen is still here."

Forty Six

Sunday breakfast was Virginia's favorite; a mashed avocado with a few drops of lemon juice, salt and pepper, spread on slices of whole wheat toast; freshly squeezed orange juice, by me, and strong black coffee from a drip through filter.

She kept a plastic container of kibble and dog biscuits under the kitchen sink, so Rocco got his usual, minus a small portion of canned food that I mixed in at home. When we finished eating, I went out to inspect a pile of firewood at the side of the house, knowing that I was likely to help stack. Virginia had already started a few days earlier. There was not much more than maybe a half-cord left on the ground.

We talked about the coming week, her schedule for classes, and counseling students in an Advanced Environmental Legal Research course. I said that it was likely that I was going to drive to Massachusetts with the hope of finding a man who *might* know something about the old hunting fatality.

After a nice, long hug and a tender kiss, she kicked me out.

The weather was so, so. Maybe rain, maybe not. Rocco sprinted ahead, sniffing every few feet. I was sure that there were times that he didn't know that he was not wearing his alert collar. The test would come if he spotted some animal and wanted to go after it.

A phone message from Frank Marino was waiting for me. It began with a repeated thank you for the Saturday drive and lunch, then he was quick to add that prospects for a trip to Greece were even more imminent, regardless of what he learned about Selene's sister or her son.

"None of us really knows how long we have here on earth, so wasting time is not the best approach to solving this puzzle," he said in the voicemail.

I listened to it again. Something about his tone.

Does he have concerns about his health? Something he hasn't mentioned? Or is he anxious about my pacing here?

It didn't make sense to call him back immediately. I wanted to follow through in looking for Ronald Davis, the name listed as 'SHOOTER' in the old Fish & Game report from 1980. Earlier attempts to find him with an internet search had produced a total of 18 men currently living in the Bay State with that name, plus another seven obituaries for men of the same name.

One of the 'public records' websites offered some promise. It would compile all public information available on a person, put it into a report and sell it to you for a fee. What I needed to focus on were the names that appeared to be close to the age the man would be today if, in fact, he was the *same* Ronald Davis.

None of the partial profiles reflected the exact age for the guy I was hoping to find, which would be 60 or 61, according to his age listed in the incident report. There was one listed as R. Davis, last reported living in Wakefield, MA. The age shown for him was 68. Maybe close enough.

Before agreeing to purchase the summary, I read the website disclaimer:

> *Please note — we do not create any background data in this report. The information you will see has come from public records, as reported by officials at the local, state, and national level. Our reports include addresses, phone numbers, email addresses, family members, owned properties and other assets, businesses, professional licenses, bankruptcies, civil judgments, misdemeanors, felonies, sexual offenses and other court records.*

The fee was $14.99 for a one-month membership to access reports. Last time I used one of these it had been $5.95 a month for three-months. I went through the checkout process and downloaded the report.

It took all of two minutes to determine that this was unlikely to be my guy. But there were two phone numbers. *We'll find out soon enough.*

R. Davis of Wakefield turned out to be *Roger* Davis. No, he'd never had a non-resident hunting license in New Hampshire. No, he did not have any relatives named Ronald. And yes, he had once known a Ronald Davis who had lived in Saugus. He told me that that man's age was probably early 60s. But he had not seen him in more than 10 years.

So, the membership fee gave me access to more reports. Could be that my Ronald Davis now lived somewhere else. I went back at it.

The only close match that I found was one an obituary for a Ronald F. Davis, who was the right age, had he still been with us. But he had died in Watertown, New York in 2014.

Then, of course, there was always the chance that the man had changed his name. Or maybe it *wasn't* his real name back in 1980. Certainly, law enforcement folks would've been on to that.

At least one would like to believe that they would have been on to that.

Time for a little networking. I know some cops down on Cape Cod. It could be a quick call, nothing to lose. Then again, Louie knows cops everywhere in the Northeast. Find a way to plug into *his* contacts and I might learn what kind of toothpaste Ronald Davis uses.

Big Brother Ragsdale. He'll be insulted, I'm sure.

The thought reminded me that Becky was supposed to call this weekend. Nothing yet. Easy to give her cover by me calling them instead.

"Hey," I said to their answering device, "I am sittin' around with no one to talk to, hoping that I might get a little help in locating a, uh . . . *shooter* . . . last known living in Massachusetts. Brother Angler, this is for real. How about an assist here?"

Does anyone answer their phone live anymore?

Forty Seven

Sunday evening, still no return call from either Louie or Becky. My request could wait. I was sure that Marino had matters to discuss, new or previously explored.

He answered live, so there you go.

"I was planning to take a drive down to Massachusetts this week," I said. "Unfortunately, not making much headway in locating the man listed as 'the shooter' in the old Fish & Game report."

"Ronald Davis," he said immediately. "I was never able to find him."

"I don't recall everything we talked about when you gave me the summary, your essay on Callahan. Do you know anything about this Davis?"

"No. Only what's in that Hunting Casualty Report you recently got hold of. His name and age were included in the old newspaper stories, no address, just that he was from

Massachusetts," he said, then added, "But what I have always suspected — I told you this already — is that Davis was either *hired* by someone to shoot Win. Or, that there was *another person* with him the morning it happened, and that Davis was there with the non-resident license to take the responsibility."

We talked about my online search. I told him that I had reached out to Louie for suggestions. "Even if I can't immediately find Davis, some of the public records profiling might provide a hint to 'background' on the other men," I said. "Those with the same name and who are relatively close in age." I mentioned the idea that it could have been a fake name, or that he might have changed his name.

"If we come across one who has any kind of police record, Ragsdale can help chase it down," I said.

"That's all good," he said. "If we find Davis, or whatever his name might be, perhaps the person behind Win's death has another connection beyond that of one young hunter who mistook a man for a deer. Sorry to be redundant, Michael, but *somebody* wanted Win dead. They got their wish. It is connected to his intelligence work. Remember what Hilling wrote in the memoir about his conversation with Win; 'Someday you will read about my death . . . reported as an accident. Don't believe it.' And I have *never* believed it."

Frank's voice had the same glum tone that I heard in his voicemail earlier in the day.

"I'm guessing that you haven't heard anything from Athens. Your friend Maggie's granddaughter?" I said, hoping that would nudge Marino into expanding on 'imminent prospects for a trip to Greece'.

"No, I haven't," he said. "It is my understanding that Emma, Maggie's granddaughter, will be travelling on to Crete. She told Maggie that she would reply with any information she can obtain *before* they leave Athens. So, we can only cross our fingers. And wait."

"I know that this will depend in part on what she learns," I said. "But for the moment, is it your idea that any travel that I might schedule is going to be to Athens or to Crete?"

"Both are likely," he said. "If Selene's sister, or her son, are in Athens, certainly you will have to try to talk with them."

About what? I didn't say that but allowed Frank to continue.

"You asked me if I thought that Win could be the father of Selene's son. While I think that is a real possibility, I have never thought that *he* could be connected to having his father murdered. "Repetition may be a tad boring, Michael, but it is the key. Win's death was connected to his *work*. And much of his work, at least as far as Greece is concerned, was in and around the NATO installation at Chania, which is the West Cretan Naval Base at Souda."

Listening to Frank's explanation sparked a recall about an acquaintance I have with an archaeologist, a retired Dartmouth College professor, who had spent much of his career at various sites in Greece. I also recalled that his work had been primarily on Crete.

The recollection that I was dredging up from old radio interviews with the man was that Crete is the largest of the more than 500 Greek islands. And that while numerous archaeological 'digs' are scattered around the island, there are only a couple of cities of any size on Crete, at least as compared to smaller US cities.

"Okay, let's wait for the news from Maggie. Or, ah . . . Emma. We'll go from there," I said.

"Splendid idea," he said.

After we ended the call, I held the phone for a few seconds, sorry that I hadn't thought of a way to probe about how Frank was feeling.

Glum? Morose? Fatalistic? Something going on with him.

Saved by the phone again. Not ten minutes after I had finished talking with Marino, I was eating sardines, raw onion, and Longhorn cheese, drinking a beer, putting off another dive into the book *Dark Territory*. My phone vibrated.

Ragsdale, Rebecca 802-673-4265.

"Hello, Sister Rebecca," I said.

"You know a close friend of mine from middle school really is a nun," she said. "Sister Celeste."

"I think that you've mentioned her. I was just offering you a little equal treatment, same as I do when conferring with your husband, Brother Louie."

"Yes, I got it. Thank you."

"So, you have a plan about a way to distract what's-his-name?"

"Not yet," she said. "He's helping a friend over in East Haven with some barn project. He's been back and forth for three days now. I think they're almost finished."

"I left him a message earlier on your landline," I said.

"Oh. I haven't listened. I just came in. I wanted to call you before Louie comes home. You know that I told you that I am going to Arizona next week, to help my cousin Jan get settled in her new house?" she added.

"Yes."

"What we talked about earlier, you and Louie going fishing. Have you thought about that?"

"I have thought about it. *But* . . . a slight wrinkle in my current plans," I said. "For the past couple of weeks, I've been doing some work for a new client. Mostly background research so far, no 'bang, bang stuff' as Louie calls it. Now . . . he's about to send me to Europe," I said.

"*Europe*. Really?"

"Yeah. Specifically, to Greece."

"When are you going?" Becky asked.

"Uncertain. But on the phone this evening I had the sense that he's getting a little anxious."

"The weather in Greece is probably still nice. Sounds exciting."

"Ehh, I'm not so sure. Don't know anything about the *weather*," I said, "but so far, the work I've been doing on this project could put you into a trance."

"Oh, well. Louie is just going to have to *deal with it*," she said. "It's not as though he hasn't had to take care of himself before."

"Becky. If anyone that I *know* can 'take care of himself', it is certainly Louis James Ragsdale. He'll be fine."

"I know he will. He's just been so *fidgety* since he settled on the end of December."

"When he gets home, ask him to call me. Have a good time in Arizona. When are you leaving?"

"Flying out of Burlington Thursday morning," she said. "I'll be there until November 8th."

"Don't forget the sunblock," I said.

"I have a big sun hat, long-sleeve shirts. I'm all set."

"Take care of yourself."

Forty Eight

Boom. Here we go. After the tortoise-like pace two weeks running, some new information was coming into play and travel plans needed to be made ASAP.

It was Monday afternoon when Marino called again. Not only had he gotten the phone number for the woman in Athens, Selene's sister Helen, but he'd already spoken with her.

"She knows where Selene's son is. He lives in Athens, as well," Frank said. "I would like you to speak with them both. In person."

I hesitated. While Frank was clearly focused on people and past events in Greece that *may* have involved Win Callahan, I had started down the path of 'find the shooter and talk to him'.

"Frank, I'm going to have to shift gears here for a minute. You really will need to prep me on . . . exactly what I'm hoping to learn if I go there."

"Like the kids say, 'No problem.' I began making notes and writing questions as soon as I got off the phone with Helen. I assure you, Michael, before you get on any plane, I will have additional material and details on where you need to go and who you need to see."

"Okay, that'll help. What's our timeline on this trip?" I said.

"How soon can you be ready to leave?"

"Ah, couple of days, maybe. A little longer might be better."

Frank was silent. I could hear him breathing and could hear low-volume music in the background.

"How about Friday?" he said. "Can that work for you?"

"I think that could work fine. Let me get started looking at flights."

"I suspect you will fly out of Boston. You don't want to go all the way to New York," he said. "And it will be an evening departure for Europe."

"Right. What is it, a 10-hour flight? The time difference is seven hours?"

"The Western EU is still on Daylight Savings Time. You certainly will have a layover. Most likely in Frankfurt, or Munich. The entire trip over could be 12 hours or more."

"All right. I'll find out pretty quick," I said. "Let me call you back as soon as I have a flight booked. Any thoughts on how long I'm likely to be there? I would think a week, tops."

"You don't need to call me back unless there's a problem. Go ahead and make the reservation that works for you. Yes, I can't believe that you would need more than a few days, so a week certainly ought to do it. Michael, do you want to invite your friend, Virginia? Might be nice to have a travel companion. I would be happy to cover her airfare, as well."

The old bird was a step ahead of me. Then again, I was pretty sure that *he* had likely had 'travel companions' on numerous trips abroad.

"Interesting thought," I said. "I'll talk to her this evening."

"I have to call my young chum at NSA. Some things that he was going to try to track down will have to be accelerated now. It will help me get you prepared."

"It probably makes sense for me to come up to see you, say . . . Wednesday or Thursday? We can spend whatever time it takes to plan this."

"Yes, we can. And will. Why don't we tentatively say . . . Thursday?"

"Okay. I'll call on Wednesday to pin it down," I said.

"Please do that. If I'm out, I will call back."

Out. Where're you going, Frank? Chasing female staff members up Route 14?

"Got it. Talk to you then."

"And Michael, I *do* appreciate your patience. Can't be easy working with an old fogey. You will know when you're my age."

It is a wonderful idea and very sweet for you to ask," Virginia said on the phone. "As much as I would love to go, it's just impossible right now."

She went on to explain her workload, a tricky schedule at VLS still with some online teaching this semester, and that it was just "too short of a notice" to ask others to step in to cover for her. I could hear it in her voice — genuine disappointment about not being able to make the trip.

"But as soon as you have your reservation, let me know. I'll fix dinner for you before you leave. Maybe another pie," she added.

Bummer.

Ragsdale had failed to return my call from the previous evening. Becky had said that he was helping a friend with a barn project. Maybe up to the top of his waders in cow shit.

Calling Louie's 'emergency' cell number might get him all cranked up. But this *could* be considered an emergency. He answered on the second ring.

"Yes?" was the non-committal reply. I'd heard this at least once before as Louie never knew who might be on this phone.

"Hey, tell me if this is a bad time," I said.

"Hanlon. No, it's an OK time. What's up?"

"Where are you?"

"I'm about to get in my truck and head home. Been helping a friend put rafters up for an addition to his barn."

"Becky says that you've been at it for a while."

"Yeah. Took longer than we thought. All finished now. So, what's shakin, Jerry Lee. Sorry I didn't call back last night."

"No big deal. I was just feeling sad, lonely and ignored."

"Save the bullshit, Hanlon. You wouldn't call me on this number if you didn't have something going on," he said.

"Wanna go to Greece?"

"*What?*"

"My guy in Williamstown. He's pulling out the stops. Lining up some old woman and her nephew in Athens for me to talk with. Gotta be in person and gotta be soon."

"This still part of the same old hunting incident where his friend took a bullet?"

"Still the same," I said.

"Bob Seger, 1978."

"And thank you for that. Wait a second, let me make a note."

"*When* are you going?" he asked.

"Probably leaving end of this week. I've been looking at flights from Logan. All of them are evening departures, between 5:20 and 9:10."

"You know that Becky is going to Arizona. She put you up to this?"

"Brother Ragsdale, sorry to be unkind, but you are my *second* choice. Virginia can't go."

"How long?"

"Maybe a week. Could be shorter. Marino is putting together details about other people that I might need to see on Crete."

"Isn't that where your pal goes every summer, the Dartmouth guy?"

I was impressed that Ragsdale remembered a long-ago conversation about the archaeologist. "Yes. And as soon as I have this trip locked-in, I'm gonna call him."

"You're serious. You want me to come along? Afraid some Greek Mafia type is going to obstruct your activities?"

"Something like that. They lay eyes on you, it's off to piss in the olive groves. By the way, is your passport up to date?"

"Hasn't changed since we went to the Bahamas. 2016. Thanks to you, pal."

"Think about it," I said. "Could be good for you before you have to bear down the last couple of months on the job."

"When will you know for certain about reservations?"

"I'd like to wrap it up tomorrow."

"I'll call you."

"No, Becky did *not* put me up to this." A small lie. Click.

Forty Nine

Nikolaos Andreadakis was back to having cigarettes an hour apart, a minor concession while his granddaughter and her friend were staying in Matala.

Nikos arranged for the two to stay with a woman named Effie, a seasonal employee who prepared dinners served at the taverna during the busy tourist months. The American, Emma, knew little Greek and Effie spoke passable English. Melissa told her grandfather that they would get along fine.

The plan was to tour parts of the island on day trips, with Matala as their base. Emma had rented a car for the week. Today was their first full day on Crete and they were having an early breakfast with Nikos.

"The weather is good today. Where are you going?" he said in English, directing the question to Emma.

"The National Park. Samarian . . ." she hesitated.

"The Samaria Gorge," Melissa interjected. "I have not been there since I was little." She touched her grandfather's arm and added, "You took me there, Papouli. Do you remember?"

Nikos nodded. "That is a *long* drive," he said.

"The directions say that it's just under five hours," Emma said, lifting her iPad from the table, tapping the screen.

Melissa laughed. "You saw the road down here from Heraklion. This will be even slower," she said. "I remember all of the goats in the road the other time."

"Many goats," Nikos said. "You must be careful in your driving. There will be many places where goats . . . *shit* on the road. Then it rains!"

"These are not highways such as you have in America," Melissa said.

"I know. You said that when we were driving at home," Emma said.

"Or like the road from the airport in Athens," Melissa added. "That is the best road in all of Greece."

Nikos grunted. "When Melissa was small . . . it has been perhaps 20 years," he looked at Melissa, then continued, "before the Olympics."

"Two-thousand-four," she said.

"Our government spent *too much* building the road for the Athens airport. No funds for *here*," he tapped the table and waved an arm out to the bay. "*Millions* of Euros to build roads for more cars."

When they finished eating and were standing to leave, Nikos touched Melissa's shoulder, then motioned with his eyes and a slight jerk of his head for her to wait. She came back to him.

"I have something to discuss with you," he said in Greek. "When you come back."

"It will be late," she replied, also in Greek.

"Not tonight. We can find time . . ." he glanced toward the American woman, "just you and me. It is important."

"Of course, Papouli." She gave him a hug and kiss on the cheek.

"Be careful the *katsikakia*," he said to Emma.

Emma looked at Melissa.

"Kids. The goats," Melissa explained.

"Thank you. I will be very careful," she said to the old man.

Fifty

The shooter talked to three different real estate agents by phone. He provided his address, some basic information about the house and told each of them that a visit could be scheduled the following week.

"I have some tidying up," he'd said. "When that's finished, I will call you. No need to call back until I'm set."

What he already knew was that older, modest, two-bedroom homes were being advertised for sale at prices between 399-thousand and 600-thousand-dollars. According to a newspaper ad, a similar house one street over recently sold for four-twenty-five. Not one to converse with neighbors, he didn't bother to ask.

It was also likely that a few nearby residents would show interest in purchasing *his* home. The two-acre lot was unusually large for the neighborhood. Having lived in the house for more than 30 years, he was confident that it would not be on the market long.

His immediate task was to arrange for a rental truck to drive the crates of firearms to Stoneham. It was a short run, he could make a round-trip in the same day, even allowing for a couple of hours to show the guns and provide their history, specifically as it related to his ownership.

What he would *not* do was entertain new talk about pricing. The thoroughness of the list that he'd already provided — along with the condition of the weapons that he'd already shown — got them to this point and the handshake agreement.

Buy 'em all. If you can mark them up even more, good for you.

Armando Ramos was an experienced, shrewd and well-connected gun dealer. The small, private business of Weapons, Ltd. did not have a high profile with the general public but functioned as one of the 'go to' firearms resellers in the Northeast.

Since the initial meeting with the man offering to sell a small cache of shotguns and rifles, Armando had used the man's inventory list selectively. Conversations with a few of his best customers confirmed that it all could be conducted in a neat, clean and profitable manner.

The preference was to resell the entire lot of 31 weapons to one buyer. That was a strong possibility. On the VIP list were two serious collectors — one in Chicago, the other in Texas — both of whom had indicated an interest in acquiring all of the guns. The clincher would come with individual photos, Armando's opinion on their condition, and possibly an in-person visit to inspect the collection.

A deal could be consummated within a week.

Fifty One

It was as if I had encountered a *new* Louie. The old Ragsdale — 'I don't like flying' and 'what's the point of travelling outside New England?' — had apparently slipped into a phone booth and changed his uniform.

I wonder if there are any phone booths still around?

The trip to Greece was on and . . . Louie was going. Amazing! Once he told me that, I proceeded to book two seats on Lufthansa. We'd settle up later. Most likely, *Becky* would write me a check for Louie's airfare.

It was an 11-hour flight from Boston scheduled for Friday evening, departing Logan at 8:30, with a brief stop in Munich to change planes. Estimated time of arrival in Athens: 2:30 in the afternoon.

When I got Frank Marino on the phone to let him know, per our previous discussion, we agreed that I would go see him Thursday afternoon. He said that that would give him sufficient time to finish preparing notes, questions and a short 'to do' list for the trip.

Next, I found the email address for the Dartmouth archaeologist, the guy who I knew had spent a lot of time in Greece over the past 40 plus years. At a minimum, he might offer lodging suggestions and other 'tourist tips' for both Athens and Crete.

It had to be some planetary alignment. An hour after I sent the short email, Professor Jacoby Rudner replied. He told me that he was, in fact, in Greece at this very moment. I looked at my watch; 11:40 a.m. That meant 6:40 p.m. there.

Rudner was attending a conference in Athens and would be there for two more days. His plan was then to visit colleagues at dig sites on Crete for three days, before traveling to Chania for a couple of days, before heading back to New Hampshire via Athens on October 24th. He added that he was more than happy to offer advice on hotel accommodations and asked that I email my itinerary.

Still disappointed that she could not make the trip, Virginia nonetheless was happy to keep Rocco while I was gone.

I didn't want to rush Frank about the prep work, so I resigned myself to the likelihood that anything new from him would have to wait until I saw him in person. Whatever questions sprang from his latest directives could be addressed then.

What did we do before the internet? It is mind boggling — unless perhaps you're under 45 — at just how much you can find online. Yeah, yeah, consider the source, I know. I did that each time I clicked on another new link to travel, history, food and culture in Greece. In all, I spent almost two hours online and decided that I would stop at the Quechee Library to get a couple of guidebooks. Unfinished homework on spies could wait a few hours.

It occurred to me that the so far unsuccessful search for the *right* Ronald Davis in Massachusetts could be farmed out while I was away. I called a police chief I knew in Sandwich, MA. We talked for a few minutes, I filled him in regarding what I was working on, asked for any assistance or suggestions that he might have and said that I would call again when I got back.

As I had not discussed this with Louie, I sent a text with the same information about Davis and his approximate age, 61, and asked if he could put out feelers to his law enforcement pals while we were gone.

Surely, if this guy was still using that name and had been involved in any serious incident since the 1980 hunting casualty, it would have been on file somewhere.

Then again, was Davis himself still alive?

Fifty Two

"The most disturbing bit there," Frank said, pointing to the four typed pages that he'd just handed to me, "is the period between 1953 and 1955."

We were in his living room for the pre-trip briefing and to discuss the contact information that he'd compiled. I held the pages on my lap and was reading over the cover sheet.

"Those are all the dates and countries where we can be sure about when and where he was on assignment. The dates highlighted are when he was in Greece," Frank said. "What I didn't know," he went on, "is that Win had a probable connection to CIA activity in Guatemala at the end of Eisenhower's first term. Perhaps a revisionist perspective now, but not a shining moment for the US."

Scanning the first two pages, double-spaced, I saw dates listed, followed by a country, followed by an agency designation — CIA, NSA and US AID.

"Agency for International Development?" I said, not looking up. "Correct."

In all, of more than forty periods that were covered on the list — some over multiple years — five showed Greece as the location: 1946, 1951-52, 1964, 1971 and 1974-75. Frank had used the term 'on assignment', yet according to his own early history, Callahan had been a young US soldier in Athens in 1940 when Frank was a child.

Flipping to the third page, I saw that several paragraphs followed under the heading, TIMELINE: GREECE AFTER WW II. Again, some dates were interspersed with the text. About a third of the way down the page, I paused to look at Frank. He was sitting quietly, legs crossed, watching me read.

"I have to ask . . . where did you get all of this? None of it was in your essay 'Not an Accident'", I said.

"No, that I first wrote just for myself. It was in my desk for years. Only later did I edit and make revisions before giving it to you. Of course, I hadn't yet *picked* you, had I? It was intended to be, shall we say, a persuasion narrative. Whoever agreed to take this on needed a grounding in *why* I believe that Win's death was intentional."

I waited a beat, then tapping the pages I held in front of me, said, "So this is a supplement, I get that. Did you compile this list previously, or are you, ah . . . getting assists from, whatd'ya you call him, the protégé still working full-court?"

"A little help, yes. I told you that I had a fair idea of where Win had been throughout my years in Washington, while he was still working. We often discussed assignment locations in general terms." He again pointed at the pages I held, adding, "Those specific dates and the locations, while not all *technically* declassified, are still considered to be privileged information."

My suspicion was correct: Frank had somebody currently in DC passing him the ball. Maybe frequently. At least enough to make his shots at the basket more accurate.

Standing up from his chair, he looked down at me. "Let me get us something to drink," he said. "What we need to go over are the last two pages. Would you like coffee, tea or something else?"

"A glass of water would be good," I said.

He went to the kitchen, and I kept reading.

By the time I was ready to leave, we'd covered questions that Frank had written for me to ask Helen Stavrakis, the old woman living in Athens, as well as some questions for Selene's son, should I actually be able to locate him.

"I've spoken with Helen. She knows that you are coming," he concluded. "I think that it makes sense for you to visit her on Sunday. That is what I told her. We should confirm that after you arrive in Athens. I will call her to settle on the time."

"I told you that Louie Ragsdale is going with me?"

"You did," he said. "You can add his airfare to our final tally. And, when you get back, we'll have to make a plan for me to meet him. And your friend Virginia, too."

"She's really bummed that she couldn't go."

"I can imagine. It is a beautiful country. Wonderful people, great food."

"Yeah, I think that might've been a deciding factor for Louie."

We shook hands, he wished me safe travel and good luck, and repeated that he would wait to hear from me when we got to Athens.

Before pulling out of the parking lot, I sent a text to Louie confirming that he should be at my house by 4 p.m. tomorrow.

Fifty Three

The young American woman drove slowly through villages — some with only a few homes — and was on alert for the goats that she'd been warned about. Top speed on the narrow pavement was 65 kilometers, or approximately 40 miles per hour, a pace that would have provoked a lot of horn-blowing back home.

They had been talking about Nikos. Melissa was providing an abbreviated account of her grandfather's life, as she knew it.

"He moved to Matala long before I was born. My grandmother wouldn't stay. She came back to Athens and lived with us until she got sick. All the time that I was growing up, he came only once to see her. She died later the same year after my father drowned.

"I started coming here to visit first with my mom when I was five or six. When I was older, every summer I would come for a month. He would let me help at the taverna," she said.

Emma laughed. "What did you do?"

"I helped in the kitchen. Effie was very patient with me. Most of the time I spent with her. After I started high school — Papouli had a car — we would go for drives, and I spent more time with him. In the past two years, he's become what my mother calls 'melancholikos.' Depressed. He doesn't talk the way he used to. Smokes too much. I'm really the only one he wants to spend any time with."

"Was it your grandmother's death and guilt over not seeing her?"

Melissa shook her head. "I don't think so. They talked about each other as though they were strangers. I'm sure he feels some guilt. But my mother says that he has always been cold and distant with her, too."

Nikos had the old photograph spread out in front of him again. He would show the print to Melissa. Right at this moment, he wanted to study the American's face. Taken 74 years ago, the image still offered better detail than he recalled in the wallet-sized snapshot he'd taken with him on his last visit to the US.

That snapshot, along with a handwritten letter from his uncle, Nikos presumed, had long ago been destroyed. Examining the soldier's face in this group photo, he dredged up memories from the old letter.

Composed in English by someone other than his uncle, the contents had been confusing, almost as though it were written in code. He remembered the letter alluded to meetings and businesses in Philadelphia, Pennsylvania. What Nikos could recall was that a man's name had been written above the name of a town in New Hampshire — a place he had never visited but had seen on a map. He knew it was not far from Boston.

The man's identity would not come back to him. Since the afternoon just weeks ago outside the chapel at Preveli, Nikos had tried in vain to bring up a name.

Everyone was dead. It was unlikely that anyone in this old photo was still alive, Now Pavlos was dead, too. Any details of what the old man had been up to with Nikos' uncle back then were now lost.

Staring out across the bay, forcing his mind to go in another direction, Nikos struggled to recall the faces of all the young tourists and hippies in Matala from almost 50 years ago. He could clearly recall Yvette, the girl from France. The others were all mixed in what could have been a beach crowd from just this past season.

Placing the rubber band around the photo, he stubbed out his cigarette, pushed his chair back and shuffled back inside the taverna.

Fifty Four

Virginia Jackson had an inspiration. Shortly after moving from New York City back to Vermont and during her first semester teaching at VLS, she had had a student from New Jersey who was bright, talented, cocky, and very funny.

The whiz kid had spent much of his social time in South Royalton spinning outlandish tales about his Greek American heritage. One of his fellow students, a young woman from Massachusetts, had regularly and good-naturedly challenged the veracity of his stories.

Late one evening at a local brew pub, a few days before the class graduation ceremony, the student from New Jersey had distributed copies of a phony tabloid that he'd printed. Included were doctored photos of classmates, fake headlines and newswire photos, inserted collage-style, and a full-page of bullet-point items that he *claimed* had been fact-checked.

Virginia went to a filing cabinet in her office, opened a drawer where she rummaged through folders and school-related pamphlets. Near the bottom she found it. The Masthead was written in the Greek alphabet, translated to English — according to the author — it read 'ALBANIANS DON'T KNOW SHIT. AND THE TURKS ARE NOT SO NICE, EITHER! Reading it again, she laughed at some of the photo captions.

Exactly what Hanlon needs to take with him to Greece.

Ragsdale finally convinced Becky that he was not pulling her leg. Yes, he was really going on this trip with Hanlon.

"So terribly sorry that I can't go with you to Arizona," he'd said. "But then I wasn't invited, was I?"

Becky was certain that Michael had made some outrageous plea, or a promise, or perhaps a *bribe* related to a future fishing trip, that had persuaded her husband to get on an airplane for the second time in five years. Not just get on a plane but fly *across the Atlantic* and spend time in a foreign country. He'd always grumbled that it wasn't fear, stating that he genuinely "just doesn't like to fly."

Then again, Becky considered that Hanlon's client and the 'research' that Louie was to be helping with, might be a more serious matter than her husband let on. It would not be the first time that he was non-communicative about work.

"Will you be paid for your time?" she said. "And what will they say in Albany?"

Albany, NY being the geographic headquarters for the interstate counter-drug law enforcement endeavor for which Louie had been employed going on 11 years.

"In the army," he said, "when you are this close to finishing your tour, you are thought of as a short-timer. While Albany may have been happy that I stayed around for as long as I have, I'm pretty sure that it's not breaking their hearts that I will be outa there in two months. I am . . . a *short timer*. They might even give me a hat and a coffee mug. *And* the training for the newbies that I'll be running doesn't start until November 16th," he added. He did not comment on the question of 'will you be paid for your time?'

For the rest of the afternoon while Louie took care of some tasks around the house, and then brought his rolling duffel up from the basement to pack, Becky shadowed him like a mom anticipating a teenage son about to leave on a class trip.

Finally, trying not to show concern, she said, "How about I fix spaghetti and meatballs tonight," she said. "We can eat early."

"Or, we could have a glass of wine and eat later," he said.

"Deal."

Fifty Five

Light traffic through southern New Hampshire into Massachusetts. We had left on time, so making it to Logan Airport two hours prior to the flight looked good. I expected that we'd have time to spare.

Louie was driving while I reclined in the passenger seat reading and laughing my way through something that Virginia had given me. It was a 'mysterious dossier' as she'd called it, prepared by one of her students from a few years back. She claimed that — aside from some silly and raunchy allegations the author had written about classmates — the document *did* have a mix of 'small, bite-size historical facts about Greece, along with an admittedly biased slant on Greek immigrants to the US during the 20th century.' I dog-eared a page in the creative 'dossier' and shoved it back in my carry-on bag to read later.

"So, I said that I would fill you in about who, what, where and when for the trip," I said.

"Geez. I was hoping that I might get turned away by the screeners at the airport and not have to listen to any of that," Louie said. "Yes, you did say that you would fill me in. So, let's hear it, Ace."

"Athens for two days, three at the most. Once we, or possibly just me, have talked with a woman by the name of Helen Stavrakis, there's a chance that we'll also get to speak with her nephew, who reportedly lives in Athens as well.

"That part's still a little fuzzy. Frank came up with a separate line of questions for the nephew. And he wants me to take some photos of each of them." Louie kept his eyes mostly on the driving but gave me a quick glance.

"I can only imagine that this is going to thrill these people beyond words," he said. "Here comes this American gumshoe, who is *nothing* like what they have seen in movies or on television. And Gumshoe Gus 'just wants to chat a little' and take a couple of snapshots, if you don't mind. Would that be OK?"

"Didn't we agree a long time ago to drop the phrase gumshoe?"

"Yeah, yeah. PI, private dick, wandering liberal, whatever. Why don't you just practice your pitch on me? I'll help you not screw it up," he said.

"Do you actually want to hear the itinerary, or would you be satisfied to keep kicking my ass?"

That got the smirk without additional comments.

"When we're all finished in Athens, we book a flight to a place called Heraklion. It's the largest city on Crete. About a one-hour trip, I'm told. But we will have at least one full day to do tourist-type things in Athens. Frank was adamant that we at least trek up to get a look at the Parthenon.

"Then same thing in Heraklion," I added. "Spend a day, visit their museum, go see an archaeological site nearby, maybe see a guy."

Another quick glance from Louie and an eyeroll.

"Your sure old chum Marino there isn't tied into some tourist scam?"

"Visiting the museum and the site are at the strong urging of the Dartmouth Prof, *not* from Frank. But if we do wind up 'seeing a guy', that will have been arranged by Frank."

"O-kay," he said. "I forgot about your buddy the Prof."

"That would suggest that you *also forgot* that my buddy the Prof is responsible for having selected the hotel in Athens where we have a reservation, smack in the center of the old part of the city."

"Right. You told me that. And he's there now, yes?"

"No, he'll be gone by the time we show up," I said.

"I thought we were gonna see him."

"Maybe. But it will be at the *end* of the trip. A place called Chania. That's where we're booked to fly home from, again via Athens and Munich."

The traffic picked up the closer we got to Boston. Ragsdale is nothing if not a good driver; alert and quick. He turned on the radio, tapped the seek button, then locked in on an oldies station. They were playing Marty Robbins' *Devil Woman*.

I went back to reading, this time a guidebook about Athens. I knew that at any moment, if a track came on the radio that Louie deemed to be 'classic', he would crank up the speakers. Maybe open the windows.

Frank Marino made another phone call to his former associate in DC. Could he supply contact information for the present commander of the base at Souda Bay? Yes, he could. It would be a US Navy officer in charge of the NATO facility, located at the western end of Crete on a Greek Air Force Base.

"Check your email in thirty-minutes," the man said.

Following up on an earlier discussion with Hanlon — with a particular interest regarding Win Callahan's numerous visits to the base in Chania — Marino's latest thought was that it was *possible* that somewhere, buried in the archives of the Navy's 65-year residency at Souda Bay, there could be useful information.

The idea for the expanded military base had come at the end of the war, even though construction did not begin for another 10 years. Were there names of groups or individuals who had opposed the US presence on Crete? *Win had not been going back to Crete out of nostalgia.*

One key ingredient of the accelerant fueling Marino's belief that someone from Callahan's past was responsible for killing him was a memory of conversations they'd had when Marino was a young man at the beginning of his own career.

Callahan had had stories about his travel, a lengthy roster of 'unnamed' characters with whom he had regularly interacted, and certain 'projects' that had stretched on longer than originally anticipated. One of those projects had been in Greece — possibly rooted in Athens, but much of the focus had been on Crete.

From the beginning of his determination to prove or disprove that the shooting was 'not an accident', Marino had convinced himself that information could be found in the Hellenic Republic known to most of the world as Greece. He'd further persuaded himself that there was a connection to the military base just outside Chania.

Callahan's lifelong affair with Selene Stavrakis, her son currently living in Athens, and Selene's still living but very-aged sister were simply loose threads. He didn't really believe that they would unravel the mystery, but he did think that speaking with them in person would give Hanlon a broader perspective than just reading an eight-page essay and some old newspaper stories.

Fifty Six

The plane pushed away from the gate at 8:32 p.m. Following the advice of my archaeologist contact, a veteran trans-Atlantic traveler, I'd managed to get two aisle seats directly across from each other. Better for conversation, as well as going to the restroom.

"How many passengers you think we have?" I said, stretching my neck to glance around the Economy Class section of the plane.

"Why don't you get up, walk around and count 'em?" Louie said. "Then you can put it in your report. Could be important."

Ignoring him I stood up, and in an attempt at nonchalance, slowly panned the interior of the cabin. After a long minute of extending my arms, cracking my knuckles and then placing my hands behind my head, I decided that the flight looked to be approximately sixty percent full.

"Approximately 200. A lot better than a few months ago, I bet."

"And you arrived at the number how?" he said.

"You told me that this a 747-8, right? And you said it has 364 seats. Is that something you looked up on your own, or Becky do it for you?"

No reply.

"I'm counting . . . probably 150 empty seats that I can see. More in the back of the plane, maybe a couple in Business Class."

"We could move up there," he said.

"I don't think so."

Settling back, I adjusted the seat belt and snapped it closed. A man and a woman were to my left. Louie was on a center aisle, and the row of three seats next to him was unoccupied.

We'd been in the air for less than 30 minutes when a voice on the overhead announced — in German and English — that we had attained cruising altitude and that flight attendants would be coming through the cabin with beverages and snacks.

Louie had headphones on. The seatback screen in front of him showed a map of the US and Europe with our flight path dotted across the Atlantic. Placing my own headphones on, I scrolled through the choices of videos and selected a National Geographic documentary on park rangers in the Smoky Mountains.

The seven-hour flight was smooth, delivering us to the Franz Josef Strauss International Airport in Munich at 9:40 Saturday morning. Our layover was shy of two hours before the connecting flight to Athens, which took another two-and-a-half -hours. The cab ride to the city center was 30 minutes and got us to the hotel at 2:45 in the afternoon.

"We'll check in, then walk," I said.

"Yep."

More travel advice from the Prof; beat the jetlag by *not* resting on arrival, get out, get some air and exercise.

Hard to miss the Acropolis from the middle of Plaka, the old section of the city. Right up there above everything, in the same way you see the Lincoln Memorial from afar, especially if it were positioned on top of a hill like this. Pretty impressive.

The Adams Hotel had complimentary city maps. The desk manager marked the spot of where we were, then using an orange felt-tip marker, sketched a short route around the neighborhood. He marked a spot where I could purchase a good map of the country, including Crete and the other islands.

Following narrow cobblestoned side streets, we walked across an open area past a fenced-off excavation site, up other residential streets of tightly packed four-story buildings, and eventually reached a point where we could look out over the sprawl of Athens. The entire urban area is home to 4 million people. The city center, 15 square miles, has a population of just over 660,000 — greater than all of Vermont and approximately 19,000 people per square mile, three times the density of Boston.

After two hours of walking and gawking, we found a taverna with outside tables — the place is crammed with such establishments — and settled in for a beer and to think about dinner, or perhaps more sight-seeing.

"What's your guess, how high is that?" I asked, pointing up at the Acropolis.

Louie stared at the columns erected on the rocky hilltop, took a drink of his beer and said, "Maybe 500 feet. Could be a little higher. I don't do meters."

"And the elevation here?"

"Above sea level?"

"Yeah."

"From what I saw on the approach before we landed, the drive in from the airport, I would say that we're probably close to 250 feet right here, give or take."

"The elevation in Quechee is 580 feet," I said. "Mount Ascutney is over 3,100 feet. Mansfield is, what, 4,400 feet? *That*," I pointed again toward the ancient citadel, "looks higher than 500 feet from here. It's sure as hell higher than the hills around my house."

Waiting for our dinner to be served, I pulled out my phone and tapped in the number Frank had given me for Helen Stavrakis. Five full rings before she answered.

Explaining who I was and that I would like to visit with her tomorrow, if possible, we agreed on 10 o'clock in the morning. I told her that yes, I had the address and that I also had a map of the city. When I told her where my hotel was, she said that the walk to her apartment was a short distance. Her English was accented but perfectly understandable. Mentioning that I had a friend travelling with me and asking if it would be all right for him to come along, she said that she was fine with that.

241

While Louie and I ate — shellfish linguine, fried calamari, and a Greek salad — someone up at The Acropolis had turned on lights for our benefit. It gave the appearance of a gigantic, luminescent twenty-five-hundred-year-old spaceship that had just landed on a high plateau.

After a second glass of beer, it was going on 9 o'clock, middle of the afternoon back home, we were ready to let the jetlag kick in. Walking back to the hotel was slow, easy, and quiet. As soon as we arrived, Louie called Becky to let her know that all was good and that they could talk again on Sunday before we left Athens and before she left for Arizona.

Fifty Seven

Helen Stavrakis was a short woman who reminded me of a high school teacher I'd had in Pennsylvania nearly forty years ago. She opened the door to her apartment, invited us to come in and to be seated at a table in her small kitchen.

She had a plate of baklava/fig tarts/sweet pastry on the table and served us what she called 'sketos', black coffee with no sugar, although she produced a small bottle of milk should we want to add some to the coffee.

I had reviewed the written observations and questions Frank had provided a few days earlier. I removed the pages from the side pocket of my cargo travel slacks and smoothed them flat on the table. Hoping that it might serve as an icebreaker, I began with, "Mister Marino has many fond memories of your sister."

Helen smiled and lightly patted just above her heart.

"Selene also loved 'little Franklin' very much," she said.

I laughed. "Little Franklin," I raised my left hand up high, "is not so little. He is well over six feet tall. For a man his age, he still towers above some of us." I glanced at Louie hoping that he would not smirk. He didn't.

"He is my age," Helen said. "Eighty-four."

"I believe that he might be a year older than you."

"My father was married to Selene's mother, who died when she was young. He came to Athens and married my mother. I was born much later. Selene was fifteen years older than me."

She talked for a few minutes about family, growing up in Athens, never having been married herself, and how much the city had changed during her lifetime. As she went on, Louie took his coffee to the window and looked out from the third-floor kitchen at the traffic and the pedestrians below.

"Frank wanted to be sure that I remembered what to ask you," I said, again smoothing the type-written pages in front of me. I *didn't* say that he'd added, 'You can tell so much more face to face, much better than over the telephone. Watch her expression when she answers the questions.'

"First, and Frank knows that this was personal and if you are not comfortable talking about it, that's OK. He said that the last time he visited with Selene, it was here in 2004, that she spoke of another man that she knew very well."

It was not exactly a glare that Helen was giving me, but a pretty cold stare. Eyes locked on mine, no blinking, mouth shut tight. She let me go on.

"Do you know about that man? Were they close? Do you know his name?"

I sensed Louie turning to look at me, almost conveying some admonition like: '*Take it easy hotshot. This woman's not running for office.*'

Helen shifted in her chair, sat up a little straighter, and closing her hands together rested them on the edge of the table.

"She was close to an American, yes. And for many years, there was a younger Greek who wanted to marry Selene. She was a young woman still. And beautiful."

I sipped my coffee, said nothing, and tried to indicate understanding. For what I was not yet sure.

"You know that Selene had a child. Franklin has told you this," she said. I nodded. "Yes, he did tell me."

"My sister . . ." she paused and looked over at Louie by the window, then turned back to me, "she was forty-one when Theo was born. It was a miracle. She thought that she was too old for children."

Helen's expression seemed to be a mix of awe and a bitter-sweet memory. She stayed quiet for a few seconds, then smiled before continuing.

"She was a wonderful mother. All those years, until the day she left us." And continue she did, for another twenty-five minutes, in what seemed like a year-by-year account of her sister's long life as a devoted mother.

"Still . . . in the last days before she died, Selene was proud of Theo." she added.

Frank's interest in the son and his whereabouts in Athens were among the final questions on my list. They could wait.

But I was not sure if Helen was taking a break, or if this was as far as she was prepared to go.

After what seemed like a full minute of silence, she again offered a weak smile, which I took as a signal that that part of the story was at an end.

"The American man, he was the father of Selene's son?" I asked.

The sad smile remained. More silence. No answer.

"The Greek you said wanted to marry her. What was his name?"

Helen offered a barely audible, dismissive grunt. Unclasping her hands and pushing back from the table, she slowly got up from the chair. She held up a right index finger and waggled it back and forth. The smile had turned into a scold, her eyes slightly enlarged almost in surprise.

"You will wait," she said, then turned to go into what I presumed to be her bedroom. A minute later she returned clutching a handful of letters. She placed them on the table in front of me, opened one, removing a sheet of paper, then gave it a harsh tap with the same index finger.

"That is his name," she said. She pushed the letter closer for me to see.

Most of the writing was in Greek with a few words in English. There was a single name handwritten at the bottom of the page; Hektor.

"He is longtime dead also," Helen said. "I am told that his *other* family, in America, they are . . . what I believe you call . . . gangsters," she said, the tone expanding on the grunt from minutes earlier.

"I will give you the address for Theo. I have not seen him for a time," she said. "Only a few visits since Selene has gone. He was living here still," she added, handing me the sheet of paper with Theo's name and an address written on it, something she'd apparently done following the phone conversation with Marino and in anticipation of my visit.

I started to copy the man's name signed on the letter Helen had just shown me, but she picked it up, folded it and placed it back in the envelope.

"You take these," she said, handing me the letters. "They are of no use to an old woman. I will be gone soon. Who will know what to do with them?"

"What about Theo?" I asked.

"Yes. You may give the letters to him."

Fifty Eight

Before we left her apartment, the only additional piece of information offered by Helen was her belief that Selene's son might be the only one alive who knew the real identity of his father.

Walking back toward the center of the old city in the direction of our hotel, Louie was uncharacteristically quiet. I had the envelopes containing the letters and had placed them in my pocket along with the piece of paper with the address for Theo Angelos. That visit could wait.

Arriving at an intersection that we recognized, I pointed to the right and we headed that way toward the Acropolis. A few minutes later in a large cobblestoned plaza surrounded by an iron fence, we were at the entrance leading to paths up a hillside to one of the world's most iconic structures.

Saturday morning and there was a crowd, perhaps as big as one sees on opening day at the Champlain Valley Fair. A lot of people, many wearing face masks. Tickets and guide map in hand, Louie walked across the plaza to purchase a couple of bottles of water from a street vendor and we began the ascent.

For the next three-and-a-half hours, we must've acted like the ten-zillionth tourist to have climbed up, thru, under, and around amazing architecture and stonework. According to my guidebook, the earliest habitation on this spot has been documented as dating to the Early Neolithic period — seventh millennium BC — more than 8,000 years ago.

Nearly intact, or remnants of, twenty-one different structures and statues spread across approximately seven acres of a mostly flat, rocky outcrop looking down on the modern city of Athens. I read about many of the military confrontations that have wreaked so much damage to the buildings, the most serious having occurred during a siege by Venetians in the late 17th century. The guidebook showed the earliest known photograph of the site, a daguerreotype dating from 1842, as well as a summary of recent restoration efforts dating back to the mid-1970s.

When we had finished our time on the mount, unfortunately, we had less than an hour to hustle through the Acropolis Museum and get a quick look at some of the ancient artifacts on display.

"Makes you wanna sign up for the full Rick Steves trip, eh?" I said.

Louie looked at me. "The guy on Vermont Public TV?"

I nodded. "I think he has an audience beyond the Green Mountains."

"Really?" he said. "Be sure to let me know when you book a tour. I'll check my calendar."

That evening I got a text from Jacoby Rudner telling me that he was on Crete at a dig site and would be going to Chania on Friday, leaving there the following Tuesday. Over a late dinner — seafood, more Zeos Blue Mak lager and a tiny glass of Raki with dessert — we spent time studying a Nakas Road Cartography map of Crete. We'd already decided to fly to Heraklion, spend one full day there, then head west with a rental car.

I knew that Frank was working to get us an appointment at the NATO base in Chania, either on Friday or Saturday. That would leave us two flex days when we were ready to resume the next leg of the tour.

"So, we just have to find this Theo guy tomorrow," Louie said. "Then we fly over to Crete."

"Yep."

"Need reservations?"

I shook my head. "Not according to The Prof. He says there are multiple flights every day." Reaching for my phone, I swiped the screen, typed in Aegean Air, brought up the schedule and saw that there was a morning flight, two in the afternoon and two more late in the evening.

"If we can see Theo in the morning," I said, holding my phone for Louie to see the screen, "We can try for the 1:30. It's less than an hour flight."

"Sounds good. Hotel?"

"Again, The Prof. He gave me the name of a place he says is clean, quiet, low-key and not likely to be busy this late in the year."

Louie looked at his watch. "I'm going to call Becky. Back in a few minutes," he said. He went out to a bench on the street in front of the hotel from which I had made my calls earlier in the day.

Sunday morning, we checked out, arranged to leave our bags for later, then went looking for Theo Angelos. The address Helen had given us was a 10-minute cab ride.

In a neighborhood known as Kato Petralona, the cabbie pulled up in front of another multi-story apartment building and we got out. As I started to pay the driver, it occurred to me that it might be a good idea to check first. Maybe Theo wasn't here or had moved. I gave the man a €20 note and held up my hand.

"Can you wait for a couple of minutes? I'd like to be sure that he's home."

"No problem," he said in passable English.

Inside, the building was close to being decrepit. In the small lobby I could smell cooking, perhaps all the meals prepared over the last two years. The address listed on the paper Helen had given me showed the apartment as C-44. We took the elevator.

A woman, maybe in her fifties, came to the door. She opened it just enough to see us.

"Hi. My name is Michael Hanlon. I'm looking for Theo Angelos." No idea if she understood English. I was up the creek if she did not.

She shook her head but said nothing.

"I'm here from the US," I said, pulling a business card from my wallet. "I am running some errands for a man who was a close friend of Theo's mother." I handed her the card.

"Theo is not here. He went to Crete," the woman finally replied as she studied my card.

I turned and looked back at Louie. He gave me the raised eyebrows and a tap to the side of his nose. Reaching into a pocket, I pulled out a pen.

"May I leave a note?" I reached for the card, she handed it back. While I held it against the door jamb to write, I told her why I was there.

"Frank Marino is a man back where I live. Vermont," I said. No response. "He's getting along in years now, but when he was very young, he lived in Athens with his grandparents. Theo's mother took care of him then. And he was here to see her not long before she died," I added.

When I finished writing Frank's name, I circled my cell-phone number on the front of the card and handed it back to her.

"Do you know when he's coming back?"

She shrugged and shook her head. "He does not tell me. Maybe two days, maybe one week." Another shrug.

I thanked her and asked that she let Theo know that Frank would love to speak with him. She nodded and started to close the door.

"Do you know where on Crete?"

She hesitated, offered another shrug, then said, "Heraklion. Maybe Matala. I am not sure."

"**Nice gesture** there," I said to Louie when we were outside. "You give that little nose tap signal to rookies? *Sniff it out*, like a good bird dog?"

"Everly Brothers, 1958. Look it up."

I shook my head and opened the cab door for him to climb in before me.

The driver was happy to take us to the airport. We stopped for our bags at the hotel along the way, and for another €60, a twenty-five-minute drive. Not much traffic on a warm Sunday morning.

We were able to get tickets for the 1:30 flight, which left us a couple of hours to kill. The Athens airport is like that of most of the other major hubs that I've seen — lots of shops and food establishments — with still many of the workers and passengers wearing face masks.

Shoulda gone back to the Acropolis Museum. Too late.

Fifty Nine

Melissa and Emma were now back in Matala planning to explore the caves, but not before Melissa and her grandfather had spent a few minutes lingering over coffee.

Nikos pulled the rolled-up old photo from a pocket of his jacket and placed it on the table. Melissa watched him as he removed the rubber band and slowly spread the photo open. He used a coffee cup to hold down one end, while his right hand prevented the other end from curling back.

Once fully open — it was wider than the table — Nikos held it in place. He raised his eyes to look at his granddaughter.

"Wow. That is really *old*," she said. "Who are these men?"

Nikos tapped an image of one of the young boys in the photo. "This is my uncle, Hektor."

She leaned closer, placing a finger on the image. "I see the resemblance," she said, rubbing the boy's face. "It's his nose," she added.

Nikos made a sound that was a mix of a laugh and a cough.

"We *all* have that nose," he said. Touching her left cheek, he added, "I believe *you* have it, agápi mou."

She reflexively pinched her nose. "Maybe not as . . . *large*."

Now he did laugh. "When you are my age. You will see."

"And the eyes," she said, getting closer to the photo. "You have those eyes." Sitting upright, she ran her left hand slowly across all the men in the photo.

"Where was this taken? And *when*?"

Nikos told her a story about the young boys working with a construction company in Chania shortly after the end of World War II. He told about one of the other boys in the photo, Pavlos, who had recently died. Speaking softly, with frequent pauses, as though he was uncertain of details, he told her what he'd learned from Pavlos very recently.

After several minutes Nikos stopped talking. He leaned back in his chair, rubbed his eyes with both hands, looked directly at Melissa, then back to the photo. He tapped the image of the American soldier standing near his uncle.

"I believe that Hektor had this man killed."

Melissa put a hand to her mouth and sat back. "*Why?*" she said.

Nikos nodded. "I do not have proof. I am not sure of . . . why. But . . ." looking toward the bay as though he expected to see a boat arriving, or perhaps Zeus coming ashore, he lightly touched his breastbone and continued. "I am the one who arranged for this to happen."

255

She stared at her grandfather. *Was he saying that he had directed someone to kill a man?*

"Killed him in the war?" she said.

Nikos shook his head. "I was a little boy during the war. No, this was much later." Again, the gaze out across the water. "Forty years ago. My uncle sent me to see a friend in the United States. A friend from Athens; a bad man. It was that man who helped me to hire an *American* . . . who was paid to kill him."

He tapped the area where the American soldier stood next to the boys, but Nikos was not looking at the photo now. He lifted his right hand and moved Melissa's coffee cup in its place.

"Why?" Melissa said. "What did this man do?" She placed her hand on the photo.

"Hektor did not tell me. He did not say that it was to be a murder. There was money that I took to a meeting. In Philadelphia. That is when I met. . . the Greek gangster. He made a phone call. It was something that he and Hektor had talked about before my trip." Nikos paused again.

"Then I was sent to meet *another* man, younger than me, in Boston. I gave him the money. And a name with an address for this man." He tapped the photo, letting his hand rest on the image of the American."

They sat in silence. Nikos fondled the cigarette package in his pocket but did not smoke in front of his granddaughter.

"Does anyone else know about this? My mother?" Melissa said.

"No," Nikos said in an urgent tone and with a vigorous shake of the head. "When we visited the Monastery, the last time you were here. There was a young American, with a woman and a little boy."

"I remember," Melissa said. "They were on the bench outside the chapel, near where we sat."

"Yes. The little boy was climbing on his mother, excited about the peacock. And the goats behind the fence. The father was laughing, trying to hold the boy. I watched the father for a long time.

"That night I had a dream, about this American soldier." His left hand lay flat on the photo, only his thumb moving slowly up and down when he spoke.

More silence.

Finally, looking around to see if Emma had returned, Melissa pushed her chair back to get up. Nikos watched her.

"Papouli, are you going to . . . *tell* someone about this?"

"It was so long ago . . ."

"Yes. But what about this man's family?" she said, stretching a hand back to the photo. "Maybe you could write a letter to . . ." Nikos cut her off.

"I am telling *you*." He looked up at Melissa.

Placing her right hand on his shoulder, she bent forward to kiss the top of her grandfather's head.

"Papouli, we have to tell someone about this. If not in Athens, then . . . the police in . . . Philadelphia. Or in Boston."

"I would like to go back to the Monastery," he said.

She let her hand rest on his shoulder and watched him in silence. He was staring out at the bay. They stayed like that for a long minute.

"Yes, we can go," she said. "I will talk with Emma. She would like to see the Monastery."

Sixty

The shooter drove the rental truck onto the delivery access street directly behind the office/retail complex in Stoneham. Armando had told him about a rear entrance to Weapons, Ltd.

Pulling the passenger side tight to the building, he put on the four-way flashers and climbed out of the cab. It was 11:30 on a Monday morning. He presumed that Armando was already inside.

Three doors at the back of the building; one at each end and one in the center, which was the entrance that he'd been told would be unlocked. He tried the handle, the door opened.

Inside was a narrow corridor. Worn commercial carpeting, generic wallpaper above wainscoting, emergency power lights and smoke detectors, and six doors along one wall approximately 20 feet apart. He let his eyes adjust to the dim overhead lighting. Armando had instructed him to knock on the door numbered Unit Two.

Ten seconds of small talk and the two men went back to the exit door. Armando pushed on the handle and found a rubber wedge to keep the door open. Bright light flooded that section of the hallway. The shooter went out first.

With the rear door of the box truck rolled open, Armando could see the three crates aligned in a row, strapped to the floor to prevent movement. The gun safes were behind them, also a hand truck, and two smaller cardboard moving boxes were strapped to the left side panel.

"What's in the boxes?" Armando said, pointing to the smaller containers.

"A lot of ammunition that I no longer need," the shooter said. "All yours now."

They carried the smaller cartons inside first, then made three trips for the wooden crates, followed by a trip for each safe using the hand truck. When they had finished, Armando went back to remove the rubber wedge doorstop.

"Move the truck?" the shooter said.

"Yes. You'll find a space out front to park. I'll let you in the front door."

They took two hours to go through the crates, examining each gun — some more closely than others — then replaced the weapon back into its individual case. Only three weapons were left uncased. Armando wanted them for a zoom video session that he had scheduled for later in the afternoon.

Walking to his office, Armando picked up a manila folder from the desk and removed a check. He handed it to the shooter.

A cashier's check in the amount of $135,000.00.

The agreement was for seventy-five percent payment on delivery, balance to be paid within seven days.

"Good," the shooter said, folding the check and placing it in his left shirt pocket.

"I don't anticipate any issues," Armando said. "In all likelihood, my buyer will overnight a check and I can mail you the balance as early as Friday."

The shooter held up his right hand in a pause motion.

"No mail. *Call* me. I will come back and get the check in person."

"Okay. That'll work."

The forms were completed and signed with the real estate agent; the documents dated for the listing to go on the market at the end of the week.

Reiterating his original instruction, he told the agent that she could begin showing the house as early as the coming weekend. Regardless of how long it took to sell, she would have the keys and it was all on her now. Any future transactions would be arranged by fax or electronic signatures over the internet.

While he had the rental truck, the shooter hauled several boxes of household items, hand tools and articles of clothing to a Goodwill store in Newton. The power equipment from the basement workshop would go to a man that he knew from his former manufacturing job. Truth was the shooter planned never to spend another day using his hands for any form of gainful employment.

This time next week, he would be on the road to Arizona.

Sixty One

The port city of Heraklion is the largest municipality on the island. It functions as the administrative capital of Crete. First impression is that it is similar in size to the Burlington, Vermont metro area.

Ragsdale and I were here for three reasons: one, to visit the Archaeological Museum and check out the faience statuettes of the so-called Snake Goddess from about 1,600 BC, as well as the Phaistos Disc, reputed to be 4,000 years old but discovered only a century ago; two, to visit the Bronze Age palace of Knossos to see the ruins; and three, to pick up a rental car. We decided to handle number three first.

Hoping to avoid the experience in Athens with an early closing time, we visited the Heraklion Museum before dinner. Suffice it to say that for a couple of woodchucks, it was impressive.

"You need to purchase a replica of the disc," I said. "When you get home, have Becky take a look at the website. She's gonna be jealous as hell."

"Right. Should I buy the mini-statue of the snake woman, too?"

"Sure. Wave it around, razzle a little voodoo. Scare some of your drug pals. But I'm *serious* about the disc. You know that I'm getting one for Virginia."

"It looks like a *bagel*."

"I think the gift shop has a bagel version. Including all the little symbols."

"Why don't you get Virginia a t-shirt? She'd look great in it," he said.

"And shall I tell her you said that?"

Our next hotel lived up to the billing of being quiet, low-key, and moderately priced. A bonus was that several neighborhood eateries were within short walking distance. We picked a family restaurant called Merastri. Slow-cooked lamb with oven potatoes and stuffed zucchini, a noodle dish with fresh seafood, then a knock-your-socks off chocolate cake with a fruit platter. A bottle of dry Greek red wine was nice, too.

It was an easy stroll back to the hotel. I needed to check in with Frank Marino and gave him a call as soon as we arrived in the lobby. Middle of the afternoon in Vermont; I hoped that he was not taking a nap.

"Michael Hanlon, you are a man of your word," he said by way of answering.

"How's that?"

"You always call me when you say you will. Where are you?" he asked.

"Heraklion. Arrived this afternoon. Just finished dinner a few minutes ago."

"Thank you for the email summary on the visit with Helen. Since then, I've been in touch with my colleague at Fort Meade. He came through with a couple of names and phone numbers. The US Navy Captain in command at Souda Bay, and the Public Affairs Officer there," he said.

"Great. Can you send them to me?"

"Yes. And I've already drafted questions that pertain specifically to things they may be able to help with. You need to pin down precisely *when* you will arrive there. I want to call them in advance. Two or three days from now would be my preference."

"You heard my message that Theo Angelos was not in Athens?" I said. "According to a woman at his apartment, he's somewhere on Crete. She mentioned a place called Matala."

"Is the woman his wife?"

"Didn't ask. She was giving a vibe that did *not* indicate any eagerness to tell me much. Might've been the language barrier. I did leave my card and asked that she let him know that I'd like to speak with him."

"I don't believe it matters all that much," Frank said. "He is, for my way of thinking, not at the front end of what we're looking for. That could change, subject to what you learn in Chania."

"I need to study a map I bought. We're going to visit the Palace of Knossos tomorrow, then head west. I'm told that the roads are OK, but driving is slower than we're used to in the states."

"May depend on where you are driving," he said. "Last time I was there, the highways were much improved."

"At this point, my plan is for us to reach the western end of the island sometime on Thursday."

"As soon as you get my next email, try to give me a better idea. Might make sense that I place a call to Souda Bay and inquire about setting up a meeting for you on Friday," he said.

"Yeah. If it needs to be sooner than that, I can adjust the sightseeing."

"You will enjoy Knossos. Fascinating how much they've been able to preserve from 4,000 years ago."

Frank went on for another minute about what he knew of the Minoan ruins and mentioned a famous monastery that we also might consider trying to visit. I said that I'd call again in two days and that he should text me if I needed to check in sooner.

Turns out that it was a British archaeologist, Arthur Evans, who made the discovery and along with others, began excavation of the site at Knossos. Or at least what is now referred to as the 'Palace Period'.

Beginning in 1900 and continuing for thirty some years, all kinds of pottery, bronzes, seals, tablets, wall paintings — the list goes on — were unearthed at the site. The mythical figure of the Minotaur is rooted at Knossos. It is believed that people began arriving at this location by boat more than 8,500 years ago.

Ragsdale and I had seen some of the frescoes from the palace at the museum in Heraklion. Now — up close and personal — we were able to get a sense of the scope of the site. It is believed that at its peak the ancient city's population was between 20 and 50,000. Remnants of the palace, the throne room, gigantic storage jars, the royal family courtyard, a theatre for 400 people, all on three acres with the palace alone covering 150,000 square feet.

"Unbelievable," I said, standing atop the palace court and watching a few other tourists meandering below.

"Do you know how *large* the biggest Walmart or Home Depot is?" Louie said.

"Don't have a clue."

"C'mon, Hanlon. Give me your best guess."

"Okay. How about . . . a hundred-and-forty-thousand square feet," I said.

"Over two-hundred thousand on one level, for the big super centers. This place has *four or five levels* just on the east side of the court."

"Yeah, and you don't get paintings like that." I pointed back toward the fresco reproduction of a man leaping over a bull.

"Think they did that at the first Olympic Games?"

We could have circled around again, especially to have a closer look at the stonework. Instead, we found a taverna across the street from the palace, got a table on a second-floor open deck and had a beer with a Greek salad and some green peppers stuffed with feta.

"Too bad the car doesn't have GPS," Louie said. I had unfolded the road map of the island and was running my finger slowly south from where we were at that moment.

"Prof Rudner says that we wanna drive down here, through the olive groves, then go west." I flipped the map over and traced a route that eventually would take us north again, toward the Cretan Sea and out to the western end of the island.

"The only stop we have for sure," I continued, "is right here." I tapped a spot near the southern coast on the Mediterranean. "It's the Holy Monastery of Preveli. We'll get a room in one of the nearby villages."

"Right. Where they hid the allied soldiers during the Battle of Crete," he said.

"Yep. Then . . ." I ran my finger back up the map toward Chania, "this is where we wind up."

"How far?"

"Ah-h-h, I'm guessing from here to Preveli, maybe four hours. Then from there on to Chania, maybe another two hours."

Louie studied the route I had been tracing with my finger. He leaned in closer to the map.

"Tell you what, Brother Ragsdale, you are the primary driver here. Better look that over carefully. I have to hit the restroom." I got up from the table. "Don't spill beer on the new map."

"Never," he said.

268

Sixty Two

Following a slow, leisurely drive through small villages and across the Messara Plain — its vast expanse covered by olive groves, some trees had the circumference of a Vermont border maple — we came to an intersection.

"See the sign?" I said, pointing.

Louie pulled to the side of the narrow road. "Yes. What about it?"

Giving me the 'Are you serious?' smirk, he shut off the engine and pulled the hand break.

"So, what, I should let you out and you walk around shouting his name? Do you have a photo? And we don't know if . . ." he pointed at the sign, "*Matala* is the size of Averys Gore or . . . Heraklion."

"Yeah, we do." I opened the map. "Looks pretty small. But never mind. Just an idea. Turn right. It says 63 kilometers to Preveli."

We'd barely gone one kilometer when Louie gave me a laugh and tapped the side of his head just above his right temple.

"63 kilometers. That's close to 40 miles, yes?"

"Sounds right."

"Duane Eddy, 1959. *Forty Miles of Bad Road*. Look it up."

"How do we *know* the road will be bad?"

"Would you like to drive now?" he asked.

"You're doing swell. Straight ahead."

Ragsdale's oldies nonsense prompted me to turn on the radio. I fiddled with the dial and found a surprising number of FM stations. After scanning for a minute, I stopped the dial at Fly FM 88.1. The promos were in Greek *and* English! To spite Louie, I punched up the volume on some *really* bad Europop electronic noise they were passing off as music.

"*Really?*" he said.

"Hey, taste is subjective."

The 'music' sounded more like telemetry, or maybe a digitally enhanced busy signal.

"See if you can find a station that plays Vangelis," he said.

The name was vaguely familiar. "And what was *their* biggest hit?" I asked.

"He/him. Just one guy. Greek composer. Lot of movie stuff. *Blade Runner. The Bounty*, I think. But his biggie was *Chariots of Fire*. Made it to number one. Back about the same time your guy got, ah, whacked . . . in the hunting accident."

"What?"

"Early 80s."

"Speaking of that, let me try something out on you. All the reading on spies that Marino has had me doing."

"Yes?"

I turned the radio volume down to barely audible.

"Far as I can determine, this cloak and dagger bit — now it's mostly cyber, unless you count Russians having people poisoned or assassinated — there is some *serious* competition and maybe more than a few fragile egos skulking around among the US agencies."

"Hard to believe," Louie said.

For the next twenty-minutes, I brought him up to speed on my slowly evolving hypothesis that perhaps Win Callahan had been 'disposed of' at the request of someone in another US service, for something that he might have done a long time ago, years before the hunting incident in the White Mountains.

"He did tell a friend that 'one day you will read about my death, and it will be reported as an accident.'"

"What does Marino say?" Louie said.

"Maybe. But he's mostly on the trail of someone outside the US. We may learn more when we get to the Naval Base. He's trying to dig up information on Callahan's numerous trips there over a period of forty years or more."

"Guess that's why we're on tour, huh?"

"Yep."

We arrived at Preveli and spent a couple of hours going through the buildings, walking the old stone-paved terrace on the upper and lower levels, watching animals behind fences — goats, cows, chickens, sheep, a peacock — and then we went inside the chapel.

Neither of us considers himself a 'religious person'. And while we both have been inside churches and cathedrals, we agreed that this seemed to be different. Small interior, no windows, dark to the point that it takes a few seconds for your eyes to adjust; a gold cross reputed to have pieces from the True Cross; iconic paintings and lighted candles at different stations.

We left the chapel by the same door we had entered, walked across a stone terrace and looked out at the Libyan Sea. A few other people were here on a sunny, blue-sky afternoon — normal weather for this part of Greece 90% of the year.

Driving back up to the main road, we stopped for a closer look at the memorial that featured a monk holding a rifle. The armed Abbot of Preveli Monastery, with a plaque showing the flags of Greece, the UK, Australia, and New Zealand, alongside another statue, this one of an allied forces soldier from 1941.

Back in the car it was my turn to drive. We skipped the radio entertainment. Louie began a slow, quiet delivery on what turned out to be, for him, a lengthy and solemn commentary on things that most people just don't know about if they've never been in a military battle.

Hanlon. Keep your mouth shut.

Ragsdale's personal experience had been during the Gulf War in 1991 with the US Army. Rarely did he talk about it. And he wasn't reminiscing on that now.

"We see all the movies, the documentaries and some of the clips on the History Channel. That stuff gives you a taste of what it was like. But read the real histories, the first-hand accounts of battles," he was looking out at the rock covered hills as we drove along, "it is almost impossible to imagine . . . what people *went through*. What they had to do just to *survive*.

"That's one I knew nothing about," he went on. "But you can bet I'm gonna read up on the Battle of Crete. Thanks for asking me to come along. And for making that one of our stops."

After I concluded that he had finished, we continued traveling at between 50 and 70 km per hour, mostly in silence, watching out for goats or people on bicycles.

Another hour and a half to Chania.

The time difference between Vermont and Greece slipped Frank Marino's mind. His first call to the Naval Support offices at Souda Bay had gone straight to voicemail. Now, Wednesday morning 08:45 in Vermont, he got a return call from the Public Affairs officer at the base; "How can we help?"

Marino first told the PA officer about his own career with the agencies in Washington — if the man already knew he didn't let on — and then explained what he hoped might be in files somewhere at the base.

"I know that material with any merit has been scanned and by now has likely settled to the bottom of all the digital files. This is a lifetime ago, early 1950s. What I'm after, are there names of groups, allies, individuals, *anyone* on record at the time, who opposed the establishment of a base? Or particularly didn't like us and the men we kept sending over there?"

"Let me see what we have, sir," the officer said. "Should I call you at this number?"

Marino said yes, then also gave the man his email address.

"And please offer my congratulations to Captain Facundo. He doesn't know me, but I know about his naval career. The new assignment must be an honor," Marino said.

Marino was confident that the new commanding officer at Souda Bay would be momentarily curious and possibly flattered. This tact had worked in the past and might help to facilitate Hanlon's visit.

Sixty Three

Walking the beach at Matala, coming back from exploring the caves, Melissa told Emma about the earlier conversation with her grandfather. Not in detail — mostly because she didn't have any — but about the guilt and worry that she saw bearing down on the old man.

"He has this photograph from a long time ago, a large group of men. One of the men was his uncle. He said that another man in the picture, an American, was killed. And that he, my *grandfather*, was involved with making the arrangements and delivering the money to pay someone to murder the American."

Emma stopped walking and touched Melissa's left arm. "Do you believe him?" "Why would he make that up?" Melissa said. They stood looking at each other, no one else on the beach.

"My grandfather went to America at least twice when he was young. My mother learned later that the only reason he came back was because my grandmother was pregnant with her. And, according to my mother, they never got along. All my grandmother's family lived in Athens. Papouli moved here to Matala before I was born. His family is from Crete."

They proceeded without further conversation. The taverna came into view a hundred-fifty meters off. After a minute, Emma stopped walking. As soon as Melissa realized that her friend was behind her, she stopped.

"What are you going to do?" Emma said.

Melissa walked back to where Emma stood at the edge of the water. She looked down at her feet, slowly moving one sideways to touch the other, then repeating the motion with the opposite foot, giving the appearance of a person testing her coordination and balance.

"I asked him if he was going to contact the police in America. Or tell someone here. He wouldn't answer. *But* . . . he wants to go to the monastery. We were there the last time I visited, this summer."

Emma put a hand on Melissa's shoulder. "Then we should go to the monastery. You wanted me to see it anyway. Tell your 'Papouli' that we can take him tomorrow."

Nikos Andreadakis had ferreted through his memory time and again since the dreams first began. Brief images of men's faces came but faded quickly.

No one's name had been provided, but he could recall the meeting place; a restaurant in Boston not far from the stadium where the baseball team played. It had been crowded. Two younger men were waiting in a booth. They had apparently known who he was and had been expecting his arrival. One of the men stood and motioned for him to join them.

Nikos had a photo and the letter which contained a man's name and an address, a place in New Hampshire. He also had the money, ten-thousand-dollars cash. The conversation had been brief, and he was out of the restaurant only minutes after he'd arrived.

What he did recall was the name of the man in Philadelphia as it was well-known back in Greece — Patanzis. Nikos' uncle had known Stefanos 'Steve' Patanzis before the man had moved from Athens to the US in the late 1960s. From his memory, Nikos had calculated that Patanzis had likely been in his early 70s when he'd met him that summer of 1980. He would not be alive today.

Rummaging through a handful of old books and papers in the back of his bedroom closet, he found a small cardboard box. Inside the box were personal letters and photographs, some postcards, and a few family greeting cards that he'd received over the years. One of the postcards had been from his American friend.

He would ask Melissa to help find out if the man was still alive.

The smell of the sea on a cool evening and no customers for dinner at Pithari. Nikos had Effie prepare dishes just for himself and the two young women.

"Mister Andreadakis," Emma said, hesitating. "Melissa has told me about the monastery . . ."

Before she could finish, Nikos raised both hands as though cautioning her about saying more. "Yes. You would like to take us there," he said. "I know this."

"I would," Melissa said. "Could we go tomorrow?"

Nikos looked at his granddaughter. She patted the old man's hand but said nothing.

"It would be nice for you to drive us to Preveli. It is not far," he said.

Reaching for a bottle of retsina at the center of the table, Nikos filled their glasses. He proposed a toast, first in Greek, "stin ygeia." He repeated it in English, "To health," then added, "To friends . . . and to our history."

It was 9:30 the following morning when they left Matala for an hour-and-a-half drive to Preveli. The sky was clear. Sheep, goats, and other tourists not yet in sight.

Melissa insisted that her grandfather sit in the front.

"You know where all of the goats are," Emma said, clicking her seat belt and checking the outside mirrors on the small rental car.

"Too many goats," Nikos said.

Melissa reached forward and gave an affectionate tap to the back of his head. "More sheep than goats, Papouli? They don't walk in the road."

Conversation during the drive was primarily between the two women, each of them making the effort to draw out the old man. When he did respond, comments were short and without elaboration. Finally, Emma seemed to have struck a chord.

"Do you know any of the monks?" she said.

Nikos glanced over at her, then attempted to look over his shoulder at Melissa, suspecting that she had put her friend up to this question.

"I knew an elder. He is gone now."

"We learned about his death when we were here the last time," Melissa said.

"I'm sorry," Emma said.

"He was from my family's village. He was a good man," Nikos said.

What he did not say was that the previous visit to the chapel — and learning of the old monk's death — had precipitated all of the mixed emotions now tangled up in reflections on three-quarters of a century being alive.

Younger than Nikos, the old monk had dedicated his years to religious service. His long stay at the monastery had been vastly different than Nikos' life. It was one of the recurring thoughts that he had now; *what* were the events in their youth that had led to such divergent existences?

Sixty Four

With still another recommendation from Prof Rudner, we found a small eight-room hotel located just inside the old town section of Chania.

I had to park the rental car outside the city walls — fortifications dating back to the Byzantine Empire a thousand years ago — and make our way through narrow streets to an antique wooden door set back from the curb, which took us up to the third floor. Two compact bedrooms and a shared, efficient small bathroom at the end of the hall.

After ten minutes to wash up and put on a clean shirt, we headed for the port area to scout out a place for dinner. Along the Venetian harbor — dating back to the 14th century — there had to be at least 20 restaurants offering outdoor dining within 15 feet of the water. We settled on a place called Stis Annas, hidden away in a side alley one street back from the harbor.

As soon as we were seated, after a quick glance at the menu, Ragsdale threw me a changeup. "You know what, Hanlon? I think this meal's on me. But *you* choose for both of us."

"Really?"

He nodded. "You have the inside dope from your archaeologist pal. Didn't you say he told you about this place? Go ahead, surprise me."

I ordered a half-carafe of house red wine and another of the house white. When he returned with the wine, the waiter brought appetizers — fried tomato croquettes, homemade flatbread and a bowl of mixed olives.

Fully intent of giving Louie the 'surprise' that he'd asked for, I held the menu up for the waiter to see what I was pointing at and indicated that he should bring enough for us to share, then said, "And a large Greek salad, please." He nodded, smiled, took both menus and disappeared up the stairs into the kitchen.

"So, the plan is that we head out to the naval base in the morning," I said.

"How far is it?"

"Maybe 10, 15 minutes. We'll look at the map. And I'll bring it up on my phone and get a better sense of getting from here to there"

"Of course. The phones will get a signal here," Louie said. "I thought some spots in Vermont are bad. After we left Heraklion, I don't think I had a signal three times during the entire drive."

"Marino set us up to see the PA officer. Apparently, he has a couple of folders that we can look at. Callahan had visited here several times during his years working what the spies call humint" I said.

Louie stopped eating and gave me the smirk. He took a sip of wine and wiped his mouth with a napkin.

"You know," he leaned in closer, "it ain't just spies who call it that. I think if you go back and watch early episodes of Rocky and Bullwinkle, they probably used that term." He stared at me for a beat, then added, "*Hume*-int . . . *sig*-int. Got it?"

"Sorry. Had to be my upbringing. Wasn't until I met you that I learned that 'undercover' is something *different* from what we tried to do with girls at MYF camp."

Now the smirk, raised eyebrows and hands up, as in, 'I am confused'.

"MYF – Methodist Youth Fellowship. You don't know what you missed," I said.

Finishing off the appetizers and most of the wine, we yakked for several minutes, speculating about what it must be like on a NATO base for those serving there and wondering if it was just US and Greek military, or if other countries were represented.

When the entree arrived, we watched as the waiter dished portions onto clean plates. It looked good and smelled great. Louie had a fork in his hand before the waiter had turned from the table.

I glanced at my watch; 8:50 PM, which meant 2:50 back home. Marino was likely to send another email or text knowing that I would see it before going to bed.

"**What's the name** of this dish?" Ragsdale said. I half expected to see him begin licking his fingers. We were nearly finished with the meal.

"Imam Bayildi," I said. "The Prof says it's also known as 'the sultan fainted.' Not bad, huh?"

"I might faint," Louie said. "This is *really* something."

"Glad you like it." I looked around the room at the other patrons. Those eating seemed to be enjoying their meals, perhaps not as much as Louie was enjoying his. I could not recall ever having heard Ragsdale rave quite like this about food.

The waiter returned with another half-carafe of the red wine, topping off our glasses. He removed the empty olive bowl and the bread platter.

"Efcharisto," I said. The waiter nodded, smiled, and went to another table. Louie stopped chewing long enough to give me the smirk.

"It's all Greek to me," he said.

"Yuk, yuk."

"Remind me when we get to see this pal of yours," Louie said. He took a sip of wine, then added, "And do you think he knows anything about Vangelis?"

"If it works out, we might get to meet him late tomorrow afternoon. He's across town attending some gathering with

283

archaeologists from the UK and Germany. Been here since Wednesday and said that he expects to be free after 3 o'clock.

"And I don't have a clue if he knows about your Vangelis, he/him."

The latest email from Frank confirmed the time of our appointment and the name that we should give when we arrived at the gate.

That's where we were going now, 15 kilometers east of the old town to the head of Souda Bay. Passing through the port village we could see a military base not far from the harbor. Higher up from the bay an air traffic control tower was visible in the distance. That was our destination — the US Naval Support Activity HQ — part of the Hellenic Air Force Base in the center of the peninsula.

Two guards were at the entrance checkpoint, both sporting the flag of Greece on their uniforms, a white cross with alternating blue and white horizontal stripes. They gave the rental car the once over: open the trunk, mirror on steel rod to look at the undercarriage, and a slow walk-around to check the interior, front and back.

I gave the names that Frank had listed in the email. We showed ID, passports and driver's licenses. In less than five minutes an American sailor driving a military grade ATV escorted us to a parking area. He pulled ahead at an angle and pointed to the space where I should park.

"Which name do ya' think triggered the 'enter' button?" Louie said. "It sure as hell wasn't Public Affairs Officer J. Kraft."

"You don't know, Mister Cynic. A good PA Officer can have a lot of influence."

"Right. As long as he is in the good graces of the Commander of the base!"

"Actually," I said, "Lieutenant J. Kraft is a woman." That was not true, but it caused Ragsdale to give me the eyeroll as he unbuckled his seat belt.

The sailor walked us through a door that led to a security scan station, much like those found in courthouses or museums; empty your pockets and proceed slowly. When we cleared the other side, we were greeted by a man in a short-sleeve dress white uniform, shoulder boards reflecting his rank and a right-breast blue name plate that read KRAFT.

"Gentleman," he said, stepping forward and extending his right hand.

Kraft took us to a small meeting room adjacent to his office — an oval table and six chairs. On the table were two black file folders; each looked to be perhaps a quarter-inch thick. A white lined pad of paper and a pen was on the table next to the folders. We declined an offer of coffee.

"Captain Facundo sends his apologies," Kraft said, standing at the open door. "He left earlier this morning for Washington. He also wanted me to tell you that he *did* speak personally with Mister Marino."

He pointed to the folders on the table. "Some of the information is incomplete, but it corresponds to the dates and names that were requested. Let me know if you need anything, I'm right next door."

We pulled chairs away from the table and sat. I separated the folders and gave the bottom one to Louie.

"Anything that refers to Callahan," I said. "Flag it and we'll look it over."

"Aye, aye, Ensign. Do I focus on *hum*-int . . . or *sig*-int?"

On the drive to the base earlier we'd puzzled over why an old hand like Win Callahan, reputedly a spy looking after *people*, had had any connection to a facility that must surely be involved with *signal* intelligence, in addition to its strategic location in the Mediterranean.

Nearly two hours later, including brief exchanges over a particular document in one of the folders, I had identified five separate pages that could warrant further review. All five sheets had piqued my interest, but the real test would be with Frank Marino's interpretation.

Lieutenant Kraft made copies of the documents. When I thanked him as we were ready to leave, I commented that nothing in either folder had been redacted.

"Unclassified," he said. "If you had filed a Freedom of Information Request, we would have scanned these and sent you a PDF."

"But we weren't exactly sure *what* we were looking for, were we?"

"True. And these," he held up the five pages, "aged out a long time ago. All declassified."

Sixty Five

Armando called to say that the sale had been completed and the second check was ready, forty-five-thousand dollars. The shooter could pick it up anytime on Saturday between 11 and 4:30.

Proceeds from the gun collection would be deposited to a credit union account, less five-thousand cash for short-term travel and living expenses. Aware of the federal Currency Transaction Report required of banks, the shooter and Armando had agreed on a personal check that would make the deposit exempt.

Almost sixty-two years in Massachusetts — all his life experiences to date — and it was about to be left behind. No further employment obligations, no family that he cared about, no real friends that would miss him, or that *he* would miss.

For weeks, everyday news had been consumed with speculation on so-called 'next phase variants' of the Coronavirus pandemic. The shooter was ready for the next phase of his life. At least that is what he'd been telling himself for more than a year. And that it would be the *final* phase, no late in life 'second wind' laps for him. He knew his own body and knew his family history of men not reaching the US average life expectancy mark of 78 years for white males.

The sureness and efficiency of how he had handled the sale of the firearms had produced only one surprise. Nearing the conclusion of the transaction had provoked in him a re-examination; *how did I get from there . . . to here?*

Much self-reflection had occupied his hours in the basement workshop and during the drives back and forth from Weapons, Ltd. Now, about to make the last run to that discreet little shop in Stoneham, the shooter had managed to organize his life's events in chronological order. Exercising self-discipline as though it was a new daily health habit, he routinely maneuvered and realigned the introspection from each decade all the way back to elementary school.

Shining like some late-night beacon from the tallest building in Boston, visible from all approaches, he had come to focus on the one milestone that placed him here, *today*. It had been an act of youthful stupidity and greed. And it had been a calculated move that resulted in deception, a murder, and self-sacrifice.

The shooter had arrived at another decision. He knew exactly what he needed to do to absolve himself from guilt for the event of forty years ago.

On Crete, the bus ride from Heraklion to Matala took two-and-a-half hours. Theo Angelos was one of only a few passengers for this late season run.

A phone call out of the blue from a cousin was the reason for the trip. Angelos had not been on the island for a long time. He had not seen the older relative in more than 20 years.

Nikolaos Andreadakis was the son of a brother to the man who claimed to be Angelos' father. Hektor Andreadakis, long dead, *may* have fathered a son, or a daughter, possibly in Greece or in America. But it was not Theo.

Certain that Nikos remained under an impression that he accepted that Hektor had been his real father, Theo had yet to dispel that illusion. The old man had sounded confused and desperate in his phone call asking Theo to come to visit him in Matala.

The bus slowed as it approached the seaside village. A half-dozen cars were parked behind a concrete barrier opposite a strip of vendor kiosks. During the peak season of August, there could be a hundred parked cars lining the roadway, with crowds heading for the beach and browsing the pop-up businesses catering to tourists.

Off the bus, Theo went to a woman at a souvenir stand. A minute later, he was walking toward the bay and the Pithari Taverna.

The trip to the monastery had been a pleasant outing for the two young women, but not so much for the old man.

Sitting on a stone bench, waiting, observing people go in and come out of the small chapel, Nikos couldn't get beyond his self-reproach. Watching Melissa and her friend in the distance offered momentary relief. Each time that his granddaughter visited Matala, some of the 'good days' from his own youth were rekindled, causing him momentarily to see the present in a more favorable light.

It never lasted long. A new thought, or a recurring rumination appearing like an ominous cloud in a perfectly clear sky, would instantly overtake him. And there were frequent lapses in his short-term memory, triggering confusion and frustration. The sight of a stranger — almost *any* man who did not appear to be a Greek — would pull Nikos back into despair.

Now the two women helped him walk back to the car. Suffering from sleep deprivation, he moved slowly. When they arrived at the vehicle, he asked to sit in the back for the trip home.

The American woman, Nikos could not recall her name, drove. Melissa talked to the woman in a soft voice. They were playing music from the radio. It faded in and out.

Five minutes on the highway and Nikos fell into a slumber.

Sixty Six

A man was seated at one of the outdoor tables at the taverna. It was late, no other customers around. He watched Nikolaos Andreadakis shuffling toward the entrance. The old man had not spotted him.

Having assured his granddaughter that he would be fine and that he would see them in the morning, Nikos was exhausted, physically, and mentally. As tired as he could ever recall being in his entire life.

Hesitating, Nikos turned and looked at the man sitting perhaps three meters away. The man didn't speak. He was smoking a cigarette. It was the smoke that had caused Nikos to stop.

"We are not serving dinner this evening," Nikos said in English.

The man stubbed out his cigarette and rose from the table.

"You wanted me to come to see you," the man replied in English. "So here I am."

Nikos stared, uncertain, he studied the man's face. The only light came from a string of small white lights wrapped around a fence that encircled the café tables. The man stepped forward. "It's Theo, your cousin. You don't recognize me?"

No, he didn't recognize him, even as the man now stood less than a meter away.

"Nikos, you *called* me. A week ago," Angelos said, switching to Greek.

He had called him. It was coming back now. It had been following Nikos' visit to Opsigias, after he had visited with Pavlos, who had then up and died the very next morning.

"Theo," Nikos said. "Syngnomi," he said in Greek — I am sorry. Then he stepped toward him to offer an embrace. "It has been so many years."

They sat outside the taverna talking for a long time. Nikos had placed a bottle of ouzo on the table. Each man had drunk two small glasses during the conversation, and now both abstained.

"I want you to see something," Nikos said, again speaking in his accented English. He rose slowly, shuffled back through the kitchen area to his bedroom, retrieved the old photo and brought it to Theo. Removing the rubber band — as he had done many times now — he unrolled the print to spread it across the table. The ouzo bottle was a good weight to hold down one end of the photo.

Theo leaned closer to look at the print. Nikos watched him.

"Who are these men?" the younger man said.

The old man tapped the monoprint near the end where the teenaged boys stood. "Look closely," he said. The light was not great.

Theo shifted his eyes to the left end where Nikos had indicated. He bent forward to get a better view. He smiled.

"This is Hektor," he said.

The old man nodded. "Yes. He was just a boy."

"And *this* . . ." Theo added, touching the image of the American soldier, "is my father."

Nikos stared at the photo. Slowly lifting his head to make eye contact with Theo, he placed his left hand over his mouth as though to prevent himself from speaking. Elbow on the edge of the table, holding the hand covering his lips, Nikos gave a barely perceptible nod.

His eyes shifted downward again as he looked at that American soldier in that group of men from 75 years ago.

With little contact over three decades, Nikos had concluded long ago that Theo knew that Hektor had not been his biological father.

In the early days, it had been Selene's family who perpetuated the lie. They may have believed it. When the boy was young, Hektor had played along. Then a few years before his own death, Hektor had gone to the US, remained there illegally for a spell, and had had no direct contact with family back in Greece.

Nikos again placed his left hand flat on the edge of the photo to hold it fast to the table. After several seconds, he looked back at Theo who was also studying the photo.

"Your mother told you about this man?" Nikos asked.

Theo leaned back in his chair. Folding his arms across his chest, he cocked his head slightly and offered a bemused smile. "Yes," he said.

Nikos looked down again. He ran his right hand on the photo, tapping two fingers near the image of the American.

"There was an old man who lived in the village next to mine. He knew Hektor, and my father. I went to see him and showed him this," Nikos said, again tapping the photo.

"Pavlos. *This* boy." Nikos pointed to one of the others in the photo. "He told me that he and Hektor went to Chania for work. It was after the war." Nikos rolled the photo far enough to show the writing on the back; Chania, 1946.

"This was part of what became the military base.," Nikos said, running a finger along the building in the photo. "Much bigger now," he added.

Theo leaned forward, his face only a few inches above the photo. Moving his head slowly to take in the building behind the group of men, his eyes settled again on the American.

"I met him once. He came back to Athens. He died many years before my mother," Theo said.

Nikos kept his gaze on Theo. Finally, he managed to ask the question that had prompted the phone call of more than a week ago, the call that Nikos had forgotten.

"You met your father? And you know his *name*?" Nikos said.

"Yes. My mother called him by a nickname, Win. His real name was Stephen Callahan."

Sixty Seven

A phone call bumped our travel plans from the '*headed home*' routine prep stage, to a '*not quite so fast*' holding pattern. We were just a few hours from going to the airport.

It was Sunday morning. Ragsdale and I were having coffee and eating bougatsa at one of the outdoor restaurants in old town Chania. As soon as the caller identified himself as Theo Angelos, acknowledging that I had visited his Athens apartment only four days earlier, I was all ears.

"Could you hold on a second, please?" I said, pressing the phone to my chest and looking at Louie. I pointed to my left ear, then toward the water. It would be better to get away from people close by and their conversations. Standing, I started walking across the paved boardwalk. Out ahead of me at the mouth of the harbor was the stone lighthouse dating from the end of the Ottoman Empire.

"Yes. Thanks for calling," I said. "I am working for an old

friend of your mother's. I spoke earlier with your aunt, and she gave me your address. Do you know the name Frank Marino?"

"My mother took care of him when he was a small boy. His family lived in Athens," he said.

"Yes. And he was able to see your mother, apparently not long before she died."

"The summer of the Olympic Games, 2004. A time when . . . she was confused about many things."

I was getting accustomed to English with a thick accent, like outtakes from the old *Zorba* film with Anthony Quinn, or most of the men in the bride's family of *My Big Fat Greek Wedding*.

"Frank has retired and is living near me, in Vermont. He doesn't travel much and . . ."

"Bernie Sanders from on television," he interrupted. "I know of Vermont. He was going to be your president."

Until a few days ago, if you had held a gun on me, I could not have told you the name of a single politician in Greece. *And this guy knows about Bernie. Okay.*

"Yeah, that didn't work out last time," I said. "The main reason that I am in Greece is to get some information on *another* man, who was also a friend of your mother's. Did you ever hear her speak of a man by the name of Win Callahan?"

There was a long pause. I held my phone out to look at the screen, thinking that I might have lost the call.

"Hello?"

"My mother wanted to marry Stephen Callahan," he said. "He went back to America, but he visited Greece many times after the war. And he visited my mother frequently. But he was married to an American woman by then.

"Stephen Callahan was my father," he added.

Theo Angelos continued, speaking slowly, recounting the only time that he'd met Callahan and of subsequent discussions he'd had with his mother.

I leaned my back against the wall at the base of the lighthouse and listened.

After a few minutes, he paused again. This time I could hear what sounded like him lighting a cigarette. I looked back at the table where Louie was still seated watching pedestrians as they strolled by.

"Mister Hanlon, it is interesting that you should be here asking questions about my mother and Stephen Callahan. Perhaps a coincidence," he added, "I had a long conversation with a man that I have known all my life. We talked about my father also.

"Nikos, it is what everyone calls him. He is like a cousin to me. He has been to your country, a long time ago. Nikos tells me, just last night, that he believes that Greek gangsters in America arranged for the murder of Stephen Callahan."

I had to restrain myself from butting in too quickly. He was on a roll. The shifting between 'my father' and 'Callahan' was a bit puzzling, but if the information was credible, Theo was providing a real leap forward. It was the first *serious* movement in the case since I had sat listening to Frank Marino three weeks earlier.

"You are still in Athens? How long will you be in Greece?" he said.

"No, I am in Chania. I am supposed to fly home this afternoon."

"*Chania*? You are not far from where I am right now. Do you know where Matala is?"

"I saw it on the map when we were in Heraklion, then a highway sign. It's on the coast?"

"South from Heraklion, yes. A famous beach. And the hippie caves. Nikos lives in Matala. He owns a taverna here."

Ragsdale was up and walking along the water coming in my direction.

"I would like a chance to talk to this man," I said. "I will have to change my flight. Can I call you back in, say . . . an hour? Two at the most."

Silence. In my head I counted to three.

"The bus to Heraklion is at four o'clock. I was going back to Athens," he said.

"Let me see what I can do," I added. "Will Nikos talk with me?"

"My number is on your phone ID, yes? Call soon, please."

"Thank you," I said.

"I believe that Nikos, yes he will speak to you. I will wait."

Sixty Eight

Changing flights was much easier than expected, a surprise considering some of pandemic-related travel restrictions. *Then again, fewer people flying, eh?*

A questionable roll of the dice with this man Nikos, certainly. Instead of leaving today from Chania, we were able to get seats on a flight tomorrow afternoon.

When I called Theo Angelos, another break. He told me that the old man had been pestering his granddaughter to take him back to a monastery which happened to be about half-way between Chania and Matala.

"Preveli," I said.

"*Yes,*" he said, an inflection of surprise in his voice.

"I was there two days ago."

Angelos proposed that we meet there. He said that he would do all that he could to get the old man to tell his story.

Already checked out of the rooms, we only needed to return to the hotel to get our bags. At 11:25, we were back in the rental car and headed east. The Holy Monastery of Preveli was approximately 90 minutes away.

The trip took us back through villages that we'd seen coming west earlier. Louie volunteered to drive. Partly sunny with temperatures predicted to hit 22 Celsius, according to the weather app on my phone, or in the low 70s Fahrenheit.

Three different radio stations, I read a guidebook for half-an-hour, then we got into a discussion speculating about spies, this time including talk about foreign-born gangsters, and the different levels of law enforcement in the US.

With his retirement just weeks away, I decided that this was not the time to press Ragsdale on views about recent urban police department controversies, defunding and citizen protests. I already knew that he held strong views about 'bad cops' and 'stupid, unnecessary fuckups that cost lives.' We had talked about police training in the past and I suspected that we would again, just not on this trip.

Up ahead on the highway before the turn-off was the statue of the monk holding the rifle. A better view coming from this direction.

Louie slowed down as we passed, turning his head. "Warning, yahoos. No scammin' around here," he said louder than necessary.

"There's a real story about Preveli," I said. "One of the guidebooks I read after we were here, talked about the first monastery going back a thousand years."

"*Yeah.* I read the plaque last time. What's their scoop on Father Bolt Action?" He motioned with his head toward the monk.

"From the bit I read, people around here — at least for the past few hundred years — have had periodic skirmishes with *somebody* on a fairly consistent basis. The Venetians occupied the island going back to the 13th century. The Turks showed up and got nasty in the middle of the 17th century. Later on, the Turks called in some Egyptians.

"The Balkan Wars, 1912, I think. Along comes World War I. More backyard brawls and ongoing nasty events for another 25 years. World War II cranks up." I pointed back in the direction of the statue. "That guy commemorates the Battle of Crete, spring of 1941."

"Yep. That's what it says on the plaque," he said.

We arrived at the parking area above the monastery. Ragsdale switched off the engine and rolled his window down. He looked at the conclave below.

"Gives new meaning to 'count your blessings,' huh? Come for Sunday service, bring your gun," he said.

Two men sat on the stone bench in the courtyard. The younger man, possibly late 50s: dark hair, thin build, dark blue polo shirt. The other man might be in his 80s: close-cropped gray hair going to white, weathered face, banded-collar black shirt. Angelos had told me that we could meet in front of the chapel.

"I think these are our guys," I said, pointing to the men.

Engaged in conversation, the pair paid no attention to others. We walked down the steps and moved in their direction.

"Excuse me," I said. "Theo Angelos?"

The younger man stood. "You are Michael Hanlon?"

"Yes." We shook hands. The old man watched but made no effort to get up, no effort to say anything.

"This is Lou Ragsdale," I said.

Angelos extended his right hand and gave a quick nod. They shook hands.

From my back pocket, I pulled out the letters given to me by Helen and handed them to Angelos. "Your Aunt Helen wanted you to have these," I said.

He looked at the letters in my hand, accepted them and said, "Thank you" in the thick accent. After a couple of seconds, he placed the letters inside his waistband.

"Nikolaos Andreadakis," he said, gesturing to the old man still seated.

"Thank you for coming to meet us," I said.

The old man reluctantly shook my hand.

"There is a table, by the trees," Angelos said, pointing beyond a knee-high stone wall surrounding the courtyard. "We can be in the shade."

He helped the old man stand. All of us moved in the direction of the table. It had a bench on each side. As soon as we were seated, I was aware that the old man had kept his eyes fixed on me.

"Nikos," Theo said. "The story you told me last night. About Hektor, your trip to America. And Stephen Callahan. Mister Hanlon would like to hear it."

Watery, blue-gray eyes but an unwavering gaze, the old man's lips trembled but no words came out. He pulled out a handkerchief and wiped at his mouth.

"We can wait over there," Angelos said. He glanced at Louie. They both walked away from the table and sat farther along on the stone wall. The old man waited, then looked back at me.

"My uncle, Hektor . . ." he began, tilting his head slightly and dabbing at his eyes, "he went to America. Almost fifty years ago. He had friends, from Athens. They left Greece before the junta got them . . . *Aprilianoi.*"

Short, halting delivery, as though he was searching for the correct words in English. After a few seconds, he resumed.

"They were gangsters in Athens. They became gangsters in *your* country," he added, returning the gaze.

"Later, after Hektor was back in Greece, he sent me to America to . . . to make arrangements. It was not my first trip. I had been there when I was younger.

"There was an American who Hektor had known from a long time ago. When the man had been here in Greece." He gave a slow shake of the head before continuing.

"Hektor hated this man. He had done something. With the gangsters, they wanted to assassinate the American."

Sixty Nine

Nikos' story went on for what seemed like half an hour. I offered an occasional, brief, verbal prompt, or a nod to encourage him. I held the questions. And I did not look at my watch.

At one point, I saw Louie get up from the stone wall, walk around, but he made no attempt to rejoin us. I couldn't tell if he and Angelos had been in conversation.

This meeting was another instance where I regretted not having my hand-held digital audio recorder. Using my phone occurred to me later, but there was the fear that it might put Nikos off.

Almost at the first minute into the tale I started taking abbreviated notes using the inside back cover page of a guidebook. Nikos had watched me do this and apparently had no objection.

As his account of the long-ago events was winding to a close, Nikos took longer pauses. Then he would add another detail or attempt to correct a date that had been mentioned earlier. Finally, when I presumed that he was finished, I waited a few seconds before asking a question. His answer would be crucial in the report I planned to write.

"Nikos, are you willing to . . . *voluntarily*, go through this again and permit it to be recorded?"

The same rheumy eyes studied me. He looked tired and extremely sad. Before answering, he turned to look over at Angelos sitting on the wall next to Ragsdale.

"I will tell this to the police. Melissa has asked me to do this also," he said.

Melissa, I knew, was his granddaughter. She and a friend were somewhere nearby, as they had driven the two men to Preveli for this meeting.

As we were about to leave, I asked Nikos and Theo if they minded if I took some photos. They had no problem with the request.

Again, the smartphone could have worked, but I had already taken so many shots with my camera that it made sense to use it here. While I removed the lens cap, Theo turned from his sideways position to face the camera and stood behind Nikos, who sat up straighter and tried to improve his posture.

"The camera, it prints?" Nikos said. "It is a Polaroid?"

"*Eh-h*, I don't think people use those much anymore." I adjusted framing the shot to get the men centered. "But this one makes really good photos. You can see them instantly and you can send them over the internet."

When I finished taking three different shots, including close-ups of each man, Theo raised a hand to wave at someone. I turned to see two young women standing in the courtyard next to the bench outside the chapel. They began walking in our direction.

Theo made introductions and we talked for a few minutes. I learned that the American woman was from Virginia and was *stunned* to find out that it had been her grandmother — the woman I'd met in Burlington two weeks ago — who connected her with Frank Marino, who then had dispatched her to visit with Selene's sister and to try to locate Theo Angelos in Athens.

After getting their permission to take another photo, Ragsdale surprised me by suggesting that he take group photos, with me and the two women, and another with the three of us standing behind Nikos and Theo.

Nikos slowly pushed himself up from the bench, resting his hands on the edge of the table. He looked at his granddaughter.

"I would like to go to the chapel," he said.

She put an arm around his neck and kissed him on the cheek. The American woman joined them crossing the courtyard.

"Do you mind driving a while longer?" I asked. Louie pulled the key from his back pocket and tapped it on his right temple.

"Gotta write some of this stuff while it's fresh," I added.

"Good idea."

Backing the car out to turn toward the exit, his hand on the standard-shift lever and holding the clutch in, Louie had a mischievous grin.

"What?"

"*Goin'* . . . *to the chap-el,*" he sang. "Dixie Cups, 1964. Look it up."

"Should we go tell them?"

As Louie approached the main road, I dug into my backpack for a reporter's notebook. About to get onto the highway, he stopped for a couple of seconds opposite the memorial. He gave a salute to the monk.

Continuing the drive east and knowing that I wanted to write, Louie was thoughtful enough to leave the radio off and to allow me to get to it. Using the notes from earlier, I wrote five-and-a-half pages. Reading through what I had written, I scratched out a few words, made some arrows in the margin to connect passages, and was satisfied that I could clean it up later.

Back in Chania, we were able to get rooms at the same hotel where we had stayed before. Louie was about to call Becky and I went down to a tiny room off the lobby to use the hotel's computer. I needed to compose my summary of Nikos' story.

Seventy

The patchwork tale was plausible. As far as I could determine, however, it would be difficult if not impossible to find *anyone* to corroborate much of what I had just been told.

Typing the summary in the same way I would write up any report, I used bullet points with brief observations: specific events linked to dates; direct quotations; names and places that Nikos cited during his weary disclosure.

Nikolaos Andreadakis — Oct. 25th —
The Holy Monastery of Preveli

Nikos Andreadakis was accompanied by Theo Angelos, who facilitated arrangements for the meeting. Louis Ragsdale, travelling with me, was also in attendance. We sat at an outdoor table near the courtyard of the chapel. The entire meeting lasted approximately one hour.

- 1946, Chania – an uncle, Hektor Andreadakis, then a teenager, worked for a civilian construction company contracted to handle preliminary work of the military installation that eventually became what is today the NATO hub in the eastern Mediterranean, Souda Naval Base. It was during this time that Hektor met Stephen Callahan, an American soldier on assignment at the base.

- Andreadakis stated that the two men met again approximately ten years later when Hektor moved to Athens. Callahan was back in Greece working in "some capacity as a US Government employee, not a soldier." Hektor had been renting a room at the home of the Stavrakis family, located on the outskirts of the city. Callahan had come to visit the eldest daughter, Selene, still living with her parents. He had known her from the months just before Greece entered World War II.

- Based on 'family stories' — and a more recent account offered by one of Hektor's childhood friends who had accompanied him to Chania in 1946 — what had been occasional workplace discord between Hektor and Callahan grew into full-blown acrimony. It was all about Selene. Though several years younger than she, Hektor was infatuated. The childhood friend, Pavlos Astrinidis, now deceased, told Nikos that his Uncle Hektor had wanted to marry Selene. What had been, at least in the eyes of Hektor, a promising relationship, had been torpedoed by Callahan, who reportedly had subsequent visits with Selene.

- Theo Angelos had earlier stated to me that one of those 'visits' by Callahan was sometime near the end of 1959, approximately nine months before he was born. He claims that Callahan was his father.

- In the winter of 1972, Hektor went to the US. He stayed for less than a year living in the Philadelphia area, where he worked for Stefanos Patanzis, whom he had known back in Athens. It was never disclosed exactly what kind of work he did for Patanzis, reportedly a gangster during his own days in Greece and who had been run out of the country by the military junta.

- Andreadakis' account became more focused when he described how in the late summer of 1980 his uncle sent him to the US with a 'large amount of cash and an American man's name, Stephen Callahan.' Nikos was instructed to go to see Patanzis who would help locate Callahan. "Hektor never used the word 'assassinate,' or, 'murder'. He made it clear to me that Patanzis would know how matters should be handled."

- Three days after the Patanzis meeting, Nikos traveled to Boston where at a restaurant, by pre-arrangement, he encountered two young men. "I gave them the name and an address. And cash. Patanzis added money to what my uncle sent. He also found the man's address. My meeting with the two men lasted a few minutes. Only one of them spoke. Both were younger than me. One man accepted the package and made it clear that I should leave the restaurant . . . at that very moment." Nikos made a repeated *shooing* motion with his hand as he said this.

- The story fell back into disjointed declarations of ignorance and innocence, Nikos' own marital issues and family estrangement, his eventual move back to Crete and — with financial assistance from Hektor — buying a taverna in Matala which he still operates today.

- As we were nearing the end of the visit with Andreadakis, his granddaughter and an American friend arrived. They had provided the transportation to Preveli and had been elsewhere on the grounds of the monastery during our time at the picnic table. (see photos). Brief introductions and some small talk with the American girl, Emma, was the only exchange I had with the young women.

- He says that he is willing to tell the story again. Also said that he is agreeable to allow the interview to be recorded.

After reading over the summary, I made some corrections to my typing and saved it as a PDF. From the hotel computer, I emailed it as an attachment to myself, then printed a copy before going back upstairs.

"You all set?" Louie said.

"Yep." I handed him the printout. "You can read it later. Let's go get something to eat."

For what likely would be our final meal in Greece, we walked to a small family restaurant a block from the hotel, a place that we'd spotted previously. It was nothing fancy. And, as had been true the first time we saw it, the customers appeared to be locals, including a family with small children.

I started to open the door and Louie took hold of my left arm.

"Maybe we can have a beer tonight? Or a regular white wine? Take a pass on the retsina."

"Works for me."

Seventy One

Departure from Chania was with Aegean Airlines. The Covid-19 Passenger Locator Form that we'd filled out before leaving the US was still valid. We left on time, but it was just the start of a bear of an itinerary; nearly 18 hours with the time difference; two stops and plane switch — Athens, on to Zurich — ETA Boston at 6:40 Tuesday morning. Apparently, this was unusual as most flights arrive in the US during the evening hours.

The plane was half full. My guess was most of the passengers were German or Austrian, based solely on overhearing snippets of conversations. We had adjacent seats near the front of the Economy Section. I gave Louie the window seat.

The food was good. We talked intermittently, did a lot of reading, random in-flight audio and video selections, and both of us slept for the last couple of hours. My anticipation was that any jetlag would be minimal when we got home.

After leaving Boston, we stopped in Hooksett, New Hampshire for breakfast. Just over two hours later we arrived at my house in Quechee at 11:15. It was a cool but bright morning with most of the fog cleared out. It was good to be back in Vermont.

"Always somebody," Louie said. He was sitting with the driver's door open, feet resting on the rocker panel.

"Yet another oldie that I don't know?"

"Nah." He got out and stretched. "Today it's Russian mobsters. Some places have Asian gangs. In the Southwest, Mexicans and Central American bad guys."

For a second, I thought he might start yakking about a southern US border wall. But he was onto the story from Nikos Andreadakis.

"We've always had the Italians, with a lifetime of stories about the Mafia. It was your wine buddy Coppola who really seared *that* into our culture. And Boston has had its Irish mob. But who knew anything about *Greek* gangsters here?"

"I'll bet you talk to cops in Philly, maybe a few other cities with large concentrations of . . . *bad guys from Europe* . . . it probably ebbs and flows with who's coming here and who can they take power from. We live in a *bubble*, Louie. You're the one got me onto that."

"I'm afraid change is on the way, partner," he said. "And it's not like we don't have our share of home-grown bad guys, huh?"

"Sure you wanna retire?"

"You betcha. Just have ta' crack the whip on young hotshots we're about to train. Do the *right* thing."

"Wasn't that Spike Lee? I don't remember any chart hits from the movie."

He was back in the truck ready to leave when I motioned to hold up.

"Hey, Marino wants to take us to dinner sometime. He made a point of saying that he would like to meet you."

"Let me know," Louie said. "Becky's not coming home for another week."

Back in Athens, it was apparent to Theo Angelos that he should visit his mother's sister and clear the air. They had never been close. He suspected that Helen viewed him in much the same negative way that she had viewed his reputed father, Hektor. As far as Theo knew, at the time of his mother's death anyway, Helen was still accepting that story. But now she'd sent along the old letters.

No good reason for keeping the secret any longer. His aunt might be around for years or could be gone tomorrow. He wanted her to know — and believed that his mother at long last would want her to know — that Win Callahan had been his father. And he wanted her to know how he died.

The beach at Matala was quiet. A waxing gibbous moon hung above the bay, some stars out. Off in the distance, tiny lights of a ship were visible on the horizon. Nikos sat alone, smoking.

Before she left the island with her friend, Melissa assured her grandfather that she would go with him when he spoke to the police, most likely in Athens. They had left it that Theo, in Greece, and Michael Hanlon, in the US, would handle contact with law enforcement officials and present the story. The Greeks might have an interest, but doubtful jurisdictional standing in the matter.

Seventy Two

Two-hundred-fifty-one towns and cities in Vermont and I wondered why Marino had chosen Williamstown in which to spend his final days on earth.

A small state with 23,000 miles of rivers and streams, 800 lakes and ponds, approximately 640,000 people in an area of some 9,600 square miles. Quite the contrast from having spent most of your adult life in the metro Washington area encompassing the District of Columbia.

Scrolling through photos on my camera to refresh my memory, I popped the SIM card so I could insert it into my laptop and show them to Frank on a larger screen. He wanted to see the Knossos and Preveli shots, too.

It was twenty after ten. He'd said that I should get there at noon. We could have sandwiches and "discuss what you have uncovered." Depending on what he thought of my summary of Nikos' story, plus the photos, and observations from my visit with Helen, all of this would influence what he asked me to do next.

I had a hunch about 'next'. If I was on target, it would all go straight to the FBI. Probably involve some cops in Greece, possibly a historical incident review by New Hampshire F & G.

Didn't matter. It would not be my call.

Rocco was eager to go along, so up onto the backseat and we were ready for the one-hour drive north. He could stay in the car while I met with Frank.

Before leaving, I sent a text to Ragsdale and left a voicemail for Virginia, same message:

Dinner invitation from Frank Marino for Sat evening. I'll call you.

When we spoke on the phone earlier, Frank sounded tired but perhaps a bit relieved, sorta like a person mellowed-out after a lengthy exercise workout.

But he was enthusiastic about wanting to host a dinner. I wondered if he planned to prepare it himself or get some help. Good thing Becky wasn't here. The dining area of his apartment could barely accommodate four.

The shooter sat at a guestroom desk of a Residence Inn on the outskirts of Granville, Ohio. Writing on hotel stationery, he composed a short 'To Whom It May Concern' letter, addressed to the New Hampshire Fish and Game Department.

In November 1980, at the urging of a friend, I went on a hunting trip to your state. Records will show that I was *involved in an incident that took a man's life. November 21, 1980, in the town of Bethlehem. My punishment was a $500 fine and the loss of hunting privileges for 10 years. I did not pull the trigger. The man who fired the shot is now dead. For the protection of his family's name, I <u>voluntarily</u> accepted responsibility.*

The slate is now clean.

Ronald Davis

Checked out of his room, the shooter dropped the envelope in a USPS box just outside the hotel lobby prior to resuming the cross-country drive to Arizona. Rather than settling a long-ago incident, he suspected that the letter would be the basis for authorities to take a new look at an old case.

The shooter had no intention of hiding. If they found him, he would cooperate. This was simply a matter of setting the record straight — on his own terms — and a final, necessary step in his departure from New England.

It should not have surprised me when I learned that Frank — after receiving the email summary of Nikos' story two days ago — had already been in touch with "some people I know" at NSA and the FBI.

"I believe that I told you," he explained, "Win was a rare bird for the times, in that he worked across agencies. Very unusual. Not everybody loved him, but he knew a lot of people, had seen plenty of 'not good' activities, and he was committed to serving his country."

We'd just finished tuna fish sandwiches Frank had made. Another opera CD was playing at low volume. I was about to open my laptop to show him the photos from Greece. He kept talking.

"Aside from the Andreadakis' story and the enduring animosity between Selene's jealous suitors, there really were Greek-born gangsters in the Philadelphia area for a number of years. Naturally, the FBI had a role in busting it up.

"And we may never know for certain, but some of my friends believe that Win played a part. Identifying — perhaps even interrogating — known criminal figures from Athens who wound up here in the US. The most likely culprit in putting out the order for a 'hit' was Patanzis," Frank said, then adding, "A fair chance that he wanted Win dead just as much as Hektor did."

"So, what happens now?" I said, my laptop screen ready for the show.

"Things will move along, slowly and quietly, no doubt. And yes, someone will be heading to Matala for a talk with Nikos. I may not be around when they're ready to file their report. But the bureau will chase every detail."

This had to be maybe the tenth time in a month when I'd heard some variation from Frank alluding to 'I may not be around.'

I looked at him and he studied me. Neither of us spoke. His expression would qualify as one signifying marginal contentment.

Then, as though he'd received a minor electrical jolt or had just remembered something, he sat up straight and placed both hands flat on the table.

"Show me your photos. And tell me about the food. It has been too long."

An hour later, with numerous reminiscences from Frank, we'd plowed through all the photos, and I had described the best dishes from the trip. This produced a transformation. He was back to that 'looks more like 65 than 85'.

We walked slowly to my car and let Rocco get out for a stretch. Before I drove home, I told Frank that I was trying to pin down both Ragsdale and Virginia for our Saturday night dinner date.

"I'll call you in the morning," I said.

"I'm looking forward to it," he said, reaching in the rear window to give Rocco a pat. "What a handsome boy."

"He hears that way too much."

Seventy Three

Williamstown, Saturday, Oct 31st – Frank, Louie, Virginia, and me, seated around an oval table in Frank's apartment. Food provided by a local caterer who is a sister of one of the staff members at the retirement facility.

A cup of fish chowder, pumpkin ravioli, Brussel sprouts, homemade rolls, a beet and arugula salad, with a bottle of Chardonnay from France for which I didn't want to know the price. Frank was pleased with the meal the caterer had prepared. Had there been an official vote, she would have scored a perfect four outa four.

The first surprise of the evening came when Ragsdale was able to identify songs from different operas.

"Tosca," he said, about five seconds into the first track. Virginia and I stared at one another. Louie offered a restrained smirk. A few minutes later, he came up with *La boheme*. After that, it was *Madame Butterfly*. And *Turandot*.

Frank had managed to extract from Louie that often, while on undercover duty in southern Maine or along the New Hampshire coast, he'd listened to a classical radio station that broadcast a twice weekly show featuring opera selections.

"The woman who put the program together really seemed to know her stuff," Louie said. "She wasn't condescending, or boring. I liked her. So, I listened a lot."

"How did we *not* know this about you," Virginia said. Louie shrugged. I didn't know what to say. Now he was flat out grinning at me and gave me a thumbs up.

"There have been a few other times I've listened to Saturday afternoon Met broadcasts on public radio, too," Louie added.

Next, he's gonna tell us that he's baking, and watching daytime soaps on TV.

I didn't say that.

Surprise number two came at the end of dinner. Frank asked if we might go for a short drive, "just a few minutes from here."

"Sure," I said.

Travelling in two vehicles, Frank riding with Louie in the lead, Virginia rode with me. It was a five-minute trip up a side road to the town high school and athletic fields.

Parking outside a crossbar gate, we walked a short distance in the bright moonlight to the baseball diamond. Along the third base line just beyond a dugout, up a steep bank, we spread two blankets on a grassy slope. I had retrieved them from the back of my car at Frank's suggestion.

There was a fence behind us surrounding a small array of solar panels. Before anyone sat down, it became obvious why we were here — a magnificent view of the full moon. No ambient light, and the temperature was slightly above what you would call cold.

"Wow!" Virginia offered first.

"Pretty impressive," I said, settling onto a blanket. Virginia sat next to me.

"Sweet," was Louie's contribution. He sat down with his legs outstretched.

Frank remained standing. "I was here late one evening in August to see the Perseid meteor shower," he said. "Barb and Pam brought me up for my birthday." I knew the two women were on staff back at the community.

Frank produced a bottle of Port and four small plastic tumblers from a canvas shopping bag. Then, more nimbly than I might expect, he lowered himself to the ground, taking a seat next to Virginia. She held the tumblers, he poured, then passed one to each of us. We sipped, sat for twenty-minutes or so, mostly in silence, and soaked in the luminescence, as though it were providing an infusion to the soul.

Before we got ready to leave, Virginia suggested a modification of the definition of a blue moon as the *fourth* full moon in any quarter, rather than just a *second* full moon in the same month. "But some will accept either definition," she added.

"One is during a given month, one is a *seasonal* blue moon," Frank said. "And that," he added, pointing, "is also known as a blood moon, or a Hunter's Moon."

Louie threw in a comment on a pop hit by a group from Pittsburgh, PA. "The Marcels, 1961," he said. "They might've played on a minor league feeder team for the Pirates."

Gathering up the bottle, the tumblers, and the blankets, we ambled along the dirt track back toward the cars. Virginia stopped, turned, touched my cheek, and gave me a surprise kiss. Frank and Louie were walking in front of us and missed the excitement. *Halloween tenderness?*

At the parking lot, Frank said, "Michael, may I ride back with you? I would like to have a word."

"Sure."

"I will quiz Mister Opera Buff here and see what else he knows," Virginia said, with a soft punch to his shoulder. Louie clicked his key fob to unlock the doors.

"By the way," Frank said, "well ahead of your 'doo wop team' from Pittsburgh, a number of crooners recorded Blue Moon." He was talking directly to Louie. "It was a Rodgers and Hart song from a film in the 1930s. Even before *I* was born."

"I think I knew that," Louie said. "Just didn't want to show off."

The 'word' that Frank needed to share was information he had received and decided not to discuss over dinner. It was about what I should expect in the coming days and weeks regarding the Win Callahan case.

"You will get a call first, then a visit. Agents most likely sent over from Albany, maybe the Boston field office," he said.

"I've been on the phone twice with DC since you met with Andreadakis. I still have some friends at bureau headquarters."

"For what it's worth, I have 'engaged' with Special Agents in the past," I said.

"And do you know why they are designated as *Special Agents*?"

"Don't have a clue."

"Everyone knows about J. Edgar Hoover. But not many are familiar with Teddy Roosevelt's last Attorney General, Charles Joseph Bonaparte — great nephew of Napoleon — who recruited former Secret Service members for a *Special Agents Force*, later the Bureau of Investigation, or BOI. It wasn't until the mid-30s that it became the FBI."

Frank segued into a short forewarning of what to anticipate when the feds showed up. Based on two previous interactions with the FBI, one in Maine and another in New Hampshire a couple of years back, I was comfortable with the idea of being interviewed by whoever came to call.

We sat in my car in the parking lot. Virginia and Louie pulled in next to us but remained in Louie's vehicle.

"What I can tell you," Frank continued, "and they may not share this, is that I have learned that the bureau did have multiple agents focused on the Greek mob in Philadelphia all through the 1970s. Win Callahan was part of that. He knew who most of the players were." After a beat, he added, "I have no doubt that it contributed to Hektor Andreadakis' success in persuading his old pals from Athens to be of service. They were eager to get rid of Win for their own reasons."

We sat in silence for bit. Despite the pleasant dinner, the wine and the opera trivia, and the trip up the hill to stare at the moon, Frank appeared to be deflating. I could hear it in his voice. He really was tired.

"Well," I said, "as soon as I hear from 'em, I will report in."

Placing his left hand on my shoulder while opening the passenger door, he started to say something but hesitated. Only when he was out of the car and I got out with him did he continue.

"I suspect that this has not been the most stimulating project that you have undertaken," he said. "Thank you for staying with it. You did a good job. And you have my deepest gratitude."

"I'd still be out there barking at the moon without you . . . *directing* me. What to read and where to go."

"I know that it was rather quick and short, but how about the trip to Greece?"

"Amazing."

Seventy Four

The first week of November got underway at a frenetic pace; phone calls, email, text messages and face to face encounters.

First up was a call from Lieutenant Heidi Murrough at New Hampshire F & G, asking if I could get on the phone with her boss, Colonel Kevin Gordon.

"We received a letter from someone claiming to be Ronald Davis, the man involved with the hunting fatality you've been researching," Gordon said.

"Really?"

"Yes. Actually, it's a short, handprinted note. An Ohio post mark. I have turned it over to our state police lab in Concord."

"Probably pushing my luck, but can I ask what the letter is about?"

Gordon was silent for a beat, then said, "Until we can verify this is legitimate, anything that I tell you is off the record."

"Yes, understood," I said.

"He claims that someone else, who is now deceased, fired the shot that killed Callahan. Says that he voluntarily took responsibility for the shooting."

"You're going to get a visit from the FBI," I said, and proceeded to brief Gordon on the information learned from Nikos Andreadakis. And I told him that Frank Marino had already started the ball rolling.

The second call came from FBI Special Agent George Calver out of the Albany Field Office. After giving him my address, we agreed to meet at my house at 10 o'clock the next morning.

When I asked if he wanted to be in touch with Louie as well, the answer was, "Not at this time."

Reading over my October 25th summary report on the meeting with Nikos, I printed a copy to have handy, then sent a short email to Frank telling him that we could get on the phone after my interview with Agent Calver.

I went through a chain of text messages with both Virginia and Louie letting them know some of what was happening. Noticing that Virginia was included in the loop, Ragsdale sent a terse response:

Heads up, Ms. Jackson. Hanlon may need a lawyer. Keep an eye on him.

The next morning, still another text from Louie.

Pretty neat moon Sat night. Look up the original — Blue Moon of Kentucky, Bill Monroe, 1946.

Veteran's Day — Wednesday, 11/11 — and the pace had accelerated, steady and quiet as far as I could determine.

With cooperation from Athens police and the Greek government, US agents had scheduled an interview with Nikos Andreadakis in Matala.

The result of an APB on his Massachusetts registered vehicle, Ronald Davis was detained for questioning in Sun City, Arizona, northwest of Phoenix — details pending.

Frank Marino was receiving what seemed like daily updates from sources known just to him. I could only speculate.

But he called me every afternoon. The latest piece of info was about a 'revisit to the Philadelphia mob scene' of nearly 50 years ago, with renewed interest in the late gangster Stefanos Patanzis and possible connections in the Boston area.

"We mostly hear about interference with elections, tax fraud, bribes and illegal kickbacks, all the high-profile cases," Frank said. "They will put this all together eventually. It would be a safe bet, Michael, that Ronald Davis will shortly be providing the name of the real shooter."

"That's what you were after. A long time coming."

"Considering that US history is replete with people being murdered by a gun, and the bureau's Uniform Crime Reporting shows that more than a third of those cases go unsolved for indeterminate periods, yes, a long time coming.

"But I am at peace with this one. Thank you."

Seventy Five

Just before Thanksgiving, Frank and I were talking on the phone every couple of days. He was back to sounding twenty years younger.

"The latest information is that 'the Shooter' as you refer to him, Davis, has provided a name," he said. "I have not learned that name yet. But I am sure that I will."

"If the Feds have a name, surely that's going to set up a new round of queries by New Hampshire Fish and Wildlife," I said. "I'll check in with Colonel Gordon. See what he's willing to share."

"As far as Andreadakis is concerned," Frank replied, "he's an old coot like me. I can't believe that any law enforcement authorities, here or in Greece, are going to come down too hard on him."

"Out of my realm of experience. Guess we'll have to wait and see." The fact that Nikos had acted as a 'courier' implicated him in some way, but I really didn't have any idea of what that would mean. Frank quickly switched subjects.

"What are your plans for Thursday?" he asked.

"Going over to Maine, Kezar Lake. Friends I haven't seen for a while."

"And the lovely Virginia, she will go with you?"

"We're negotiating that. I think she's on board."

"It's a big holiday here, I'm told," he said. "One of my girlfriends on the staff says they pull out all the stops. Even some of the cranks — her word, not mine — enjoy the meal. With everyone vaccinated, they might even allow visitors."

"Here's a thought, Frank. I'll give you Louie's phone number. You might be able to entice him to come play DJ with Music Trivia. There has to be one resident there who knows 50s and 60s pop songs."

"Swell idea. But intuition tells me that your Captain Ragsdale would be possibly overwhelmed by this crowd."

Pithari Taverna in Matala is not a venue for hosting Thanksgiving dinner. However, Nikos had been persuaded by his granddaughter to close for an entire week and come to Athens for a visit.

Part of that decision was easy. It coincided with Nikos' scheduled second meeting with police. Following a previous two-hour Q & A with detectives from the Hellenic Police, Nikos' story was kicked over to the National Central Bureau in Athens.

As part of INTERPOL, the NCB works with police forces across the globe investigating crime groups which operate on its territory and sharing intelligence. Much of their present-day work is, not surprisingly, connected to terrorism and organized crime activities on an international level.

This 40-year-old tale of a Greek citizen traveling to America as an 'accomplice' to facilitating the murder of a US citizen — while not terrorism — did involve crime groups with established ties in at least two countries.

Theo Angelos had come up with a two-step plan. One, spend a little time with his elderly aunt, Helen Stavrakis, to review the old letters and memories of his mother.

Two, a trip to the US, and travel to New Hampshire for a visit to the grave of a father he never knew. Regardless of what he might learn in any conversation with his aunt, Theo needed to do this. And he was certain that his mother would want him to do it.

Ronald Davis, The Shooter, was temporarily settled in a home in Green Valley, Arizona. He had arranged to rent the house with a Purchase and Sale Agreement in place to assume ownership in six months.

A re-opened investigation into the death of Stephen Winthrop Callahan was underway. While a small number of federal and state law enforcement officers had access to 'new information', reporters, media outlets, and bloggers, were so far unaware of what could be developing.

Louis James Ragsdale — perceived as an 'old fart' by one or two young cops in a group of trainees — was eager to help mold these new members of the *Joint Northeast Counter-Drug Task Force* into effective public servants. If their days on the road followed a route like the one Louie had traveled, they were about to assume an ever-expanding workload in getting some "really vile assholes" off the streets.

After this, come January 1st, Ragsdale was going fishing . . . somewhere.

◊◊◊

Acknowledgements

- *Golden Ring* – The Dry Branch Fire Squad – (Bobby Braddock/Rafe Van Hoy)
- *Love at the Five and Dime* – Nanci Griffith (Philo – 1986)
- *Once in a Lifetime* – Talking Heads (Sire – 1981)
- *The Catcher Was a Spy* – Nicholas Dawidoff – (Pantheon – 1994)
- *Dark Territory* – Fred Kaplan (Simon & Schuster – 2016)
- *Life Undercover* – Amaryllis Fox (Knopf Doubleday – 2019)
- *Lovely Day* – Bill Withers (Columbia – 1977)
- *Solo Piano* – Philip Glass (CBS Records – 1989)
- *The Delfonics* – (Hard-To-Find HITS – Sony BMG – 2006)
- *The Ultimate Puccini Collection* (London Records – 1998)
- *O Sole Mio* - Enrico Caruso (The Gramophone Company – 1916)
- *Still the Same* – Bob Seger & The Silver Bullet Band – (Capitol – 1978)
- *Devil Woman* – Marty Robbins (Columbia – 1962)

- *Bird Dog* – The Everly Brothers (Cadence – 1958)
- *Forty Miles of Bad Road* – Duane Eddy (Jamie – 1959)
- *Chariots Of Fire* – Vangelis (Polydor – 1981)
- *Zorba The Greek* – Nikos Kazantzakis (20th Century Fox – 1964)
- *My Big Fat Greek Wedding* – Nia Vardalos (IFC Films – 2002)
- *Chapel Of Love* – The Dixie Cups (Red Bird – 1964)
- *Blue Moon* – The Marcels (Colpix Records – 1961) Rogers & Hart song also recorded by Al Bowlly, Billy Eckstine, Mel Torme.
- *Blue Moon of Kentucky* – Bill Monroe & the Bluegrass Boys – (Columbia – 1946)

Thank you for the music, the writing, and the films!

◊◊◊

- DHMC – www.dartmouth-hitchcock.org
- Royalton Community Radio – www.royaltonradio.org
- Gina Barreca – www.ginabarreca.com
- Aspen Ideas Festival – www.aspenideas.org
- The Holy Monastery of Preveli – www.preveli.org
- Everybody Wins! Vermont – www.everybodywinsvermont.org
- Wikipedia – www.wikipedia.org

Coming in the Spring of 2023 — ***Shake It Up Baby*** — a collection of short stories. Here are two preview snippets.

◊◊◊

"Look at Domenic," Herman said. "He thinks LIFE magazine is going to come take his picture."

The only miner of the bunch who bothered to shower *and* put on clean clothes when the day shift ended, Domenic Petrucci, was the last man to arrive at the beer garden.

Ignoring the loud German American's remark, Domenic quietly took a stool at the opposite end of the bar. As was his custom, he offered a shy smile to Sarah, the woman behind the bar.

With just a nod of her head to confirm what his drink would be, she would wait until he said it.

"Iron City," the same request Domenic gave each afternoon. Served in a bottle. Beer in cans had not yet taken over.

Sarah owned the place. She knew — and generally tolerated — a noisy cluster of coal country regulars who provided much of the revenue for her small drinking establishment in a tiny back hollow mining town.

On any given weekday afternoon between 3:30 and 4, the miners would arrive, begin a ritual of drinking 'a beer and a shot', and before the third customer had a bottle in front of him, they would be trading opinions, gripes, observations on sports and current stories in the news. And exchanging insults.

(This story from a 1950s West Virginia mining town.
Lots of characters.)

◊◊◊

Ever really watch how people behave at wedding receptions?

Probably a good idea to qualify that question. Different cultures, different customs, and different times. I don't want to get carried away with generalizations.

But for *many* weddings in the US, let's say for the last 25 to 50 years, the reception is often viewed as the highlight of the celebration. Many are joyous, warm, jovial events. Music, dancing, food, celebratory toasts, stories, lots of smiles, hugs, more dancing, photos, and a happy send off for the newly married couple.

Uh, what we have in *this* story is, shall we call them 'flash-backs' from a few different people on some of their wedding reception experiences. Get a glass of champagne and let's get to it.

(This story is from California to Long Island
to Pennsylvania to New England.)

◊◊◊

Gratitude

Writing these New England Mysteries over the past few years would not have been possible without encouragement, critiques, research assistance, and overall support from friends, family, and readers. *So many people* to thank:

Karen Kayen, PJ Hamel, Priscilla Vincent, Doug Harp, Jen Fisher, Chris Boone, Pam Marshall, Janet Stanton, Andy Leckart, Donna L. Moody, John Moody, Sally and Jeremy Rutter, Gene and Jane McKenna, Dave and Linda Wallace, PK McClelland, Andrea Williams, W.D. Wetherell, Reggie Knowles, Avis Miller, Tom Pero, Sydney Lea, Ghislain Viau, and the real-life public servant and friend who influenced the character, Louie Ragsdale. Also, a bunch of Independent Bookstores throughout New England.

If I forgot someone and it was *you*, maybe give me a Moe Howard dope slap the next time we meet.

About the Author

The author is an award-winning former broadcaster living in Vermont. He began his radio career as a news reporter covering municipal and state government meetings, political campaigns, everyday community events and the incidents which frequently made the lead story of the day.

Many characters, conversations and real-life experiences have inspired much of what you read in these books, but ***the stories are fiction***.

www.nemysteries.com